TIME

AND

TENACITY

To Julie

Hannah Nale

JASNA AGM 2018

TIME

AND

TENACITY

HANNAH VALE

Colbie Gray Books

Allen, Texas

ISBN: 978-0692610978

Illustrations by Katherine Daniel
Book design by Hannah J. Vale

Cover Art and Design by Katherine Daniel and Hannah J. Vale
Cover Image: Fashion Plate (Walking Dress), by John Bell (1815)

Printed in the United States of America

To my dad, who told me to publish this thing already.

Cast of Characters

JANE FARNSWORTH- Imagine if Mary or Kitty Bennet was a shy, sensitive (and still unmarried) writer...

JANE'S ELDER SISTER, ELEANOR- Imagine if Elizabeth Bennet had never met Mr. Darcy, not yet anyway...

JANE'S ELDEST SISTER, CASSANDRA- Imagine if Jane Bennet had lived happily ever after with Mr. Bingley even sooner, thanks to the lack of a certain gentleman's influence...

CASSANDRA'S HUSBAND, MR. PHILLIPS- Imagine if Bingley was still at Netherfield Park with his young family, but starting to tire of a gentleman's life...

JANE'S YOUNGER SISTER, ISABELLA- Imagine if Lydia Bennet met a handsome and obscenely wealthy Naval officer...

COLIN DARCY- Imagine if Mr. Darcy was a 21st century college professor...

COLIN'S SISTER, BRITTANY- Imagine if Georgiana Darcy was a lively young 21st century college student...

Now imagine if they all met a time travelling rogue named RILEY GRANGER...

TIME

AND

TENACITY

Chapter One: 1815

JANE FARNSWORTH'S HEART STOPPED as the sitting room door creaked open. She tried to fold her writing paper as gently as she could into her needlework bag before her aunt saw it. She had just managed to fit the pages through the rim of her bag when a crash from upstairs startled her. The paper burst out of her hands, fluttering all over the floor.

Lady Jennings picked up a sheet. "Jane, what in the world is this?"

"It is... a letter..."

"Julia sat in bed, trying to recall her strange dream..." Lady Jennings read aloud. She crinkled her nose at the pages of Jane's fair copy, as if they were malodorous. "Jane, I thought we had this settled. Do you want everyone to think your uncle and I do not provide for you?"

"Of *course* not, Aunt Jennings."

"There you go again. It is no wonder you have failed to find a husband unlike your sisters." Lady Jennings threw the two days' worth of work into the fire.

Try not to fight... Jane told herself, her lips quivering. Any day now, if her aunt and gossipy Mrs. Watson, the vicar's wife, were right, she would be engaged to Colonel Finster and would soon be away from Reddings Hall and from under her aunt and uncle's thumb forever. Cautious relief, and hope that the colonel's thumb would be much lighter, filled her.

Alice, the head housemaid, entered the room and curtsied to Jane and Lady Jennings. "Mrs. Troughton wishes to speak with you about the turkey for dinner with Mr. and Mrs. Watson tomorrow night, my lady," she said.

"I will be there in a moment," Lady Jennings said. "Please go do something proper with yourself, Jane," she added on her way out.

Jane looked out the window. Perhaps it was time to make one possible last trip to Honeysuckle Bridge. "I think I will take a walk, Alice," Jane said.

"You know your aunt does not like you walking by yourself, Miss Farnsworth."

"My aunt does not like most of what I do," Jane muttered. "I will not go further than the bridge," she spoke up.

Alice fetched Jane's coat. "Do be prompt, Miss Farnsworth. You do not want to be late for the ball tonight," Alice said.

"I suppose I do not," Jane said. Near the stairs, one of the housemaids— Jane hated that she could never remember their names— was comforting another. Jane heard "the mirror in Miss Farnsworth's room" and stopped.

"It was like a large insect..." the crying housemaid said. "I threw a pillow from Miss Farnsworth's bed at it. The insect disappeared, but the mirror broke."

"It is all right," Jane said. "I never liked that mirror anyway. I will tell my aunt I threw the pillow because Mrs. Watson compared my face to her pug again."

The housemaid curtsied. "Thank you, Miss Farnsworth." It was only by the time Jane had made it outside that she began to ponder what sort of an insect was active in early January.

JANE RAN HER RIGHT hand across the edge of Honeysuckle Bridge, using her left to bundle against the cold air. She tried envisioning she was once again enrapturing her sisters with her stories, back in the days before Cassandra and Eleanor, her older sisters, were too busy and Isabella, her younger sister, was too insufferable.

Those days were as long gone as the honeysuckle, though. Would Colonel Finster like her stories? At seven and thirty years of age, he would probably try not to fall asleep, like he almost did last week at the Harringtons. Maybe their children would like them.

Jane made a little twirl, envisioning herself spinning her adoring children around the room, as her father used to spin her. A few larger twirls followed, the last over a patch of ice. She would have fallen into the half-frozen stream if she hadn't been caught by a stranger dressed in a purple coat and light purple breeches.

"Kind of chilly today for a swim, isn't it?" He helped her up. "You all right, Jane?"

"Yes, thank you." Jane studied the stranger. He had never been at any of the assemblies or balls she attended. His accent didn't sound like he came from anywhere close to her. Jane wasn't even sure he was the type of person Uncle Jennings would call on in the first place, with his disregard for propriety. "I am so sorry, but are we acquainted?"

"Let's just say we will be very soon." The purple-clad man pulled Jane's fair copy out of his pocket, completely intact.

For the first time she could remember, Jane struggled to find the proper words. "Is that my... my... However did you..."

The purple-clad man's face broke into a wide grin upon seeing the shocked look on Jane's. "It's easy when you have a time machine."

"A... a time machine? Whatever in the world is a time machine?"

"Imagine you wanted to have a salad with Julius Caesar or watch the pyramids of ancient Egypt be built. My machine can take you there. Well, it could if I hadn't been stranded here in the past with smallpox and poor dentistry. No offense."

"Stranded?"

"It's a long story. I'll cut to the important part. Your sister Isabella and her husband are in town and your sister Eleanor is hosting a ball for them tonight at Reddings House, if I'm not mistaken."

Everything Jane had been so carefully instructed to do told her to run away from this man, but there was something so captivating about the stranger's voice that kept her standing there and led her to respond: "No, you are not."

"There's something in Eleanor's bedroom that will help me get back to my home in 2015." The stranger handed Jane a small red cylinder with a red light coming out of the end and a clear hollow ball. "Are you listening carefully?"

"Y– yes."

"It's invisible, but it will look like reddish-gold dust when you shine this flashlight on it. The ball, when you press this button, will collect the dust. If you help me, I can take you to the future, where if you want popcorn, you just stick a bag in an oven and two-and-a-half minutes later, you have popcorn!"

Jane looked at the fair copy again. She shook her head as if to clear it out and think rationally again. A machine that could travel to different times? The man, in reality, had to be after her fortune, not as if she had a particularly large one to boast about.

"That is all right, my aunt and uncle are probably looking for me," Jane said.

"Come on! What if I told you in the future you could earn your own money if you wanted? Go wherever you wanted to go without an escort? Marry only if and when you want?"

Jane shoved his hand back in his face. "You presume to know much about what I want, you ill-mannered man."

"Jane Farnsworth, you get back here this instant!" Lady Jennings cried from a distance. Her aunt had to display her own ill manners that very moment. "You have been keeping Alice waiting!"

The purple-clad man bowed and beckoned toward Reddings. "The rest of your life awaits, my lady," he said. Jane gave him a condescending sniff and headed back. She resisted the sentences forming in her mind urging her to turn around for one last glance.

"HAVE A SALAD WITH Julius Caesar, watch the pyramids be built." Jane tried to silence the purple-clad man's voice in her head as Alice dressed her in her freshly-cleaned white gown. Anywhere would be much better than here. No, she told herself, she had a grand future as the Colonel's wife ahead of her. Still, the man's face had seemed so eager... so sincere...

"Whatever has you so down, Jane?" Lady Jennings asked, in an accent more exasperated than concerned.

"I am not so sure I want to marry Colonel Finster anymore. I know you think he is my best chance..."

"He is your *only* chance. If you were even half as handsome or selfless as your sisters, we might be able to consider other options."

Jane's lips quivered again. She wasn't *that* selfish, she told herself, for preferring her stories to conversation and dancing. She looked in the cracked mirror, tucking a wisp of her hair from her weak eyes. She straightened her glasses, if only to get a better look at the face all the ladies in town called "plain." She sighed, knowing she couldn't argue with her aunt about the first part.

EVEN FOR A TRIP of less than two miles, Jane's stomach became sick with every bump in the road Sir Francis's barouche hit. She turned to her uncle. "There was no need for the carriage. I would have gladly walked and given the horses some rest."

"Was your opinion sought after?" Sir Frances Jennings grunted before going back to his newspaper. Those were the only words anyone spoke until the arrival at Reddings House, where Eleanor had lived since her marriage to Frank Jennings,

Sir Francis's nephew and—until his death almost two years before— his heir presumptive.

Cassandra's husband, Mr. Phillips, was enjoying a warm glass of negus and talking with Isabella's husband, Captain Pym, as Thomas, Eleanor's manservant, led Jane into the drawing room. Phillips greeted Jane with a welcoming smile. The Captain greeted her with the same aloof look as always.

Jane looked around the drawing room. "Where is Eleanor?" Two streaks of red flashed through the doors past Thomas. Francis and James, Eleanor's sons, stumbled onto Jane.

"Aunt Jane, Mamma said you are marrying!" Francis said.

"Well, congratulations on your engagement, dear sister!" Phillips said.

"Thank you, Mr. Phillips," Jane said. "Though maybe you should not get too excited until he asks." Jane's heart lightened. Phillips had always been her favorite of her brothers-in-law. "How are your children?"

"The finest in England, as always."

Eleanor and Cassandra raced into the room. "Fly, you are supposed to be setting an example for your brother!" Eleanor said, grabbing James.

Little Fly slipped from her grasp. "We are hunting elephants!"

Eleanor sighed. "He has talked of nothing but elephants since I showed him a picture in Papa's old book."

Jane bent down to her nephew. "Did I ever tell you about the poor elephant whose trunk was too short?" Fly shook his head *no*. "Well, I only tell that story to good little boys who mind their mother and go to bed when they are told." Fly raced into Eleanor's arms. Eleanor mouthed "How clever of you, as always," to Jane and carried Fly and James up to bed.

In the absence of her nephews, Cassandra fretted over Jane. "Dearest, have you had anything to eat all day? Sit down!"

"*You* sit down, Cassy." Jane looked at her sister's heavily pregnant belly. It was pointless to argue. Cassandra had seized the role of mother after Mrs. Farnsworth's death, when Isabella was not six years old. Even after three— four, in a little over a month— children of her own she was reluctant to relinquish it. "Should you not be back at Woodvale Park?"

Mr. Phillips gave Cassandra a knowing smirk. "Why yes, should you not be?"

"I have another week to worry about that," Cassandra said. "I could not miss seeing my sisters."

"Isabella, darling!" Lady Jennings screeched. Isabella entered the drawing room with her usual flourish.

"Aunt Jennings!" Isabella raced to hug her aunt. Jane rolled her eyes. Eleanor and Cassandra exchanged resigned smiles. Their aunt had never made it a secret that high-spirited Isabella was her favorite niece.

"What a beautiful dress!" Lady Jennings said.

"I bought it in Bath! It was perfectly awful, but then my maid and I tore it to pieces." Isabella embraced her sisters. "Oh Jane, you missed the most *extraordinary* assembly last week! I could have chaperoned you, you know."

"That is quite all right." In the two months since Isabella had wed Captain Pym, the dashing hero of the Royal Navy, Isabella was constantly inviting her older sister to Avondale, her estate in Somersetshire, and offering to chaperon her to balls and assemblies as if Jane would ever forgot her sister's new status.

Isabella rested her head on Captain Pym's shoulders. "Cassy, Eleanor, does not my Harry look so handsome in his uniform?"

"Indeed, my love," Cassandra said, not removing her gaze from Phillips's face.

Jane looked on longingly at Cassandra and Isabella and their husbands. Even Eleanor, though a widow, had plenty to be content about with her sons; her comfortable jointure; and her own establishment, at least until three-year-old Fly was of age.

Jane remembered the "flashlight" the purple-clad man had given her. If there was even the smallest chance it were true, then perhaps there was a way out from this. Jane slipped down the hall and up the stairs to the bedroom, trying to figure out how the light came on. She bumped into a portrait of Frank Jennings, looking imposing even in death.

"Sorry Mr. Jennings," Jane murmured. A little speck of white light shone on the floor. It came from the flashlight, which she must have turned on when she bumped into the portrait. She waved the light around the room. Reddish-gold dust floated from Eleanor's bottom-right bed-knob! Jane was once again at a loss for words. She reached her shaking hands into her pocket for the ball.

The dust floated around something white and sweet-smelling. Jane pushed the button as fast as she could, but it was stiff. "Come on!" After four tries, Jane hit it. The dust went into the ball like ants going back into their anthill, making the ball glow.

Jane could hear more voices— more guests arriving for the ball— downstairs. Colonel Finster's carriage was parked outside. Guilt of abandoning her sisters and the colonel intermingled with her excitement. Jane slipped the ball and the flashlight in her gloves and returned to the drawing room.

Jane headed back down the stairs. "Jane, is everything all right?" Cassandra called out from the bottom.

"Yes, I was straightening my hair."

Isabella chortled. "As if that would make it look any less dreadful."

"Isabella!" Cassandra chided.

"She is just having a bit of amusement, Cassandra," Lady Jennings said.

"Oh yes, making sport of your own family is so *excessively* diverting," Eleanor said with sarcasm.

Colonel Finster and his sister, Mrs. Parker, had made it to the drawing room by the time Jane returned. A slightly joyful look of salutation came across the colonel's haggard face as Jane approached him. Next to him, talking to Mrs. Parker, was none other than the purple-clad man.

"Miss Farnsworth, have you had the pleasure of meeting Mr. Granger yet?" Mrs. Parker said.

"Yes, I have, actually."

"That is wonderful!" Mrs. Parker said. "He is the most fascinating young man!"

"I found what you were looking for, Mr. Granger." Jane handed him the device and the reddish-gold ball while the colonel and Mrs. Parker turned to greet Mr. Harrington. Mr. Granger stuck his thumb up in Jane's direction and stashed them in his pocket.

Couples started assembling on the dance floor. "May I have the pleasure of engaging you for the first dance, Miss Farnsworth?" Mr. Granger said.

Jane looked over at the colonel. She couldn't dance with him if she refused Mr. Granger, but she didn't want to slight the lonely colonel and lose his favor. The colonel, still in conversation, nodded that she should go ahead.

Finally, a young gentleman wished to dance with her, and he had to be so ill-mannered. "All right," Jane said, trying to restrain her sigh.

Jane could hear the whispers of almost everyone in the room while she danced with the mysterious purple-clad man. She could see a hint of jealousy in Isabella's eyes, which caused her head to swell a bit.

"I'll stay out on the bridge until half past ten in case you change your mind," Mr. Granger said.

"I told you, I'm happy where I am."

"Jane—"

"*Miss Farnsworth.*"

"*Miss Farnsworth*, I've done some research into you and

your family," Mr. Granger said. "The colonel's not long for this world. You can come with me or die in ten years an old maid, with no one by your side." What impertinence! Jane would have stomped on his foot, but knew what her aunt would say about that.

Jane raced to Colonel Finster's side as soon as the first dance finished. Here was a true gentleman.

The colonel took Jane's arm for the second set of dances. "I must be gentle with you, Miss Farnsworth, I have a slight case of the rheumatism this evening," he said. Isabella, who stood next to her in the set, giggled. Jane looked over at the handsome young Captain Pym and sighed. *I am getting much better than I deserve,* Jane reminded herself.

Jane turned back to her colonel. Instead of beaming like Mr. Phillips or Captain Pym, he looked confused. Jane turned around and realized why.

Three enormous, moth-like creatures with silver, feathery wings flew straight towards her. The other guests nearly knocked each other to the floor to get out of the room. The colonel jumped in front of Jane as one of the insects was about to land on her. The insect jerked back and spat reddish-gold dust at him, causing him to disappear right before everyone's eyes. Captain Pym came back with his hunting rifle and shot at the creatures until they fell on the floor.

Mrs. Parker raced over to the spot where her brother had been. "He always had to be the first on the battle lines."

Jane embraced her, trying to comprehend all that had just happened, and blocking out the realizations barraging their way into her mind. She looked around at the other gentlemen. There would be no others. She would be imprisoned with Aunt and Uncle Jennings for the rest of her life. Or the rest of their lives, at least, and then all would depend upon the resources and charity of her sisters. There was always working as a governess, she supposed, if she had anything of value to teach. In any situation, she would forever be a spectator of other people's happiness rather than a participant.

Maybe she should have gone with Mr. Granger after all. Mr. Granger! Jane stared at the clock. It was half past nine. She only had an hour!

"Wherever are you going, Jane?" Mr. Phillips asked. He and Captain Pym pursued her out of the drawing room, with Jane's sisters close behind. Jane brushed shoulders with Mrs. Blake, causing Captain Pym to run into her and knock her spectacles on the ground.

"Jane, stop!" Eleanor cried.

"Oh Captain, you must help me find my spectacles!" Mrs. Blake cried.

Jane's sisters and Mr. Phillips continued to chase her through the halls. Eleanor almost caught Jane in the vestibule when Fly jumped in front of her.

"Elephant!"

"Francis Jennings, you are supposed to be in bed!" Eleanor said. Fly slowed his family down enough so Jane could make it through the vestibule and out the door.

She was halfway to the bridge when Phillips's carriage began catching up to her. Jane ran all the faster. She didn't stop to keep her hair ornaments from coming loose or even to catch her breath. No... no one was waiting for her at the bridge.

Eleanor sprung out of the carriage before it could even come to a complete stop and grabbed Jane. "Jane, no, please do not jump!" Phillips helped Cassandra and Isabella out of the carriage and they ran to embrace their sister, who had now burst into tears.

"Oh, darling, things have just gone bad for now," Cassandra said. "You will see, things will look up before you know it."

"Cassandra is quite right, dear," Isabella said. "You see, I have not even told Harry yet, but I am going to have a baby in the fall. You can stay with us and teach my children to embroider cushions and play their instruments poorly!"

"Go away! All of you! NOW!" Jane screamed.

A hand attached to a purple coat clasped her shoulder. "I knew you wouldn't be able to resist," Mr. Granger said. He tapped the little ball. Reddish-gold dust came out and swirled around him and Jane.

"What in the world?" Phillips said. He grabbed onto Mr. Granger. Cassandra grabbed on to him, Eleanor grabbed onto Cassandra, and Isabella grabbed onto Eleanor.

"Mamma?" Fly must have sneaked inside Mr. Phillip's carriage.

"Fly, what are you doing here?" Eleanor cried. Jane grabbed onto her nephew the moment before everything went black.

Chapter Two

A BUZZING NOISE WOKE Jane after what felt like a few seconds. Was it those insects again? She straightened her spectacles. Coming toward her was the strangest carriage she had ever seen. It was red and it seemed to be pulling itself, without horses.

The carriage squealed as it stopped right before it was about to hit her. The front left half of the carriage opened and out stepped an unshaven man with unkempt dark brown hair and thick spectacles, wearing a thick jacket opened to reveal a blue undershirt and long blue breeches.

The man ran over to Jane and helped her up. "Are you all right, ma'am? *Ma'am?*"

There was writing on the man's shirt. It said, "Keep Calm, I'm the Doctor." The ball was now in little pieces on the ground. Jane picked them up and examined her surroundings. The park looked the same, but she couldn't see Reddings anywhere. The wooden bridge was gone. She and her sisters and Phillips and Fly were all now stirring on a wide bridge of gray paved stone instead.

"Wherever is my darling Harry?" Isabella screamed.

"Mamma!" Fly cried.

"It is all right, I am right here," Eleanor said, embracing him.

"Where are our children?" Cassandra asked Phillips frantically.

"They still must be back at Woodvale," Phillips said.

"WHAT IN THE NAME OF SANITY ARE YOU FOOLS DOING IN THIS ROAD?" the unkempt man screamed.

"There is no need to shout at us!" Eleanor said.

"Well, just get back on the set of whatever show you came from and don't lie in the middle of a road!" the unkempt man said. "Stupid actors, probably partied all night," he muttered as he got back in his carriage.

Jane had a feeling she would be at a loss for words for quite a while as she watched the man make his carriage drive away. Someone hit her shoulder gently with his fist.

"We made it!" Mr. Granger said. He was now dressed in a purple shirt with the same long blue breeches as the man.

"You mean we really are in the future, Mr. Granger?" Jane asked.

"Indeed we are, and seeing as we are, you can just call me Riley," Mr. Granger said. "We don't stand on such formalities here in 2015."

"2015?" Cassandra's face went white. "Do you mean to tell me we are *two hundred* years in the future?"

"I know, is it not wonderful?" Jane said.

"Are you playing some sort of joke on us, Jane?" Eleanor asked.

"No, of course I am not!" Jane said. If Eleanor didn't believe her, no one would. "We have really traveled in time. Have we not, Mr. Gran- Riley?"

Riley pulled a small, flat black box out of the pocket of his breeches. "We sure have," Riley said. "Just look at the screen." Riley passed the box around to everyone. On it was a picture of the seaside with *the words 7:30 A.M., February 1, 2015* overlaid.

Cassandra threw the calendar back at Riley. "Enough of this! Please take me back to Woodvale."

Riley caught the calendar before it fell. "Okay, just please be careful with my phone. My car should still be here. I hope."

Jane, her sisters, Mr. Phillips and Fly followed Riley down the hill, only Jane and Fly with any sort of eagerness. Another one of those horseless carriages— this one tall, long enough to fit several people, and blue— was parked at the bottom.

"Do not exert yourself, darling," Phillips said, taking Cassandra's hand.

"I will be fine," Cassandra said. "Let us just do whatever we need to go home."

Riley pulled at a latch on the side of the car. The side opened on its own, revealing an inside that looked even cozier than Sir Francis's carriage. Jane took a seat, with Phillips's help, on a cold leather sofa in the back between Eleanor and Isabella. Cassandra and Fly sat in chairs in front of them, while Phillips sat next to Riley in the front.

"Buckle up," Riley said. Everyone looked at him blankly again. Riley sighed and reached over Phillips for a strap. "They're seat belts. You take the strap and fasten the metal thing into this part."

"How many of these carriages do you own?" Isabella asked.

"Well, this one is just a rental," Riley said. "My real car's back home."

"Only one carriage?" Isabella muttered judgmentally. "My Harry has three. Oh, my poor dearest! He must be waking up right now and wondering where I am! We have not spent more than a day apart!"

"He will live," Jane snapped.

"Be compassionate, Jane," Cassandra said. She was probably thinking of her children, Jane realized with some regret.

Riley apparently was the coachman, as he made the carriage move around the park using various levers and a giant wheel. Reddings Hall and Reddings House were completely gone. The only part of the estate Jane could see was the New Mill Farm, which looked long abandoned.

Eleanor held Fly close. "It's like the fairies have taken it," she said. Cassandra took her hand.

"Where is Woodvale Park?" Cassandra asked.

Riley held his "phone" close to his mouth. "Okay Ziggy, we need to get to Woodvale Park," he said. The calendar turned into a small map and a lady's voice told him what roads to go straight on and which roads to turn on.

The route to Woodvale Park was the same as it had ever been, albeit not with such smooth roads, long poles with strings, or other carriages racing around them; but Woodvale Park wasn't surrounded by a large gate. A lady with long gray hair walked out from behind the gate and up to the window. "Sorry, we don't open until noon on Sundays," she told Riley.

"But this is our home!" Phillips cried.

"Very funny," the lady said. "No one has lived here since the house was donated to the National Trust in 1986."

"Where is Reddings Hall?" Eleanor asked.

"Reddings Hall?" the lady asked. "I think it was torn down shortly after World War II."

"War?" Jane asked.

"World?" Eleanor asked.

"*Two*?" Cassandra moaned.

Riley drove the carriage in a small circle and got back on the road. "We really must be in the future," Eleanor said.

"How do we get back home from this awful place?" Isabella cried.

"What makes you so sure that it is so awful?" Jane said. Cassandra sobbed quietly in Phillips's arms. Jane felt terrible for her sisters, but all the same, she had no reason at all to go back to 1815. Maybe this was an even better chance than the colonel.

"Mr. Granger, as f-fascinated as we all are to be in this tremendous place, we all want to go home," Mr. Phillips said.

"Not everyone!" Jane protested.

"The point is, how do those of us who do not wish to be here in wherever this is go back to our homes?" Phillips finished.

"There was that little time machine." Jane showed her family the pieces in her hand.

Isabella stomped her foot. "Must you ruin everything?"

"It's okay, that wasn't the time machine," Riley said. "It was more like a little bit of the fuel. Dr. Bennet has the machine."

"Dr. Bennet?" Jane asked. "Is he the man who stranded you?"

"Correct, sort of. *She* is the woman who stranded me."

"A woman doctor?" Eleanor asked.

"Yes, one of the youngest women to get their Ph.D.'s in Oxford's history," Riley said.

"Oxford," Eleanor whispered, sounding as if her panic was slowly melting into interest.

"So how are we going to get the machine back from her?" Cassandra asked.

"We just have to go to Texas and find where she's keeping it."

"Is Texas your village?" Jane asked.

"It's a state," Riley said.

"Your estate?" Eleanor asked.

"No, it's a state in the United States- um, your former American colonies."

"That will take weeks!" Isabella said with horror.

Riley laughed a small laugh and pulled out Ziggy. "Actually, thanks to the Wright brothers, we'll be there by supper tonight. Let's grab a quick bite and I'll try to get us on the next flight." Everyone stared at him like he was talking in Greek. "I mean, let's go get some breakfast and I'll make all the travel arrangements."

 BASINGSTOKE DIDN'T SEEM LIKE the same place Cassandra had gone to get her shoe-roses only two days before, with the wider streets, the shops with unfamiliar names, and the strangely dressed people. This must have been how old Rip Van Winkle from her father's bedtime story felt; only he was fortunate enough to miss only twenty years, not two hundred.

Her husband, sisters, and nephew— seemingly forgetting their manners— asked Mr. Granger questions about the shops and the people all at once. Cassandra would have joined them if the thought of Cassy, Ned, and little baby Charlotte back at Woodvale all alone did not occupy the chief of her thoughts. She couldn't wait to dry their tears and assure them their Mamma and Papa were all right.

Mr. Granger, in the meantime, drove out of the city, finally stopping in a paved field with other carriages in front of a large glass building with a sign that said "Welcome Break." Everyone got out and stretched their legs.

"I'll get breakfast," Mr. Granger said. "Why don't you go to the toilets and change your clothes so you don't look like you stepped out of some BBC costume drama anymore?" He pulled a suitcase from the back of the carriage and handed them each a long piece of cloth, each a different solid color, from inside. "Put these Chameleon Cloths on and you'll blend in."

The inside of the building looked like an enclosed village, with some of the same shop names Cassandra remembered from their drive through town. Everyone was dressed similar to the irritated Doctor who had nearly run them over. Some stared at them, a few others smiled awkwardly, and a few whispered. Mr. Granger showed them to a room in the back.

"Where is the toilette?" Isabella asked. A girl who looked to be about eight or nine, who was running her hands under a loud wind-producing device, looked at them as if they were crazy.

"It must be behind this door." Jane closed the door of a small private room, only for it to fly open again.

"Here, let me help you," the girl said. She showed them how to lock the small room, empty the large white chamber pot inside by pushing a silver handle, and wash their hands in a constantly flowing basin. "Do you work at the museum? Your dress is very lovely."

"We... are from a show," Jane said.

Another girl, who looked about two years older, stuck her head through the slightly opened door. "Kaitlyn, what is taking you so long?" she asked. "Everyone else is in the car!"

"I've got to go home now," Kaitlyn said. "It was really nice to meet you!"

The sisters all struggled in the small room to take their many layers off, as well as little Fly's. Cassandra very much regretted ever thinking Hodges, her lady's maid, was too slow. She struggled to pull the long pink cloth over her swollen body, wondering when she was ever going to wake up from this feverish dream.

"Here, we mothers need to help each other." Isabella grabbed the pink cloth and helped Cassandra pull it all around her body. Cassandra helped Isabella with her cloth and they went back to the mirror.

"I am wearing nothing but a slip!" Isabella said. She indeed appeared to be wearing a white long-sleeved dress that didn't even cover her knees. Cassandra gasped. She was dressed similarly, though her dress was pink.

"Aunt Jennings would die in fright if she saw you

dressed so immodestly," Eleanor said.

"And you wearing breeches!" Cassandra said, staring at Eleanor's green knitted shirt and blue breeches that went down to her brown shoes.

"You should see Jane," Eleanor said.

Cassandra admired Eleanor's shirt. "It is good to see you in such bright colors again." Eleanor smiled and adjusted the collar on Fly's shirt.

"Are you sure we can be seen in public like this?" Isabella said. "We are practically naked!"

"This does seem to be what others are wearing," Eleanor said. "Be patient, darling, you will be home soon."

Cassandra met Edward, who was wearing a blue collared shirt like Fly's and pants, outside of the toilets. It was like they had met for the first time all over again. A rush of joyful serenity came over Cassandra. The assembly where Mrs. Parker introduced them to each other, came back to her; back when the whole world, like her pregnant belly, seemed ripe to burst with possibility.

Jane followed Cassandra out of the toilets, wearing a yellow muslin shirt with long sleeves and long light yellow breeches. "You look very handsome, Jane, as folks from your time would say," Riley said. Jane looked taken aback. Cassandra had been called handsome plenty of times, and Eleanor and Isabella had claimed their fair share of compliments as well, but Cassandra fretted if Jane ever had. "You all look great. Well, I've got some dough-nuts, and us on the flight to DFW leaving at noon." He put their old clothes back in the suitcase and led them to the table. Ring-shaped rolls with small colorful pieces of something sprinkled on them were set out, along with cups of coffee and a bottle of milk for Fly.

Cassandra sat down, gingerly took the roll, and brought it slowly to her mouth. There was so much sugar, it made the insides of her nose hurt. She drank the coffee to wash the sugary roll down. A man at the next table was reading a newspaper. She caught a glimpse of some of the headlines: "epidemic", "murders", "war". All of a sudden, Cassandra felt numb to everything, even the coffee still in her mouth.

"This has to be the best cup of coffee I have had in years!" Edward said.

"And these dough-nuts taste so pleasant!" Jane said.

"Would you like another one?" Riley said.

"You do not need to spare so much expense on me," Jane said.

"It's okay," Riley said. "Last I checked I had almost five million dollars."

"Five million?" Isabella asked.

"Yeah, it's easy when you have- well, had- a time machine and know how to make the right investments." He backed his chair up with a screech and got up to walk towards a little shop with pictures of bread and cups of coffee in the windows. Nobody else must have noticed or cared about the newspaper.

"Are we sure we want to follow Mr. Granger so blindly?" Edward said as soon as Riley was out of earshot.

Cassandra tried to ignore the numbness. "We have to get home somehow."

Edward took her hand. "Of course we do, dearest."

"Aren't you even the slightest bit curious?" Jane asked.

"Go play with Fly if you are to be a child about this, Jane!" Isabella snapped. She beckoned over to their nephew, who was rolling his empty milk bottle around.

"Isabella, that is completely unnecessary," Cassandra said.

"Listen to her, she talks as if she is on a grand tour!" Isabella said. "I have a husband and an establishment to get back to."

"Why do we not just all go to Texas and then we can sort out who wants to go and who wants to stay?" Eleanor asked. "I am sure our houses and families will be fine until then. Other than St. John the Apostle, how many people do we know who have actually seen the future?"

Chapter Three

"ARE THOSE BIRDIES?" FLY pointed to the large metal winged machines that soared over them. "Are they going to take us to Amarraca?"

"Fly, Mr. Granger needs a chance to talk," Eleanor said.

"No worries, Eleanor," Riley said. "I enjoy children."

"I enjoy children too," Jane said wistfully.

"As do I," Isabella said. "I cannot wait for mine to arrive!" She rubbed her stomach excitedly. Jane rubbed her stomach in sadness. All she had was indigestion from the three dough-nuts.

"That was incredible," Eleanor said. "We must have traveled forty miles in less than an hour without stopping!"

Riley grinned. "Yes, Mr. Henry Ford and his friends did make the trip a lot faster."

"Is the future not wonderful?" Jane asked.

"I would like to go lie down," Cassandra said.

"You can sleep on the plane," Riley said. He drove up next to a sign with "Car Rentals" written on it. "Now, it's really important that you do everything I say."

"I traveled with my father to France during the Treaty, I should mention," Phillips said.

"Yes, but that was two hundred years ago and the slightest misunderstanding can get you arrested here, at best." Riley handed them all little red booklets. "Here are your passports. Keep them close to you and give them to who-ever asks you for them."

Eleanor shrieked. Inside was her name and picture. "How did you make these?"

"A little Chameleon cloth goes a long way," Riley said.

Eleanor examined the book. "How can a cloth trick people into thinking it is paper?" she asked, but Mr. Granger was already out of the car.

"HOORAY!"

It hadn't taken more than two minutes for Fly to find a new toy, a large metal cart that he was about to take for a ride up and down the long vestibule while Mr. Granger was pressing a picture about tickets and bags to "check in." Eleanor pulled Fly away from the cart before a mountain of large suitcases fell on him.

"Now, dearest Fly, you must behave when we are travel-ing." *He will not mind me if I cannot pay attention myself,* Eleanor thought, trying not to be captivated by the picture in front of her listing the different possible destinations: Dublin; Vienna; Barcelona; and places she had never even heard of, like Beijing or Auckland. She had dreamed of visiting other countries, like Edward, but she never thought she would actually make it much further than York, let alone in a machine that could fly.

"Okay, are everyone's pockets empty?" Mr. Granger said. "We're going to go through security now. Just hand your passports to the security agents; smile as much as pos-sible, but not too wide; and say 'Have a nice day.'"

It all went according to Mr. Granger's plan until Fly caught a glimpse of people walking into a glass enclosure. Fly clung to Eleanor's leg. "What is that thing?" he whimpered.

"It's okay, it won't hurt you," Mr. Granger said. "It just wants to look under your clothes." Fly burst into tears right in front of the security guard. Everyone behind them in line groaned. A few even shouted some very nasty words.

"What is it with today?" the man behind Eleanor said. His eyes looked almost afraid when he saw Eleanor. Eleanor had no idea why the man was staring at her in that way until she recognized the writing on his shirt. It was the same unkempt man who had nearly hit them with his carriage earlier that day.

The man took a deep breath. "May I go before your son?" he asked. Eleanor nodded. The man walked backwards into the machine. He smiled and stuck up his thumbs at Fly. "See it won't hurt you a bit." Eleanor nodded her thanks to the man and went through the machine. She tried to make out the character of the man, who was now hastening away as fast as he could. Despite his inelegant appearance, perhaps he was actually a gentleman.

Mr. Granger yanked Eleanor away as she was grabbing her shoes. "Come on, they just announced the final boarding for our flight," he said. He pushed everyone through the crowded airport.

"Oh, look at that dress!" Isabella said.

"Come on!"

"Look at all those books!" Jane said.

"Come on! You can see lots more later!"

Mr. Granger continued to push them through a long windy hallway. "Where is the birdie?" Fly said.

Eleanor picked up Fly. "We will see." They walked into a noisy, narrow carriage. A woman shoved Eleanor to get to her seat.

"Okay, Eleanor and Fly are right here," Riley said. "Cassandra, Edward and Isabella are behind them. Jane and I will be in the aisle near the back." Riley said. Eleanor sat Fly down, trying to keep him from squirming or bouncing.

"Excuse me, I think I have that window seat." The unkempt man stared at Eleanor, shaking his head in disbelief.

"Hello again... again." He turned to Fly, forcing a smile. "Have you ever been on an airplane before?"

"No, we traveled through time!" Fly said.

Eleanor grabbed his shoulder. "Fly, please do not..." She did not exactly know why or if they needed to keep their time travel such a great secret. Perhaps, not unlike Edward, she harbored some mistrust of Mr. Granger herself.

"Well, would like to sit by the window then?"

"That is so kind of you, sir."

"My pleasure," the man said. "Anything to make this flight less insufferable," he muttered under his breath. "Would you let me stow my bag overhead?" He struggled to push the heavy lump of cloth in. As uncouth as he was, he had helped Eleanor, so Eleanor decided to return the favor. A piece of paper was attached to the handles of the lump.

"Colin Darcy? Is that your name?"

"Yes, and yes, that's my actual name, I promise; it's not just something I use to pick up ladies." He laughed nervously and shifted his head.

"It is a pleasure to meet you, Mr. Darcy," Eleanor said. "My name is Eleanor Jennings." Eleanor could hear her aunt lecturing about how she was supposed to be properly presented to a man before addressing him. Maybe it was time to test how different things really were in the future. Mr. Granger had presented himself to them without any reservations, after all.

"Nice to meet you, Eleanor," Mr. Darcy said. "Though if you want to be that proper, it's actually Dr. Darcy."

"Oh, yes, your shirt."

Dr. Darcy looked perplexed. He looked down at his shirt. "Oh yeah. My sister gave it to me last year when I got my Ph.D."

"What did you..."

Before Eleanor could ask him what subject his doctorate was in, Dr. Darcy grabbed a phone like Mr. Granger's, only smaller and flatter, out of his jacket pocket. It was the same blue color as his shirt with a white two-pronged tail. He put the ends of the tail into his ears and spread out over the seat, like Frank's younger brother Richard when he had had too much to drink. *I must have made him out all wrong,* Eleanor thought. She grabbed a glossy magazine from the seat in front of her to distract Fly.

The plane slowly moved forward. "I thought this thing was supposed to fly," Isabella said.

"Give it a while, it's still on the runway," Riley said. He helped Isabella fasten her seatbelt. People in a moving, talking picture in front of her sang about "flotation devices" and "emergency exits."

"Landing *in the ocean*?" Cassandra said softly. Eleanor reached over and held her hand.

A uniformed woman walked up to Riley. "Sir, please take your seat, I'll help them," she said. Riley took a nervous look in Eleanor's direction and quickly complied.

Finally, the plane ascended into the air. Eleanor held on to Fly, both of them frightened and excited.

"Are we going to heaven? Are we going to meet Papa?" Fly asked so loud that everyone in the plane could hear. Eleanor shushed him. Dr. Darcy gave a disgusted sigh and turned over. Eleanor looked up to the clouds. It did seem for a moment like they could meet Frank. Eleanor could imagine him embarrassing her in front of her friends or lecturing her like she was a little girl once more.

 JANE PAGED THROUGH THE colorful Sky Mall catalog, wondering what noise-canceling headphones were. The woman in the picture was resting so peacefully. Jane realized she had never really gone to bed in between the ball and finding herself in the middle of the road that morning. She yawned and struggled to adjust the flimsy pillow on the stiff seat. The "Dr. Pepper"

the flight attendant had given her was starting to make her nerves feel tight.

"Having trouble sleeping?" Riley asked. He handed her a blanket and a thin head brace like the "headphones" in the catalog. "Watch the movie with me, it's kind of cute. It's one of those cartoons for kids." Jane could hear talking come from the ends as he helped her put them on. It matched up with the mouths of the people on the moving picture.

Jane intended to watch a bit, but she ended up enchanted by the images on the screen. It was even more captivating than any of her stories. It was the story of Princess Lily, an adventurous princess who turned into a bird after touching a magic feather and got lost in a forest as a blizzard approached. Princess Myrtle— her more reserved, fearful sister— turned into a bird as well and had to learn to fly with the help of an enchanted prince, some fairies, and a flying squirrel in order to rescue her sister. Jane wiped a few tears from her eyes as the words *The End* came on the screen.

"Remind you of your own sisters?" Riley asked.

"When we were younger, perhaps," Jane said. "Not now, and probably never again. Do you have any brothers or sisters?"

"Nope, only child," Riley said. "I had a friend I met studying at Oxford— his name was Nate— who was like a brother to me. He was English like you, from Kent. He was getting his doctorate in history, so he was kind of like the historical adviser on Dr. Bennet's time travel project."

"Project?"

"Yeah, I built the time machine and the three of us did scientific and historical research together, until Dr. Bennet left both him and me stranded. I don't even know what era he's in. He could have been eaten by a dinosaur by now for all I know."

"Why did she ever do such a horrible thing?"

"Time travel takes powerful stuff, and great power is pretty darn desirable."

Another movie showed up on the screen, this one about a man and a woman from the former American colonies who bought houses to fix them up and sell them to others. Jane's nerves loosened with Riley around. She looked out the window at the vast, sparkling ocean and fell asleep.

A FEW ROWS AWAY from Jane, Cassandra stirred. Edward, barely awake himself, kissed her hand.

She would have known by now, he realized. He wanted to tell her after the ball; to give her one more night of untainted joy.

"Darling..." Edward loosened his stiff feet. "Remember when I said I needed to tell you something?"

"Yes, what is it?" Cassandra said.

"Fly!" Eleanor cried from the row in front of Edward and Cassandra. Fly was playing with a blue phone he had taken from the now-no-longer-sleeping Dr. Darcy's hands.

Edward unbuckled his seatbelt and grabbed the box from Fly. "Why don't you give your mother a chance to rest? You can sit next to Aunt Cassy for a while." Eleanor nodded her thanks; she and Cassandra helped Fly to Edward's seat.

Edward turned the phone around to find a screen with words. It was a poem by Walter Scott, who Edward noted had become *Sir* Walter sometime in the intervening two hundred years.

"How wonderful!" Edward said.

"Yeah, it's okay," Dr. Darcy said. "The battery life is pitiful. You thinking about buying one?"

"Yes, I am," Edward said quickly. "May I take a look at it?"

Dr. Darcy's mouth went rigid, like Cassandra's whenever anyone asked to hold their children, but he finally relinquished it. Edward pressed a small arrow in the corner and rows of miniature artworks appeared on the screen. He pressed a picture of a young man and a young lady writing to each other titled *The Gate of the Year*. Another story, one about a young girl named Maggie working on a farm, popped up. He touched the right side of the screen and it changed as if he had turned a page in a book.

"How fascinating!" Edward said. Hoping he wasn't opening himself too much to awkward questions, he quickly added, "The story, I mean."

"It's not one of his better works. Andrews was a lot better writing history than fiction. You like David Andrews?" Noticing Edward's hesitation, Darcy added: "Yeah, he's not as famous as Tolkien or Lewis, but he's probably my favorite of the Inklings. His account of the Battle of Hastings was brilliant." Edward was still hesitant. "You've never heard of the Inklings, either."

"I have heard of the Battle of Hastings." Edward remembered Mr. Hartnell's, his tutor's, engaging accounts.

"The Inklings were a group of authors who met at a pub in Oxford and read each other's works."

"How interesting." Edward had always wanted to go to Oxford, but his family had decided he should tour Europe instead. "May I read this?"

"I can do even better." Darcy reached into his bag and gave Edward a hard copy of the same book. Edward handed the phone back to Darcy in return. Darcy put his headphones back on and clutched the phone close to him.

Edward read the first ten chapters in thirty minutes. It turned out Maggie lived on a farm in the Cotswolds in 1941 because of some war, and had found a way to write to Peter, a young man who lived in the same house in 1965, through her diary, which had been granted some powers of time travel through her floorboard. Edward's mind became slightly unnerved as he read, wondering how time travel had become such a major part of his life all of a sudden. What if it wasn't a random occurrence that they had met Mr. Granger?

The flight attendants were coming toward their row with trays full of hot food. "I had better get back to my seat," Edward said.

"Oh, yeah," Darcy said. Edward handed him the book back. "It's okay, I have two more copies. I don't even remember where I got this one from."

"Thank you so much," Edward said.

"No problem, anything for a future Andrews fan."

Edward sat back down next to Cassandra. "So what was it you needed to tell me, darling?" she asked him.

"Oh... just that I have the finest wife in England, that's all."

Cassandra laughed and kissed Edward's cheek. He should wait until they were alone to tell her after all, he told himself. For now, he had a fascinating book to read.

Chapter Four

ISABELLA TOSSED AND TURNED in her uncomfortable seat, trying to rest her head on the flimsy pillow. Her dearest Harry probably had to put up with worse in his days on the ship, though she was hardly naval material.

She must have finally fallen asleep, because for a moment she thought her beloved captain was shaking her awake, to tell her it had all been a horrible dream. It was one of those awful flight servants instead.

"Miss, we are about to land," she said. "Please stow your tray."

"That's *Mrs.* Pym, please," Isabella snapped. The servant had already moved on.

Isabella looked out the window. Beautiful green spaces of land were flanked with some of the most massive buildings she had ever seen. She arrested her fascination by reminding herself that Harry wasn't enjoying the sight with her. She closed her eyes and imagined him holding her hand.

"Have you ever seen anything so amazing?" she asked him in a whisper.

"No, I have not." It was Mr. Phillips, not her Harry, who had replied. Isabella regained her composure.

Isabella shifted her feet as the plane touched down on the ground and pulled up to another long gate. Everyone hastened to get off as soon as the flight servant told them they were free to. Isabella would have joined them if she didn't pride herself so much on being a lady.

Isabella rushed past her family through another noisy tube. "This way," Mr. Granger called to her. They went all the way down a long hall only to find yet another line behind three men in glass boxes. The baby would be walking by the time they got out.

"Next please," the man in the middle box finally said.

"Okay, let me handle im-." Mr. Granger started, but Isabella charged ahead.

"Passport?" the man asked.

"Oh yes." Isabella pulled out the passport Mr. Granger had made.

"British girl," the man said. "What brings you to Dallas?"

"I am trying to return to my husband," Isabella said.

"Is he an American?"

"No, he is..."

Mr. Granger quickly pulled Isabella aside. "He's been living here for a while."

Finally, after the man stopped asking Mr. Granger so many forward questions, they made it through the gate into another crowded terminal. Isabella was too tired to look at the shops this time. Bath's were better anyway, she was sure. She and her family, once Eleanor got a hold of Fly, followed Riley to a large concrete room of carriages where another horseless carriage, this one red and bulky with a large open trunk, was parked.

"Sorry, everyone except Cassandra is going to have to squeeze in the back of the truck," Mr. Granger said. Isabella shrieked as Jane and Eleanor, with Fly on her lap, crushed her to let Phillips in.

"Are we going to see Dr. Bennet now?" Isabella asked impatiently.

"Do you not want to rest awhile?" Edward asked.

"Do you not want to see your children?" Isabella snapped back. "I have had enough rest to last a lifetime."

"Well, I can't just go to the woman who left Nate and me stranded and say, 'Hey, give me my time machine back,'" Mr. Granger said.

"Well, then why do we not just take it from her?" Isabella asked.

"That would be stealing, Belle," Eleanor said.

"Papa was the vicar, not you," Isabella said. "She left poor Mr. Granger stranded. I do not see why we must play fair."

"The machine is protected by a device that scans people's eyes," Mr. Granger said. "I can't access it, but you and your sisters might, seeing as you're her family."

"Her family?" Isabella asked.

"Dr. Bennet just so happens to be your great-great-great-great-great-great granddaughter, Isabella."

Isabella rubbed her belly in shock. The baby inside her would one day be the father or mother (or aunt or uncle-- she and Harry were going to have a large family after all) to someone who would be the father or mother to someone else &c, and she would be meeting this descendant?

"All right, where is this... great-great-great-great-great niece of mine?" Cassandra asked, shivering herself at the thought.

"She's about a forty-five minute drive from here," Riley said. He pulled out onto the widest road Isabella had ever seen.

"We're not going to her now, are we?" Jane asked.

"Of course not," Riley said. "She does research at a local university. You can stay at my place and we'll figure out how to get to her and the machine."

"SORRY THERE'S ONLY ONE bathroom. And not much to eat. Or a working clothes dryer." Riley led Jane and the others through the door of a house the size of the drawing room at Reddings Hall to what must be the house's own drawing room, or at least where the sofas were.

"It is perfectly delightful," Jane said. She ran her fingers across the keys of the pianoforte and then turned to look out the front window where she could see a tree-lined lake— which she believed Riley had called "White Rock Lake" as they were passing it in the car— and the enormous buildings of Dallas in the distance. "Is this your house?"

"Well, actually it's my landlady's, Mrs. Milner's," Riley said. "She's on a cruise in the Bahamas with her sister. I live out in the back in a garage apartment. There wouldn't be enough room for all of us to stand, let alone sleep."

"Why do you live in such a small place if you have so much money?" Isabella asked.

"I've found it's best not to flaunt it. People ask too many questions that way." Riley showed them through a small, plain dining room into a room with light brown stone floors; cabinets of all sizes, shapes, and colors topped with what looked to be marble; and strange devices like Jane had seen in the magazine on the airplane. Jane turned off and on the sink under the window, like in the toilets where they had changed clothes. Fly pushed a button on the base of a glass cup, setting off a loud whirring noise.

"Careful, that blender's brand new," Riley said. "So, this is the kitchen if you ever want a drink or snack. It's probably changed the most since you last went in one, if you've ever been in one."

"Not since helping my mother in the vicarage," Eleanor said. "Where is the fireplace?"

"Right here," Mr. Granger said. He opened the door of

a large metal cabinet and turned a knob to turn the fires on.

"I do not know what my cook would think," Eleanor said.

"Yes, I'm sure she would either cry or faint." Riley led them down a narrow hall to a bedroom with a medium-sized bed. "Cassandra and Edward can sleep here." He pointed to bedroom next door. "Eleanor, you and Fly can sleep on the trundle beds in the guest bedroom. Jane and Isabella can sleep on the couch in the living room."

"There is a *living* room?" Jane asked. Riley led them back to the drawing room and pointed to the ragged brown sofa.

"How are Jane and I to fit on that?" Isabella asked.

Riley took the seat of the sofa off in two pieces, tossing them over by the piano, and pulled out a thin bed. Isabella sighed. "It does not look very comfortable."

"You are not this rude to your hosts in Somersetshire, are you?" Jane asked.

"At least I get invited," Isabella said.

"Is your cook preparing dinner?" Eleanor spoke up with a measure of weariness.

"No cook, but I'll go pick up some barbecue from the place down the street," Riley said. "And it looks like we made it in time for the Super Bowl."

"What is the Super Bowl?" Jane asked.

"It's the championship game for professional football teams." Riley turned on a picture frame like the one on the airplane, except this was one was larger, flatter, and more rectangular. A woman slicing a cake came on the screen. He pressed some buttons on a small, long black stick and some numbers and dashes appeared on the top of the screen.

"What is Foot Ball?" Cassandra asked.

"It's a game... you Brits would probably call it American football... except you don't since it won't be invented for about another hundred years from you..." The picture changed to a movie of bulky men throwing a brown, oddly shaped ball to each other.

Riley pulled his phone out of his pocket and pressed some buttons. "Here, Wikipedia should help you catch up on the last two hundred years." He handed it to Cassandra. "Here, just type in whatever you want to know and press the 'Okay' button on the screen... it's that small gray one."

"Oh, look up 'Henry Pym'!" Isabella cried happily. "My darling Harry must have books written on him!"

Cassandra looked at the "Wikipedia", feeling numb once more. "What am I supposed to do again?"

Riley tried to keep his grin as he sighed. "This is like teaching my grandmother. Here, first press the button that says 'H'- it's right there in the middle- no, it's that one over there- don't forget to shift... actually it doesn't matter that much..."

After much trial and error, Cassandra typed in "HenRy pym" with the miniature letters and pressed the gray box on the screen. "All I can find is a fellow who goes by 'Ant-Man'," she said.

"Well, unless your captain is a comic book character who can talk to ants, I don't think that's him," Riley said. Jane tried not to laugh. Cassandra, tiring of a device she could not understand, handed the phone to Jane and instead propped her legs up on the couch along with Isabella . Jane didn't know where to begin. What other sports did people play? Who was the king of England? What was Dr. Bennet's first name?

"Why are all the people cheering?" Cassandra said.

"That guy's just about to make a touchdown," Riley said. The picture changed to an image of a dog chasing its tail while disembodied voices laughed and changed again to a ticking clock.

"Fly, stop that!" Eleanor cried. Fly had found the same set of buttons Riley had pressed earlier.

"Elephants!" Fly cried. A bunch of elephants were grazing on the screen, while a Scottish man standing somewhere in the distance where Jane couldn't see him talked about their habitats.

"Fly, let Mr. Granger watch his game." Eleanor gave him a stern look.

"This is fine too," Riley said. "I've always wondered about where elephants live."

"La, I am so thirsty!" Isabella cried. "Riley, can you ring your servant for a drink?"

"Sorry, no servants here, we're all about self-service here at Casa Milner," Riley said.

"Then you fetch me a drink, Jane."

"You heard what Riley said!" Jane said indignantly.

Isabella simpered. "When you are having a baby, I will fetch your drinks."

"You wicked thing!" Jane bolted from the couch and to Eleanor's room. She slammed the phone on the table so hard, the screen cracked and the image became scattered colors.

"Well, it's a good thing I just paid that off," Riley said.

"Oh, for heaven's sake, I will fetch the drinks!" Eleanor said.

Eleanor followed Mr. Granger to the kitchen, where he showed her to a large white humming cabinet where green metal cylinders with "Canada Dry" written on them were stacked inside.

"It's probably none of my business, but why do you let Isabella walk all over you guys?" Mr. Granger asked.

"Why would we ever let Isabella walk on us?"

"Oh, um, I mean why do you allow Isabella to be so..."

"Indulged?"

"Yeah."

"I do fail to see how that is any of your 'business.'"

"Sorry."

Eleanor examined the drinks. "She was always sickly as a child. I suppose we were too afraid of losing her, and losing another piece of my mother along with her. Cassandra especially could not say no to her after my father died. I am probably too much of the same to my sons."

Isabella screamed from the living room. Eleanor knocked the cans on the floor. She and Mr. Granger met Jane as she was racing from the bedroom, and the three raced into the living room.

Everyone else was huddled behind a chair; Fly and Cassandra crying. "It's another one of those insects!" Isabella said.

"That's not an insect, it's a drone," Riley said. The insect shot reddish-gold dust straight at Riley. Riley stepped out of the way, but the dust hit the TV screen, causing it to disappear like Colonel Finster had.

"Well, it's a good thing Mrs. Milner doesn't watch a lot of TV," Riley sighed.

The drone turned in Isabella's direction. Jane grabbed a large wooden stick with "Texas Rangers World Series 2011" written on it that was lying against the pianoforte and beat the drone with it until it crashed to the floor.

"Nice job, Jane!" Riley said. Dust swirled around the drone, making it disappear. "Don't touch it!" Riley told Eleanor.

"Why in the world are there drones after you?" Cassandra said.

"Well... it may be that another two hundred years down the road, some folks don't take too kindly to time travelers," Riley said. "So they send these drones here to round them up and destroy them."

"Destroy them?" Cassandra asked. "Is that what

happened to poor Colonel Finster?"

"Unfortunately yes," Riley said.

"How grand," Isabella said. "You could have not just stayed at the ball, Jane?"

"Why is this my fault?" Jane said. "You did not need to come along."

Cassandra's face fell. "You mean you would have gladly left us all forever without a second thought?"

"Why not?" Jane said. "You all left me."

"So now it is our fault for not remaining at Reddings Hall with you?" Isabella snapped. Cassandra trembled for a moment and grabbed her belly, crying again. Jane lay her head down, silently chastising herself for once again for her thoughtlessness.

"Why don't you all sit down and rest?" Riley said. "I'll go ahead and grab dinner." *I will be more considerate after I eat,* Jane told herself.

"I suppose I will go dress *myself* for dinner," Isabella said.

"Why, what's wrong with what you're wearing now?" Riley said.

ISABELLA AND HER FAMILY sat on the couch for the next half-hour, quietly drinking their ginger ales. Finally, Mr. Granger arrived with a large brown bag. "Dinner's here!" he cried.

Jane hastened to the front of Isabella as the family entered the dining room. Isabella cleared her throat to remind Jane of her new position. Jane sighed and took her place behind Isabella.

"Why are we all here, Mr. Granger?" Isabella asked once everyone had served themselves.

"Well, once upon a time there was a brilliant scientist named Gillian Bennet who grew up in Moseley, Birmingham listening to a neighbor's stories about little pockets of energy that, almost like magic, could transport people and things to the past and the future. She devoted her whole life to finding as many of the little pockets as she could, even though many of her colleagues laughed at her and dismissed the scientific validity of her work..."

Isabella tried hard to focus, even though the spices in the sauce were burning her mouth. "Mrs. Chapman would never massacre a pork roast this way," she imagined Harry saying. Isabella ate another roll and pushed the rest of her plate aside.

Jane, meanwhile, listened intently to Riley's every word. "She went on to get her Ph.D. when she was only twenty-four," Riley said. "With the help of her research assistants, she looked all over the world for the little pockets, collecting them in little orbs like the one at Reddings House."

"Wait a moment, one of them was at Reddings House?" Eleanor asked. Jane looked down at her pulled pork.

"As I said, they're everywhere," Riley said. "Well, anyway, I worked with her to develop a machine. She had collected enough pockets that she could travel virtually anywhere she wanted. But then she took my machine and left me and Nate stranded in the past."

"So how are we going to going to find the machine?" Cassandra asked.

"This might be a good starting point." Riley handed her a piece of paper. On it was a drawing of a black-and-white dog and someone's messy handwriting:

My dearest C, E, J, & I,

Please go to Willis Hall room 333 as soon as possible. There is something in my office I need you to bring to me.

Yours &c, G. B.

"Willis Hall?" Edward asked. "Is that her home?"

"No, it's a building at the university," Riley said. "She wants to meet you in her office."

"But what if I don't want to find the machine?" Jane said.

"You have to help us, Jane!" Isabella said. "Cassandra, tell her she has to help us!"

"Please do not involve me, darling, I am getting a splitting headache."

"I do not see any reason why Jane has to help us," Eleanor spoke up. "I am rather curious myself to see more of the future while we're here."

"She is just jealous because I have descendants and she does not."

"How do you know I will not?" Jane asked.

Isabella sniffed. "You are almost four-and-twenty. You are practically an old maid."

"You're only 23?" Riley asked. He laughed as Jane nodded yes.

"Isabella," Eleanor reprimanded with a whisper.

"No, it's just... you're hardly an old maid, at least not in 2015," Riley said. "Lots of people don't get married until they're in their thirties or even forties."

"But I will die one, as I believe you said," Jane said.

Her sisters and Phillips looked at her in shock. "Jane, dear, are you sick?" Cassandra asked.

"No, I am fine, he just said if I didn't go... I would die an old maid in ten years with none of you by my side." Even Isabella looked taken aback.

Riley took her hand. "That's not going to happen now. The important thing is that you are here." Jane looked in Riley's face, wondering if he meant more than mere comfort.

"I had better clear the table," Eleanor spoke up. "Fly, would you pick up the forks?"

"How about a brandy and a nice game of whist?" Phillips said.

"I can round up some cards, but how about Dr. Pepper instead of brandy for now?" Riley asked.

"There is that pianoforte in the living room," Eleanor said. "I have not practiced in years, but I can see if I can play a bit for you."

"I will put on some tea," Cassandra said.

"*I'll* put on some tea, Cassandra, you sit down," Riley said.

Eleanor sat down at the pianoforte and played her father's favorite song. Edward helped Cassandra sit down on the couch. Jane was about to take a seat next to them when Riley took her by the hand and bowed to her. Jane curtsied back.

Isabella sulked. "Why do I not get a dance?"

"When you are not having the baby, you can dance," Jane said.

"Jane!" Cassandra chided, but she couldn't help letting out a small laugh as well.

Riley led her down the room. Jane tried to ignore the glare on Isabella's face and tried to focus instead on the beaming on Eleanor and Cassandra's. Her instincts were telling her Riley was too good to be true, not after all the hurt she had caused. Still, she couldn't ignore the joy she felt being near to him.

Chapter Five

FOR THE FIRST TIME, Jane missed something back home: a comfortable bed. She tossed and turned on the rigid mattress that Riley had pulled out from the couch, covering her head to avoid Isabella's incoherent sleep prattling.

"How does the Captain tolerate this?" she muttered under her breath. Someone stirred on the other side of the wall. She got up and followed the light to find Riley in the kitchen looking around the shelves.

"Hey, impeccable timing! Want to see that microwave popcorn?" Riley stuck a flat bag in what looked like the television, but had a handle and was hollow inside. He pressed a few buttons, making the inside of the machine light up and hum. The bag expanded within minutes. Riley pulled out the bag carefully when it beeped and, as he had said, popcorn came pouring out of the bag when he tipped it into a purple bowl.

Jane took a handful and examined it. "This is amazing." She put some in her mouth and sat down on the small kitchen table.

Riley handed her a thick book with a shiny brown cover. "I found my old world history textbook from college. Maybe this will help you catch up."

Jane read the book until the first hints of dawn slipped into the kitchen window. She couldn't believe all that had transpired since 1815. There had been horrible wars and devastating tragedies, but also amazing innovations and brave men and women who had worked tirelessly to make the future a better place for everyone.

A noisy bird outside the kitchen window awakened Jane from her sleep. It took her a few moments to remember she was in 2015, and laying her head on the table. Someone had draped a blanket over her. The clock right across from her said it was almost 1 p.m. Jane lifted her aching head and made it over to the door by the hallway where a long mirror hung. Her Chameleon Cloth now looked like a yellow sleeveless dress with a light yellow opened sweater.

"Yellow is definitely your color," Riley said. He handed her an elastic ribbon. "Here, you can tie up your hair with this." He gently took her hair and put the ribbon around it.

"Do you do women's hair too?" Jane asked.

"Well, I tried to cut my cousin Audrey's hair once, when I was seven," Riley said. "I don't think she appreciated it."

Isabella slumped in. "What is for breakfast?"

"Just leftover pulled pork," Riley said. "We need to get going if we're going to be there in an hour-and-a-half."

"I think I can wait," Isabella muttered. "How soon can we leave for the university?"

"Let's see if your sisters and brother-in-law are ready," Riley said. Eleanor came in, trying to manage Fly while pulling her hair in another of the elastic ribbons. Cassandra and Phillips came in hand-in-hand, Cassandra struggling with her hair as well.

"I must give Hodges a raise," Cassandra said.

"What are we going to do today, my dearest Jane?" Eleanor asked.

Jane looked over at Riley. "There are a couple of pretty nice art museums on the college campus," Riley said. "The Egerton's actually having a special exhibition of art from the Regency period, as a matter of fact."

"Would you like to see a museum, Fly?" Jane asked.

Fly rubbed his stomach. "Hurts."

Riley looked in his pantry. "Ah, I guess the mystery of what happened to all the Twizzlers and Chex Mix is solved."

"Francis Jennings!" Eleanor cried. "Jane, dear, I am sorry, but I suppose this means I cannot go out with you."

"All right," Jane said, trying hard, and most likely failing, to conceal her disappointment. Even though Eleanor was the closest distance-wise of her sisters, being still on her uncle's estate, Jane hadn't been able to see her often since Fly and James were born.

"I will stay home with Fly," Phillips spoke up.

"Are you sure you can manage all by yourself, darling?" Cassandra said.

"Cassandra, dear, he is a child, not an elephant," Edward said. "I think I can manage." As eager as he was to see things himself, he wanted to be useful. Anyway, he had stayed up late himself reading *The Gate of the Year*, and was almost at the end.

RILEY PULLED THE CAR into another huge lot filled with carriages. "Okay, I'll go buy some groceries and a new TV. Meet me at that coffee shop across the street at four." He handed Jane a small box with a screen. "I went out this morning to get a new phone and got you one as well. If you need anything before I come back, just slide to unlock and press the button with my name on it and it will call me." Jane stared at the screen.

Riley sighed, trying to be patient. "Like this." He slid a green line and pressed a large button that had appeared on the screen with his name. Clock chimes sounded from within his pocket.

"Now you press the green button to answer." Jane, after a few tries, pressed it. "Now hold it up to your ear."

"Hello Jane," she could hear Riley's voice from within the

box say.

Jane laughed. "Amazing!"

"Yes, you know how to use a phone, how brilliant." A wiry woman stared at them, her face crunched up in anger. "Now, would you please let me get out of my car?"

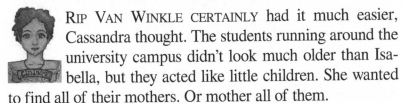 RIP VAN WINKLE CERTAINLY had it much easier, Cassandra thought. The students running around the university campus didn't look much older than Isabella, but they acted like little children. She wanted to find all of their mothers. Or mother all of them.

"There are women studying here!" Isabella said. Cassandra looked at two girls reading on a bench and realized her sister was right. There were men and women, and from all over the world too, just on this one street. Had there been another world war, an epidemic, or a famine that brought them all here? The numbness returned.

Mr. Granger walked with them into a large gray building at the end of the street. "Here's Willis Hall. Dr. Bennet's office is on the third floor. Here's a backpack in case you need to take anything." Cassandra looked up the staircase, trying in vain to fight the numbness in order to proceed.

"You know, maybe the elevator would be better for you in your state," Granger said. He pressed a button on the wall facing the stairs and a silver door opened. "Press number three when you get in that small room. The receptionist is right there when you get off."

Cassandra and Isabella clung close to each other as the room jerked up. An ancient looking woman sat at a desk on the other side of the door when they arrived. She must be the receptionist Granger was talking about, Cassandra thought, whatever that is.

"Hello," Cassandra told her. "I am looking for Dr. Bennet."

"I'm so sorry, honey, she's on sabbatical until June."

"But she left me a note," Cassandra said.

"Can we at least get into the office?" Isabella said.

"Did you leave something?" the receptionist asked.

"Why, yes, I left my- cap in there," Isabella said.

"And you don't have another one?"

"But this is the one my grandmamma gave me!" Isabella cried.

The receptionist sighed and pulled a key out of the drawer. "Fine, but just five minutes."

"It has to be here somewhere," Cassandra said, trying not to make eye contact with the receptionist. It would be difficult to find anything in this rubbish. Where was Dr. Bennet's housekeeper? Someone grabbed her arm.

"Cassandra!" Isabella hissed. She pointed to a small frame on the desk. "That's my sketching of Papa!"

"It is probably just a family heirloom," Cassandra said.

Isabella picked up the picture. A flash of light nearly blinded her. A small pink stick with a thin tail and a short piece of paper wrapped around it fell to the ground.

Cassandra grabbed a black chair with wheels, writhing. "I think the baby is coming!"

The receptionist helped her sit on the chair. "Relax and take a deep breath."

Cassandra motioned to Isabella to pick up the stick. Isabella grabbed it and slipped it in her backpack.

"Is there anyone I can call, dear?" the receptionist asked.

"Oh no, I think it was a false alarm," Cassandra immediately sprang up.

"I found the cap, Cassy, it is here in the backpack," Isabella said.

"Thanks ever so much!" Cassandra told the receptionist. They hastened back to the elevator before the receptionist could question them any further.

"USELESS, CORRUPT LEECHES, HER entire family."
Eleanor examined a portrait of a young Princess
Charlotte. "Except her." Eleanor stepped back for a
moment, as if she was anticipating a scolding from
Sir Francis about how a lady, especially a young lady, kept
her opinions to herself. It was not as if that had ever stopped
her from freely speaking her mind.

Jane tapped her fingers on her thigh, wondering if she
should tell her sister the princess would be dead from childbirth complications in less than two years, two years from
when they had come, anyway. Maybe one of them could
warn the princess and her family when they went back,
though that would mean Queen Victoria and her descendants, including the current queen of England, would most
likely never be born. Who knew how many changes could
result from that? Time travel was turning out to be much
more complex the more Jane thought about it. So Jane
simply replied, "Yes, I have always liked her best as well."

"Oh yes, good old Princess Charlotte." It was Dr. Darcy,
along with a cheerful young girl with curly reddish-brown
hair and a large silver freckle on her nose. "She was always
my favorite royal." A second woman, this one with long
brown hair and a harsh face, like someone had squirted a
lemon on it, joined them.

"How strange to see you again!" Eleanor said.

"Not that strange, I would hope, seeing as this is where I
work," Dr. Darcy said.

"Your doctorate is in the arts?" Eleanor asked.

"Art history, to be precise." Dr. Darcy looked over at
Jane.

"Dr. Darcy, may I present my sister, Jane Farnsworth,"
Eleanor said. "Jane, this is Dr. Colin Darcy."

"Nice to meet you, Jane," Dr. Darcy said. "This is my sister, Brittany, and my fiancée, Anna Kelly. Brittany is a junior
here."

"It is so nice to meet you," Eleanor said, wondering what a junior signified.

"Do you go to college here?" Miss Darcy, the young freckled woman, asked Jane and Eleanor.

"No, we are only visiting," Eleanor said. "We are... we are from Hampshire."

"Eleanor and Jane are... actors, is that correct?" Darcy said. Jane nodded.

"You're actors?" Miss Darcy asked, her hands flailing. "I'm directing the murder mystery play for the university's annual fundraiser! It's set in Regency England... sort of Jane Austen meets Agatha Christie... the script needs a little work. You should audition!"

"I don't think we'll be in town long enough, I'm afraid," Eleanor said.

Miss Darcy handed them a slip of paper. "Well, at least tell your friends that auditions are tomorrow 1 p.m. here at the Egerton Auditorium."

"Thank you!" Jane said. She and Eleanor went to the other side of the opened wall. Eleanor hoped Dr. Darcy wouldn't follow.

Eleanor tried to focus on a Constable landscape, realizing Miss Darcy had asked them if they attended the university, as if women attending university in the 21st century was nothing. "What other great changes had happened since we both made it here?" she quietly asked the painting.

"So, tell me again how you know her?" Eleanor heard Miss Kelly, the harsh-faced woman, ask Darcy in a whisper half the museum could hear.

"I'm not exactly sure I even know, to be honest," Darcy said. "I just keep running into her. It's like a bad romantic comedy or something... except for the romance, I mean."

"Should I feel threatened?" Miss Kelly teased.

"Of course not. She's not beautiful enough to tempt me."

Jane looked over at Eleanor. "Why, I do believe it is time

to meet our friend," Eleanor said.

 CASSANDRA AND ISABELLA WERE already at the coffee shop, as well as Mr. Granger, who was admiring a small stick.

"Wonderful, Isabella!" Riley exclaimed. "Perfect!"

"It was nothing," Isabella said. She took a large bite of her scone, barely swallowing before adding, "So, where is the time machine?"

Riley's brows furrowed when he opened the note.

"What is it?" Cassandra said.

"It's another note for you guys." He handed Cassandra the paper.

C.,E.,J., & I.,

Please bring this stick to the basement of Willis Hall at 3:00 p.m. on 27-10-1995. There is a pocket in the dining room at the Darcy's house that will get you there.

- G.B.

"What in the world does that mean?" Cassandra said.

"What else?" Riley said. "Dr. Bennet needs you to bring the stick to her October twenty-seventh... 1995."

Chapter Six

"So Dr. Bennet needs us to use another one of the time pockets to bring her this stick in the future?" Edward nearly missed his chair sitting down to a dinner of the enchiladas Riley had picked up from a building with a "Taco Bueno" sign in front on the way home. "Well, in the past. Well, in a further point in our future..."

Cassandra took his hand. "We know what you mean, dear."

Jane re-read the letter in disbelief. "The dining room at Darcy House. So there is another time pocket at these people's house?"

"That's what it seems," Riley said.

"I wonder..." Eleanor said. "That man who nearly ran us over back at Reddings. He sat next to me on the plane and then Jane and I met him again at the museum. His name is Colin Darcy."

"Oh, yes, his parents were William and Anita Darcy, part of one of Dallas's richest families," Riley explained. "His great-grandfather made a fortune in the oil industry. The Darcys paid for half of the buildings in the university."

"Why does this Mr. Darcy work at the university if he has such a large fortune?" Jane asked.

"His father sold the company when Dr. Darcy was seventeen when he realized the doc and his sister were more interested in art and theater. They still inherited their share of the fortune and the house. Darcy's great-grandfather built Darcy House in the 1930s based on one of the old English estates. The house isn't too far from here. It's right on White Rock Lake."

"So how are we ever going to get into the Darcy House to find the time pocket?" Eleanor asked.

"Maybe we can introduce Eleanor to Dr. Darcy!" Cassandra said.

Eleanor chortled. "Do not involve me. He is engaged and I am 'not beautiful enough to tempt him.'"

"I could call on him tomorrow," Phillips said. "Ask him more about books."

"Uh, hate to break it to you, but people don't really 'call on' people, anymore, Edward," Riley said. "Maybe one of you could get a job for him."

"A job?" Eleanor asked. "Oh dear. Aunt Jennings would say we are not beggars."

"Aunt Jennings is not here," Jane said. "I know! You could get a role in his sister's play! Everyone loved you in my plays when we were girls."

Eleanor's face colored. "Who would take care of Fly?"

"I do not mind staying home with him," Edward said.

"Oh." Eleanor tried to think of another excuse.

"Could you introduce us, Mr. Granger?" Isabella asked. "You seem to be very well acquainted with the Darcys."

"Yeah, well, Darcy's pretty good friends with Dr. Bennet," Riley said. "I bet she left it with him for safekeeping."

Of course rude Dr. Darcy and cold Dr. Bennett would be friends. "I did make a rather charming Beatrice in *Much Ado About Nothing*, did I not?" Eleanor said.

"So the play it is!" Riley said. "Hey, why don't we all go do some research? Monday nights are $1.00 at the second-run theater."

"I would love to!" Jane said. "I have always wanted to

go to the theater!"

"I would love to as well, but I am rather tired," Cassandra said.

"I probably need to make sure Fly makes it to bed all right," Eleanor said.

"Well, then that means Jane cannot go," Isabella said.

"Wait a minute, Jane's 23," Riley said. "I think she can manage on her own."

"Jane cannot go out with a man we have just met unchaperoned," Isabella said. "She is not married."

"Well, then maybe this is your chance to chaperon her, Isabella," Eleanor said. Jane and Isabella looked at each other in disgust.

RILEY POINTED TO DIFFERENT posters that lined the outside wall of the large theater. "Take your pick."

There were so many interesting-looking plays to choose from! "There is the bird story!" Jane said. "Oh Riley, can we see that again?"

"If that's all right with Isabella," Riley said.

"I do not care," Isabella muttered.

"Sounds good to me," Riley said. "Three tickets for *Winging It*, please," he told the young lady at the ticket window.

"AND THEN THE LITTLE mermaid met the prince... he was about to drown and she saved him... Francis Jennings, sit still or I will not finish the story!" Fly kept flipping the switch that turned the electric candle on the ceiling on and off. Eleanor tried to remember her father's old story. Jane could remember all the details and make it engaging. She stroked Fly's red hair. "Let's just say our prayers."

Ten minutes later, Eleanor collapsed on the couch next to Cassandra. "Is Fly all right?" Cassandra asked.

"Yes, I finally got him to bed," Eleanor said, sighing with relief. "Where is Edward?"

"In the bedroom, finishing his book," Cassandra said. She stared at the window. "I do wish I had my needlework."

"I found some yarn in the guest bedroom closet," Eleanor said. "It does not look like it has been touched in years."

"You know how to knit?"

"Mrs. Parker has been teaching me."

"What does Aunt Jennings think of that?"

"Nothing. I have not told her."

"That is probably wise. She would think you were telling everyone Reddings is in financial straits because you were making your own scarves."

Eleanor went to her bedroom and brought a pink knitting bag back. "Just wrap the yarn around the needle."

Cassandra struggled to make her loops even. "I do hope Jane and Isabella are getting along well."

"So do I."

"I almost miss the days they ran around the village together, flirting with the officers. What happened?"

Eleanor sighed. "They woke up one morning and decided they were each other's biggest competition for a husband."

"Aunt Jennings spurred them on to that, no doubt."

Eleanor nodded. She decided it was better not to dwell on Aunt Jennings. "I just hope Mr. Granger is treating Jane well."

"You do not trust Mr. Granger? He is trying so hard to help us."

Eleanor smiled. "You're just like Papa. You always see the best in everyone."

The yarn was wrapped too tight. Cassandra threw the needle on her lap. "I just want to go home to my children."

Eleanor took Cassandra's hand. "We shall, darling. Mr. Granger will get the time machine again and this will all be the past to you."

"I can only hope so." Cassandra waddled off to bed, leaving Eleanor with only the knitting.

Eleanor thought of little James, wondering if Richard, Frank's brother, and that insufferable Augusta, Richard's wife and Edward's sister, had swooped in to take him to London. In her mind, Richard and Augusta began to resemble Dr. Darcy and his awful lemon-faced fiancée. She shook her head. Perhaps sleep wasn't such a bad idea for her either.

 JANE LOVED *WINGING IT* even more the second viewing. She couldn't stop singing the film's infectious ballad, "Watch Me Soar" as they walked out of the theater.

"Spare us all your singing, Jane," Isabella snapped.

"I think it's cute," Riley said.

Jane tried to take off her jacket. "Is it still really February?"

"Welcome to Texas," Riley said. "The jacket is only an illusion, remember. It should disappear if it gets much hotter. How about we get some froyo to cool down?"

Jane had no idea what "froyo" could be, but Riley was so excited, she couldn't help herself. "Yes, let us!"

Riley drove down the highway and into a small village of shops. He parked in front of a small store with wide enough windows that Jane could see the pastel walls inside.

"My ladies," Riley said. Jane and Isabella took his arms, Jane with an eager smile and Isabella with a huff.

Inside, along the pastel walls, shiny metal bars sat below pictures of various fruits and desserts. "You have to try the red velvet." Riley pulled down a lever and a bright red string of frozen cream came out. Riley handed one to Isabella.

"I am fine, thank you," Isabella said.

After Riley paid for their yogurt, they sat on a bench outside the shop to eat. Jane and Riley sat together on the bench while Isabella walked around, trying to ward off a fly.

Jane watched the different people walk around the village, wondering what business had brought them there. "I wish..."

"What?" Riley asked.

"I wish I had a pen and paper to write this all down on."

Riley took Jane to a small store across from the fountain that belonged to a Mr. Walgreen. He led her down to an aisle that said "school supplies" and handed Jane a yellow notebook and pink pen.

"I can't believe you," Jane said three times while Riley paid. "No one's ever been so supportive of my writing since my papa bought me a writing desk. Thank you so much. I'm so glad I came."

"Really? It's so weird, there are so many people who would love to go back to your time."

"Why? There's nothing there, at least not for a woman. A woman like me, anyway."

"Well, if you really don't want to go back, and I can't say I blame you, you could always come traveling around in time with me. We'd be like the Doctor and his companion, exploring ancient civilizations, fighting threats to the universe, and... yeah, I guess that one just flew over your head like the others."

"It sounds wonderful," Jane said. Riley held out his fist in a ball of fingers. He took Jane's hand, gently folded her fingers into a ball, and bumped it into his. "It's called a fist bump."

Isabella barged in between them. "I do believe we should go home!"

"You're really going to do this to me?" Jane asked.

"Oh, that's all right," Riley said. "We best listen to dear

old Mrs. Pym." He gave Jane an impish smile.

ALL THE SUGAR MADE Jane too giddy to sleep that night. She lay on the couch, her muse running as freely as the ink from the pen Riley had given her. Jane grabbed her notebook and headed to the dining room table.

Julia walked around Mr. Walgreen's giant store, amazed at the hair products and bags of colorful candies, she wrote. *New opportunities seemed to lay before her like the items on the shelves.*

Isabella came in to get a glass of water from the sink. "Do you not think it is getting late?" she asked.

"Well, then you should probably get some sleep," Jane said.

Isabella frowned. "I do not think Riley's intentions for you are pure."

"Do you enjoy making me miserable?"

"I am only trying to return the favor you so kindly paid me, dearest Jane."

It was useless to argue with Isabella. Even though she was two years younger, she could always bend Jane to her will. Anyway, Jane had just gotten another fantastic idea. She scribbled it down before she forgot it:

Julia barely had time to miss her sisters, with all there was to do. She was sure Anne and Louisa were fine. They still had their balls and beaux, after all. It was finally her turn for independence.

Chapter Seven

THE NEXT MORNING, THE smell of bacon awoke Jane. Riley was at the stove, going between preparing a pan of bacon and a pan of eggs.

"Just for you, a full English breakfast," Riley said.

Someone had draped a blanket over her again. Jane laid it against the chair and walked over to observe Riley.

"Aunt Jennings always was proud that none of us ever needed to cook," Jane said. "It all looks so fascinating, though."

Riley gave Jane that wonderful grin. "Would you like to start with the toast?"

"Yes!" Riley handed Jane a clear bag of bread. She looked in the cabinets and drawers. "Where is the knife?"

"It's already sliced." Seeing Jane's amazement, he added: "Don't tell me, it's the greatest thing since sliced bread."

"Do I cook it over your fires?"

Riley pointed to a small black "appliance" with slots. "More like these fires. Stick the bread in the slots. Now, pull that lever down."

"All right." Small fires inside the box cooked the bread! "Is it supposed to be smoking?"

"Push the button on the bottom! It's on too high."

The toast came out blackened. "Oh dear."

"It's okay, we all have to start somewhere," Riley said. "Try it again."

Jane slipped in another piece. At the first scent of smoke, she pressed the button. "I did it! This is so much fun- I mean, this is so delightful." Aunt Jennings wasn't here to correct her grammar, she reminded herself. Riley held out his palm. Jane, to her surprise, bumped his fist back. Jane let go of her fingers.

Riley smiled. "I like it." They fist-bumped again and Riley let out his fingers, making a sound like fireworks exploding. The young gentlemen back in 1815 who looked the other way when Jane tried awkwardly to converse with them had never seemed so long behind her.

ELEANOR, ALONG WITH FLY, and Isabella were the first in the dining room. Eleanor sat down and picked up a slightly blackened piece of toast. "Oh Jane, I'm so proud of you."

"This is... delicious, Jane... thank you," Isabella said, quickly taking a bite of baked beans.

Jane chewed her toast, feeling triumphant. Phillips came into the dining room all by himself.

"Cassandra was not feeling well this morning, so she's still in bed. Do not worry, it's just the usual stiffness."

Eleanor smiled. "She should have started lying in right about now, anyway, should she not?"

"So when are the auditions?" Riley asked.

"1 p.m." Jane said. "Are you coming, Riley?"

"Sorry, acting's not my forte."

"How about you, Phillips?"

"I will stay here with Fly again."

"Well, then I am staying home too," Isabella said, patting her belly. "I am feeling sick in my stomach."

"It is just a little morning sickness, darling," Eleanor said. "Why do you not come along with us? You will feel much better."

"You do not want anything to happen to me or the baby, do you?" Isabella said.

Yes. Jane immediately prayed silent forgiveness for such a cruel thought. She knew how fortunate her sisters had been in childbirth. Cousins and friends of her family had not been as fortunate.

"I'm sure we can find a shop afterwards," Jane said.

THE VOICES OF COLLEGE students assaulted Jane the moment she and her sisters entered the auditorium. Everyone was so confident... and even more raucous than a militia at one of Mrs. Parker's supper parties. Jane's breakfast churned in her stomach.

"I think I left my notebook in Riley's car," Jane said.

"It is in your hands, darling," Eleanor said.

"Oh yes." Perhaps another excuse...

"You made it!" Jane heard Brittany cry. She turned around to find Brittany running towards her and sisters.

"Yes, it looks like we are staying in Dallas a little longer than we planned," Eleanor said.

Brittany gave both Eleanor and Jane a hug. They quite enjoy hugging in the future, Jane thought. "Well, I'm so glad you came," Brittany said. She looked over at Isabella.

"This is my youngest sister, Isabella," Eleanor said. "She is especially excited about your play."

"Oh, yes," Isabella said flatly.

"Great! Here's how the thing works: The mystery will start and end here in the auditorium. In the middle all the characters will act out the same scene for the guests while they move around the museum. Each scene gives them clues and the audience can ask the characters questions too."

"What is the play about?" Jane asked.

"Here are the scripts," Brittany said. "Take a seat. I hope to start once our lead gets here."

EDWARD CLOSED THE BOOK, feeling in a daze. He had always felt neglectful for keeping such a sparse library at Woodvale. If he could find other authors as engaging as David Andrews, maybe he could build the extensive library Susan and Augusta, his sisters, coveted so much.

A crashing noise returned his mind to Mrs. Milner's. "You seem to be feeling better," Edward told Fly. He caught Mrs. Milner's duck figurine right before it landed on the hardwood floor.

"I am hunting elephants!" Fly said.

"Is everything all right?" Cassandra asked from the bedroom.

"Yes, keep resting," Edward said. He turned to Fly. "How about we hunt some elephants outside?" He took some jackets out of the closet and struggled to put the smallest one on Fly. Edward was becoming more grateful for all Cassandra and Eleanor dealt with in raising the children. They walked across the street to a park which overlooked the lake.

"I am Mr. Elephant!" Edward waved his hands like a trunk. "Come catch me!" He barely made it two feet before Fly knocked him to the ground. Edward couldn't remember the last time he knew such joy. He wondered how it would be if Cassy or Neddy were balancing on that colorful lever or if he were pushing Charlotte on the swing…

"Bingley!" A medium-sized dog with red fur came racing towards Fly. Dr. Darcy came running close behind, screaming Bingley's name twice more. The dog reminded Edward of his hunting dogs. Edward held out his hands. Bingley came and sniffed Edward's hands, allowing Edward to grab him.

"Thanks so much," Dr. Darcy said. "You have a sister?"

"I have two."

"Well, do yourself a favor and if they beg you for a dog,

don't do it or they'll be too busy with classes and theater projects all of a sudden." A look of recognition flashed in his eyes. "You're staying around here," he muttered. "Of course you're staying around here."

Fly approached Bingley with uncharacteristic hesitation. "It's okay, he's a sweetheart," Darcy said. Fly petted Bingley as Bingley sniffed his face.

"So he's your nephew?" Darcy asked.

"Yes, my sister Eleanor's eldest," Edward said.

"Eleanor is your sister?"

"Her eldest sister, Cassandra, is my wife."

"Eleanor has another son?"

"Yes, he and my three children are still back in... England."

Colin reached into his pocket and pulled out a small blue package. "Is that Spencer's?" Edward asked. "The chewing gum Maggie keeps under her floorboard with her diary in the book. *The Gate of the Year.*"

"Yeah, it's been a real brand in England for almost a hundred years. You never... um, they don't import it anymore, so I pick it up in England whenever I'm there."

"Do you travel to England often?"

"Once or twice a year, for meetings— stockholder meetings. My father sold the family company to a British company several years ago. A friend of mine from college and her husband live in Mayfair, so Brittany, my sister, and I stay with them. I just went by myself last time because Brit got selected to direct the mystery play for the university's big fund-raiser and had a lot of prep work to do. So, um, what exactly brings you all to Dallas?"

"We have some business to take care of."

"Are you an actor too?"

"I suppose I am."

"That doesn't sound very decisive."

"My father had made a large fortune in trade, and when

he died it was the most desirous wish of my sisters to fulfill his hope of... being an actor."

"Well, it's a free country, so it's never too late to change your job." Darcy muttered "Sorry for meddling," and moved toward his pockets.

A sense of excitement rose up in Edward, the same sense of excitement he had felt right before the assembly where he first met Cassandra. It was the excitement that something unknown but wonderful was about to happen.

JANE READ THROUGH THE script twice. It was about a gentleman who was engaged to Elizabeth, the older daughter of a baronet, but in love with her younger sister Maria. The gentleman ended up murdered on the baronet's estate while multiple guests were visiting. Everyone was a suspect, even the servants.

Jane tried to imagine herself on the stage, reciting the lines. She remembered the last time they had done a play, one she had written herself for her father based on Rip Van Winkle, when she had accidentally tripped over Cassandra. The words on the script gave her a headache. She took out the notebook Riley had given her.

Eleanor glanced over her shoulder. "Are you writing again? I have always liked your stories."

"Well, there's no Aunt Jennings to throw my notes in the fire."

By the look on Eleanor's face, Aunt Jennings could very well go the way of the gentleman when Eleanor saw her next. Before Eleanor could say anything, though, Brittany stepped out.

"Okie dokie, Jane, Isabella, Eleanor and Kate, it's your turn!" Brittany led the four of them onto the stage where a young man waited.

"This is Scott Fleming, he's going to be playing our poor victim, Mr. Dawson," Brittany said. Kate looked a bit awed. Jane remembered some people in the lobby talking about how he was a famous opera star, one who sang about soap. "Okay, Eleanor, how about you read Elizabeth's lines and Kate read Maria's?"

"You waited until our wedding day to tell me you loved my sister instead?" Eleanor cried hysterically.

"Eleanor, try not to overact," Brittany said.

"I am so sorry."

"No problem, just keep going."

"You mean you could never tell?" Kate asked. She acted so natural, not overwrought like Eleanor and her sisters always acted in Jane's plays.

"I am so sorry to hurt you, but I must follow my heart!" Scott said.

"A gentleman would never end an engagement on his wedding day!" Jane spoke up. "Both he and the lady would be humiliated!"

Brittany smiled sheepishly. "Yeah, well, if people did the things they were supposed to, half of fiction wouldn't exist."

"That may be true, but you want it to be believable, don't you?"

Scott grinned in a way that reminded Jane of Riley. "I like her already, Brit. She's tenacious."

"Yeah... hey Jane and Isabella, why don't you read with Scott? Jane, you read Elizabeth and Isabella, you read Maria."

Jane's knees quivered. "You waited... until our wedding day...."

"Jane, could you have a little more expression?" Brittany asked.

Jane took a deep breath. "You waited... until..."

Scott gave Jane a comforting glance. "It's okay. Brittany doesn't shoot you if you get the lines wrong. Unlike the folks at the networks."

"You waited until our wedding day to tell me you loved my sister instead?" Jane raced through the words, trying to push them all out of her mouth as fast as she could.

Isabella simpered. "You mean you could never tell?" The role of Maria seemed written for sassy Isabella. Brittany stared at her, entranced. She roused herself and turned on a CD. Scott grabbed Isabella and danced a waltz with her. Isabella shrieked.

"Aunt Jennings would faint dead away..." Jane cried. "I mean, a gentleman and a lady would never dance so intimately. In London, perhaps, but not in Hertfordshire."

"I guess it still does need a little work," Brittany said. "Okie dokie, thanks everybody. I'll try to get back to you all with my decision by tonight."

Jane tried not to cry as they left. "I suppose I do not deserve a reward in any time," she muttered to herself.

"Jane, wait."

What further criticisms did Brittany have to give? Jane turned around to face her.

"I never got your phone number. You know, so I can reach you guys when I make my decision."

Jane held up her phone. "Number? I thought it was a button..."

"Here, can I see it?" Brittany gently took the phone. "Yeah, I don't think I've memorized a phone number since I was six. Let's see, settings... about phone... here it is!" She copied down a series of ten digits. "Thanks!"

"Thank you," Jane muttered.

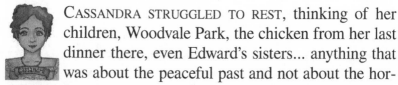 CASSANDRA STRUGGLED TO REST, thinking of her children, Woodvale Park, the chicken from her last dinner there, even Edward's sisters... anything that was about the peaceful past and not about the horrid present.

She finally seized upon a happy memory. For a moment, she was seven years old in her mind again, back in her father's vicarage.

"Eleanor, Jane, do be careful!" she called out to her sisters, who were climbing a tree. Her father placed his hand on her shoulder.

"You have another sister, Cassy," Mr. Farnsworth said. He led her into the bedroom where her mother cradled a small lump.

"This is Isabella," Mrs. Farnsworth said. Cassandra closed her eyes extra tight, trying not to forget her mother's face. She and Eleanor had never been artists like Isabella, but they had both practiced drawing their mother over the years so that they could remember her for their own children.

Loud noises from the living room shook Cassandra's attempts at recollection. She looked over at the bed. Edward still must be at the park. She crawled off the bed and hobbled to the living room.

"What are you doing?" she asked Riley.

"Setting up the new TV." Riley flipped on a switch, changing images by touching the side of the TV. He stopped when white-clad demonic figures storming down a hallway came on. Cassandra shirked back.

"Perfect, you haven't experienced the 21st century until you've seen *Star Wars*," Riley said.

"That's all right," Cassandra said, looking out the window.

Riley flipped over a few images to a grayscale world where a man talked to a small boy named "Opie". "Here, maybe we should start with *The Andy Griffith Show*."

"I am fine."

"It's about time to pick up your sisters. Want to go with me?"

"No, thank you."

"You don't have to be so afraid of new things."

"Who said anything about being afraid?" Cassandra snapped. She tried to focus back on the vicarage. It was like time travel... no, not nearly as dangerous.

 RILEY WAS WAITING FOR Jane and her sisters in his truck parked in front of the theater center. "So how are the new stars of the Dallas stage?"

"We will not know that until tomorrow," Eleanor said. *If even then,* Jane thought.

Jane's disastrous audition resounded through her mind. Every stop they made to sit at a red light gave her longer to dwell. Finally, after ten or so minutes, Riley arrived at an enormous building of assorted shops. He pulled around a small round garden and into another parking garage and handed them each five green bills, each with a picture of a man Jane recognized from Riley's book as Benjamin Franklin on them. "You can repay me when you get back," he said.

The rows of men's shirts Jane saw as they walked into Mr. Neiman Marcus's giant store only reminded her of Mr. Fleming's patronizing face. Isabella and Eleanor, on the other hand, kept proclaiming their amazement at the ready-made dresses and the bright 21st century make-up, Isabella the loudest. She eagerly dragged her sisters around the store, buying five pairs of shoes and a short red coat. Jane had never been so ready for a shopping excursion to end.

They were almost on their way out of the store when Isabella saw a blue cloth hat with a colorful ribbon. "Mrs. Watson will stop talking about her hat from London when she sees this!"

"It is rather expensive, dear," Eleanor said.

"Harry can afford it, I am sure!" Isabella said.

"I'm sure he can," Jane muttered.

Eleanor grabbed a pair of white gloves from a nearby table. "Jane, these would look so lovely on you."

Jane tried to force a smile. "Yes, they would."

"It says there is a twenty percent discount, so that is... nineteen pounds, or whatever these green things are."

"You were always the best at maths," Isabella said.

"I told you, it was all the music lessons," Eleanor said.

Across from where Isabella paid was a small shop for coffee and sandwiches. "La, I am so hungry!" Isabella said. "I will treat you both to the nicest luncheon. Though you or Jane will have to pay, I just spent my last bit of money on this hat."

Jane heaved a huge sigh. "Fine."

"Is something wrong, Jane?" Eleanor said.

"She's just upset because she is a terrible actress," Isabella said.

"You do enjoy my misfortunes!" Jane cried.

"Oh, your misfortunes are great indeed!" Isabella snapped back.

Jane almost didn't hear the sound of chimes. She looked at the phone.

"Riley?" she asked when she answered the phone.

"Jane, good, I finally reached you," Riley said. "Fly's in the emergency room."

Chapter Eight

JANE HAD NO IDEA what an emergency room was, but she didn't like the sound of it.

"Is he all right?" Jane asked.

"Don't panic," Riley said. "He just dislocated his collarbone, but I'm sure Eleanor will want to see him right away."

ELEANOR RACED THROUGH THE doors of the hospital, missing the woman at the front desk.

"May I help you?" the woman called after her. "Ma'am, may I help you?"

"I am sorry," Eleanor said. "I am looking for my son. Francis Jennings."

The woman tapped a keyboard like on Riley's laptop and looked at a screen. "He's in Room 7. First door on your right." She pressed a button by the screen and a door opened.

Edward was in the hallway. "I'm so sorry. I just turned around for a minute and he was stuck in a tree. He injured poor Dr. Darcy and himself jumping down." He led her to a small room at the end of the hall.

"It is all right, I am just so glad you are both fine," Eleanor said, hugging and kissing Fly.

"The doctor wants you to fill out some paperwork," Riley told Eleanor. "I'll help you."

"We had best not overcrowd the examining room," Edward said. He escorted Jane and Isabella back out to the waiting room.

Jane and Isabella sat on two opposite sides of the room. Edward looked at them both, shook his head, and then sat down next to Jane.

"I'm sure whatever has come between you and Isabella now will soon pass," he said.

Jane managed a resigned smile. "Whatever gives you so much confidence?"

Edward took her hand. "I have sisters too."

"ANOTHER FORM?" ELEANOR ASKED.

"Just check 'Self-Pay' and sign it," Riley said. "I'll foot the bill."

"What is this bottom form?"

"Medical history. Any heart disease or cancer in your or your husband's family that you know of?"

"My father's father had a tumor in his stomach. His mother had apoplexy, as did Frank. I do not really know much about my mother's parents. She died when her carriage overturned in the river when I was so young. I never had the chance to ask her much about them."

"Apoplexy? I'll just say 'heart attack.'" Riley checked off some boxes and handed the form back to Eleanor to sign. Dr. Jones arrived as she was finishing the forms.

"Mrs. Jennings, we were able to reset the bone without much complications," he said. "Your son will just have to take it easy the next few days."

"I will try my best." Eleanor sighed.

"Great news!" Riley said, "I'll go get your sisters and the car."

Eleanor helped Fly get his coat on. "Darling, please be more careful," she said.

"Yes, Mamma," Fly said. Eleanor picked Fly up and they walked out into the waiting room.

"Well, hello again."

Eleanor mustered her strength at the sight of the lemon-faced woman. "Oh, hello Mi..." *We are all friends in the future, apparently,* she reminded herself. "Hello, Anna. Is everything all right?"

"Yes, Colin should be fine, just a sprained ankle. He just loves children so much, what can I say?"

"When are you getting married?"

"July 25th. So you're from Hampshire?"

Eleanor nodded.

"How funny, Colin was just in Hampshire to look over the wedding venue. One of his colleagues over there got us set up with an actual castle!"

"How funny indeed," Eleanor muttered.

Colin hobbled into the waiting room. He managed a smile at the sight of Anna. He saw Eleanor sitting next to her and looked embarrassed.

Anna kissed him long and lusciously. "Are you okay, babe?"

"Let's just get home," Colin said.

Eleanor tried to move away before Colin and Anna started kissing in public again. "I'm so sorry about my son."

"It's okay, he's a good kid," Colin said. "Spirited, but a good kid. He just needs an outlet for his energy. Maybe his father can take him fishing or something."

"His father has been dead not two years."

"Oh, I'm sorry." Colin wondered if he should apologize about what he had said in the museum as well. Maybe it was better not to remind Eleanor. His grandmother's words came back to him: "You never have a second chance to make a first impression." The best he could hope for at this point is that she would return to England soon and never cross his path again.

MRS. MILNER'S HOUSE WAS fairly quiet that afternoon while Jane and her family helped Eleanor care for Fly. Riley turned on the TV to a channel that showed a map with a picture of oncoming clouds called a "radar". Except for Cassandra, who stayed focused on her knitting, and Eleanor, who was reading Riley's history book, everyone watched the screen transfixed.

Jane tried to write, but couldn't find her notebook. She looked around the house, trying to silence the voices telling her the 21st century would be as merciless as the 19th. She looked in a closet, finding a blue tub in the process. She picked it up, only for it to tip over. Little bumpy blocks of various colors and shapes came out.

Riley put one on top of another, making them stick together. "Great idea. We can build a town."

"May we call it Elephant Town?" Fly asked.

"Of course we can call it Elephant Town," Riley said. "I'll build the mayor's house."

"It will need a school," Phillips said, picking up some blocks.

"And a church," Eleanor said.

"And a library," Jane said.

"And a milliner's shop!" Isabella said.

Everyone looked over at Cassandra. "I suppose the elephants need a good watering hole," she said. They worked all afternoon on Elephant Town.

"When did we last do something like this together?" Jane asked.

"I think it was right before Cassandra got married," Eleanor said. "Remember Basingstoke?"

"And acting as if we were soldiers?" Cassandra looked relaxed for the first time since the ball. "Oh yes!"

Jane heard clock chimes and realized her it was her phone. Riley picked it up and handed it to Isabella.

"Whatever am I to do with this thing?" Isabella asked

irritably.

"Talk into it!" Riley mouthed.

"Yes?" Isabella said. "Oh hello, Brittany." Jane remembered the auditions and the trepidation returned. "You do? Oh, thank you so much!" She set down the phone. "Brittany wants me in her play!" Jane tried to join with Eleanor, Cassandra, and Edward in their congratulations. "Oh, and she wants to talk to you, Jane."

Jane picked up the phone, bracing herself for the rejection.

"Hi Jane," Brittany said. "Did you leave a yellow notebook at the auditions today?"

"I did," Jane said, only now realizing it amongst all the disorder of the last four and twenty hours.

"Listen... oh I'm being so nosy again... I took a look inside to try to figure out whose it was. You're a really good writer."

"Thank you!"

"I really need help with rewrites, as you can see. You seem to know a lot about Regency England too. Could you help me rewrite the play? I can always use extras as well."

"Yes!"

"Okie dokie! Can you come over to my house tomorrow?"

"Of course I can!"

Jane got Brittany's address and handed the phone to Riley so he could end the call. "What is it, Jane?" Cassandra asked.

"She wants me to help her with writing!" Jane cried. "I'm an actual writer!"

"How wonderful!" Phillips said.

"She wants me to meet her at her house tomorrow to work on the play."

"You mean Darcy House?" Isabella said. "Hurrah, we can go home!"

"Let's celebrate!" Riley said. "What's your favorite food, Jane?"

Jane thought for a moment. She knew Edward's, Frank's, Harry's and every previous suitors' favorite meals, but no one had ever asked her. "Lamb ragout."

"One baby sheep coming up then!"

JANE HELPED EDWARD AND Riley clear the dinner plates. "That was the best ragout I've had in years!"

"Thanks, the Internet's good for a lot of things," Riley said. He put the plates in a white cabinet that held the plates upright with small slots, closed the door, and pressed a button.

"No wonder you don't need servants!" Edward said. "Cassy, come see this!"

Cassandra looked at the dish washing machine. "Oh, it's rather loud isn't it?" She covered her ears and went back to her bedroom.

"Jane, can you come here for a moment?" Eleanor asked.

"Is everything all right?" Jane asked.

Eleanor smiled. "Fly just reminded me as I was putting him to bed that you promised him a story."

"Oh yes, of course!"

Fly was bouncing on the bed when Jane came in the room. "So you want to know all about that poor elephant whose trunk was too short, don't you?" she asked her nephew. Fly nodded eagerly. "Well, he went down to the watering hole, but he couldn't get anything to drink. A monkey and a zebra came along, but neither of them could help him. Then a crocodile came along and the elephant, having never met a crocodile before, asked for help. The crocodile jumped out of the water and grabbed the elephant's nose. The elephant tried to run away, but his nose was caught. The monkey chased the crocodile away. The elephant looked in the water and saw his nose was long enough to reach the watering hole!"

"Hoorah!" Fly cried.

"What a wonderful story, Jane!" Eleanor said. "Thank you so much." She turned to Fly and stroked his hair. "Now, we must say our prayers and go to sleep."

Jane slipped outside to meet Riley while Fly prayed. "I've always loved that story," Riley said.

"You've heard it too?" Jane asked.

"It's a fairly popular story, Jane. Or it will be someday."

"Really? My father used to tell it to my sisters and me before we went to sleep."

"He sounds like he was a great guy," Riley said.

"He was," Jane said. "Are your parents..."

"I've kind of lost touch with my whole family," Riley said. "Time traveling isn't exactly the most precise art in the world. You could come back after what you thought was only two weeks to find out it was thirty years for them."

Jane looked at Fly, wondering what it would be like to come back to Reddings Hall in the 19th century to find him running it, with James in the Navy or the church perhaps; or Neddy the master of Woodvale Park and Cassy and Charlotte wives and mothers. She couldn't imagine being away from her family that long, but going back to 1815 with her sisters and forever settling down as the hapless maiden aunt was even more vivid and painful to imagine.

"PLEASE BE WITH JAMEY and help him to come to Dalass too," Fly prayed. "Amen."

"Fly..." Eleanor started. She shook her head. How could she explain the complex situation to a three-year-old when she was only starting to grasp it herself? "Amen."

Chapter Nine

"So where is Darcy House?" Eleanor asked as she cleared the breakfast table the next morning.

Riley clicked and typed on his new phone until a map of the White Rock Lake area appeared on the screen. "Right here," he said.

"That is not too far at all," Eleanor said. "We can walk there. It's another very pleasant day."

"Is that a library over there?" Edward said. "I would like some more books about the war. Oh, and that Sherlock Holmes fellow Maggie kept mentioning."

"Yeah, I can give you my card," Riley said. "You can take Fly with you. The library has a great children's section. Children's books, that is."

"I will go with you as far as that shop," Isabella said. "I want to get some ribbon for my hat."

Eleanor examined the strange red "flashlight" Riley had handed her while they waited for a box to indicate they could cross into the park. "This button turns it on and off," Riley said.

"When you see the reddish-gold dust, collect it in the ball, right Riley?" Jane asked.

Riley grinned. "You're a regular time traveler already, Jane."

Eleanor wasn't sure if she wanted Jane traveling all over

time with a stranger. *Perhaps Jane will need a chaperon...* she thought. She imagined herself visiting the continent in a more peaceful time, perhaps a few years in the future, until she remembered Reddings Hall had been missing its heir for almost four days now. "I suppose I will have to talk to Dr. Darcy while we visit," she said. "What do people talk about in the future?"

"Weather's always good," Riley said. "Or you could always go for 'How about the Mavs?'"

"What are the 'Mavs'?" Eleanor said.

"On your left!" a woman's voice cried. Riley pushed Jane and Eleanor off the sidewalk. A woman sped through on a bicycle.

"The Dallas Mavericks," Riley said. "They're the local basketball team."

"What is basketball?"

"You run around a room and try to throw the ball in a basket."

Eleanor shook her head. "I should have gone to the library. I think I will just stick to the weather."

Riley stopped in front of a large stone gate with a white door. "We have arrived at our destination. Push that button."

"Hello?" a scratchy voice asked from the small box once Jane released the button.

"Brittany? It's Eleanor and Jane."

"Yay, thanks! I'll open the gate. Just a sec." The box made a buzzing noise, and then the door of the gate opened on its own, like in the emergency room.

Jane turned to Riley. "Are you certain you don't want to come in?"

"That's all right, you can't always be on my leash."

Eleanor was so caught up by the exquisitely landscaped plants and trees as she walked down the cobbled sidewalk that the first sight of the beautiful columned house almost startled her. A few years ago, when she and Frank had honeymooned in the North, she toured a few of the great houses. It was like one of the houses had traveled to the future along with her.

Eleanor knocked on the large brown door. Instead of a servant, an enormous red dog greeted her when the door opened, nearly knocking her over.

"Hello, darling," Eleanor said, petting his head.

"Bingley, down!" Dr. Darcy said. "Oh, hi Eleanor."

"Hello… Colin," Eleanor said. "How is your ankle?"

"Hurts like crazy."

"I know, I broke my foot a few years ago. That's actually when I- aagh!" Bingley stuck his nose between her legs.

"Brit, do something about your stupid dog!" Colin shouted.

Brittany raced in. "Aw, Mr. Bingley is just sho exshited to see his new fwiends! Yes you are, yesh you are!" Bingley flopped down on the floor and Brittany rubbed his stomach.

"That's when I fell in love with my late husband," Eleanor continued. She didn't know why she was still repeating that story. A force of habit, she supposed.

Anna barged in. "Col, we needed to have the engagement picture taken last week. Are you dressed?" Anna stared at Eleanor with a *"you again?"* look. "What are you doing here?"

"They're here to help me with the play!" Brittany said, guiding Mr. Bingley down the hallway. "The living room's this way."

"Brit, did you really have to do this today?" Colin asked curtly.

"Oh come on, you grump," Brittany said. "It's not like we'll be in your way. Can I get you any coffee or tea?"

"Tea would be wonderful," Eleanor said. "I am a bit chilled from the walk."

"You walked all the way here?" Colin asked.

"I did," Eleanor said.

"Is your car broken?" Anna asked. "I could have picked you up in my BMW."

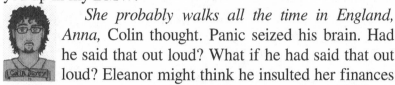 *She probably walks all the time in England, Anna,* Colin thought. Panic seized his brain. Had he said that out loud? What if he had said that out loud? Eleanor might think he insulted her finances on top of her looks. She would never believe that both had come from the broken part of his brain. He waved slightly to Anna to let her know he was going upstairs to get dressed.

"That is so kind, but I really don't mind the walk," Eleanor said. She admired the shining wood floors of the living room, then the elegant white-with-blue-stripes furniture, the classical-looking vases and the life-like portraits that lined the walls. From a large window, she could see a pool with a waterfall. She looked over to the enormous kitchen, filled with appliances like Mrs. Milner's, only larger and shiny silver. There was a hole in the wall between the living room and kitchen with a large bowl of grapes and nectarines on it.

"To be mistress of this house would be something!" she whispered to herself.

"So have you been in anything I might have seen?" Anna said. "I watch a lot of British television."

"No... We are... mostly on the stage," Eleanor said. Brittany handed Eleanor her cup of tea. Someone had painted a picture of water lilies with the most vibrant colors on the cup.

"So are you like the Redgraves or something?" Brittany asked. "Are your parents actors too?"

Eleanor sat on the white couch. "No, my father was a vicar."

"Colin, I told you *no*," Anna said. Colin came down the

stairs wearing a long colorful scarf and a floppy brimmed hat. "I want a serious engagement picture."

"I think you look lovely." Realizing she had unnecessarily inserted herself in someone else's private affairs, Eleanor quickly took a sip of tea.

Colin's face brightened for a moment. "Thank you." His face fell and he muttered something that sounded like, "Bad idea." He threw off the hat and scarf, grabbed his phone and sat down on the couch.

"Acting is a rather unsuitable position for a single mother isn't it?" Anna asked Eleanor. "I'm glad I have a steady job."

"Oh yes, a department store decorator is such a sure bet in this economy," Brittany snapped.

"Brit!" Colin said.

"You decorate stores?" Eleanor asked, stroking Mr. Bingley's head as he rested it in his lap.

"Yes, and parties on the side," Anna said. "I made the decorations for Brittany's birthday party tomorrow night."

"Tomorrow's your birthday?" Jane asked Brittany.

"Well, actually it's in March, but most of my friends and I will be too busy with the mystery play by then. Hey, you should come!"

"Brittany, are you sure it's such a good idea to invite these people everywhere?" Anna asked.

"What do you mean by *these people*?" Brittany said. "British people? You think they're going to restart the Empire on us?"

"I just meant total..." Anna caught her breath. "Colin, can't you explain?"

"Sorry, writing an important e-mail to the dean," Colin said, staying fixated on his phone. To mangle the words of Mark Twain— or whoever said it— it would be better to remain silent and look like a jerk to Eleanor and Jane than to talk and remove any doubt.

"It is all right," Eleanor said. "We have already intruded on your hospitality quite a lot." She looked at a life-like portrait hanging over the large stone fireplace. There was Colin, looking no more than fifteen and unusually relaxed, holding on to Brittany, who looked a little older than Fly. An older couple was behind them. The man looked like Colin, only with shorter hair, while the woman had his and Brittany's face, as well as tan skin and long brown hair.

"Are those your parents?" she asked Brittany.

"Yeah," Brittany said. "They died when I was twelve. Colin's pretty much raised me ever since."

"I am so sorry," Eleanor said. "Both of my parents are dead as well."

"I can't think of any bigger tragedy," Anna said. "Grandparents are so important. I'm so glad my children will have my parents at least." Brittany sprung from the couch and stormed out the back door to a chair by the pool.

Eleanor couldn't believe it. Even Isabella knew to hold her tongue when appropriate, for the most part. Eleanor and Jane quietly excused themselves to the backyard. Eleanor took a seat in the chair next to Brittany.

"I'm so glad my children will have my parents at least," Brittany said, mocking Anna's strident tones. "Good grief, can someone just drop a house on her already?"

"That is not a very kind thing to say to someone who is practically your sister," Eleanor said.

Brittany gagged. "Oh, sorry, I think I just threw up a bit in my mouth at that thought."

"But she *is* your brother's fiancée."

"Only because our mom and her mom used to joke about them getting married when they were kids," Brittany said. "He thinks he needs to honor Mom."

Eleanor tried to recompose herself. She looked through the kitchen to a room with a long table. "Jane, would you like some more tea?" she asked.

"No, I am fine, thank you."

"I think I will get some more for myself," Eleanor said. She winked at Jane.

"Is something in your eye, Eleanor?" Jane said.

Eleanor sighed. "No, I am fine, thank you." She showed Jane the flashlight.

"Oh," Jane said. "Brittany, do you want to get started on the play?"

"Sure, I'll go get my laptop," Brittany said. "The teapot's on the counter by the mixer."

BRITTANY LED JANE TO her bedroom and grabbed a flat black book off her bed. She opened it, and pressed a button. Within seconds, there was a picture like on the television— except this one was a stationary picture of a man dressed as if he were from Jane's time who for some reason was wearing a wet shirt— with a few small pictures on the side. Brittany kept clicking and typing. Some piano music came on and a box with the play script came up.

"Okie dokie, rewrite away."

Jane looked at the computer nervously. "How about you read it and I tell you what to write?"

"Of course, that's exactly the way I work best too. So everyone's gathered for the big wedding."

"Why would they spare so much expense? Weddings are- were not that big." Jane wasn't even sure Eleanor and Cassandra were even at Isabella's wedding. Isabella had been especially insufferable that day, so Jane tried to remember as little of it as possible.

"Really? Would someone tell my lovely future sister-in-law that?"

"The lemon-faced woman?" Jane clasped her hand over her mouth.

"That's pretty funny, actually. Yes, her, she's driving me

up the wall with all this 'photos' this and 'dresses' that. Okie dokie, so no wedding. How about a ball? That sounds very Jane Austen."

"Or an assembly. Almost all the gentleman and ladies would attend."

ELEANOR LOOKED AROUND THE kitchen, wondering where, or what for that matter, the mixer was. She finally found the tea pot by a large bowl mounted to a silver base. She poured more tea and walked into the dining room.

The room was entirely empty, save for the table, a cabinet with fine dishes, and the most beautiful grand piano she had ever seen. *This will be easy,* Eleanor told herself. She could hear Anna and Colin's voices from the living room as she waved the flashlight around the room.

"Where is Lucy?" Anna said. "We need that picture!"

"I'm sure it's just traffic," Colin said.

"How terrible that you have to write so many e-mails for work."

"Well, good thing it's my job and not yours then."

"Tell the dean I said hi."

"Okay, I'll tell her just like I told her for you the first three times you asked."

"Does she still have that dog- Bingley, *down*, I'm not talking about you- that hideous shaggy yellow one, like Eleanor's hair?" Anna laughed at her own joke.

"I thought Eleanor's hair looked pretty... adequate. Oh, I just remembered I need call Mayah in London before it gets too late."

"But our engagement picture!"

"Just this one last thing."

Eleanor thought she saw some dust floating out of one of the piano keys. She grabbed the ball. Colin sounded as if he was heading toward the dining room.

"Eleanor?" he asked.

Eleanor shoved the ball and flashlight into her pocket. "Colin, I am so sorry, I... saw your piano."

"Do you play?"

"Why yes, I have been playing since I was eight years old." She hoped Colin wouldn't ask her to perform. "These are such beautiful hardwood floors."

"And old. My dad had them installed the same year I was born. I tried to replace them a while ago, but Brittany put her foot down."

"Yes, sisters can be quite strong-willed, especially younger sisters." Eleanor and Colin both looked off to the side. "I should let you call your friend."

"Oh, yes, thank you." Colin fumbled around his pockets.

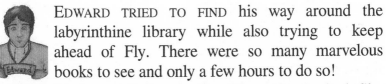 EDWARD TRIED TO FIND his way around the labyrinthine library while also trying to keep ahead of Fly. There were so many marvelous books to see and only a few hours to do so!

"Can I help you find something?" a woman asked. She wore a light wool overcoat that was buttoned unevenly and a shiny button with "Penny Smith, Librarian II" engraved on it.

"Elephants!" Fly cried loudly. Edward shushed him.

The woman in the crooked overcoat crouched down to Fly. "We have lots of books on elephants, but you need to be quiet. You don't want to scare them off, do you?" Fly nodded. Penny led them to a shelf and pulled one about elephants. "The other elephant books are right here. Is there anything else I can help you find?"

Penny was holding a book about the ancient Romans in her arms. Mr. Hartnell, the only person Edward knew growing up who wasn't too harsh or demanding, came to his mind again. "Do you have anything on how to be a teacher?"

Penny looked thoughtful. "What kind of teacher are you thinking about?"

"I don't know," Edward said. He thought about David Andrews and having the chance to read all those books. "I want to teach literature."

"Do you have a degree in secondary education?"

"No."

"Well, there's a good place to start."

ELEANOR WAS GLAD JANE was having a gratifying time writing, but she wished she hadn't left her to be the one to collect the dust. She walked back and forth between the kitchen and the living room couch, trying to think of an excuse to go back to the dining room.

"What a delightful idea," Anna said. "I think I'll take a walk around the room as well."

"Oh, no, that's all right-" Eleanor started, but Anna linked arms with her anyway. Anna simpered at Colin.

"You're not just trying to show off how fit you are, are you?" Colin asked.

"Cheeky!" Anna said, giving him a playful slap. "What am I ever to do with him, Eleanor?"

Colin went back to his phone. "I do not know, he seems to punish himself excellently enough," Eleanor said.

Colin huffed. "Just because someone doesn't socialize the way some people decided one day was the acceptable way doesn't mean they're wrong."

"Yes, but it does not mean they cannot try," Eleanor said. "I did not learn to play the piano in a day."

Colin looked like he was going to fire back, but then gave a thoughtful smile instead. "Yeah, I guess everything takes a little practice."

"Oh look, Lucy's here!" Anna said. "Just in time," she

muttered under her breath. She had never been ignored so long and she was getting tired of it.

"A MAN AND A WOMAN would never be able to go somewhere together alone unless they were married or very closely related," Jane said. "Put Miss Dawson in the scene with the vicar's wife instead. Then she can tell her how her brother would not let her marry the lieutenant."

"This is good stuff," Brittany said. "How do you know so much about the Regency period?"

"Oh, I...."

"Wait, d'oh, that's a silly question. That's what you're writing about, isn't it?"

"Of course. Why did you decide to set the play there?"

"Any excuse to dress up Scott Fleming in a top hat and cravat is a good one, right? It seems so elegant. I wish I could live there."

"No you don't," Jane interjected. "I mean... it's not always so elegant."

"Yeah, I guess it would be kind of stressful to have to marry well or be practically poor, not to mention all those diseases. Still, the guys were all actual gentlemen. Better than my worthless ex, anyway."

"I'm not sure that is true either."

"Yeah, with my luck, I probably would end up with some Wickham or Willoughby."

"Or Whitaker."

"Which book is that from?"

"Oh... never mind."

"Jane, are you almost ready to go?" Eleanor called from downstairs.

"We're only halfway done," Jane said.

"You can come back the day after tomorrow," Brittany said. "Hey, speaking of tomorrow, my party's here tomorrow night at six. No matter what Lemon Face says, I hope you come!"

JANE AND ELEANOR ARRIVED at Mrs. Milner's house as Edward and Fly were arriving from the library. Fly raced into Eleanor's arms.

"Remember Mr. Bunny, he's sorta kinda funny, yeah oh yeah oh yeah!" Fly sang at the top of his lungs. Eleanor shushed him and gave him a hug.

"I took Fly to hear the librarian read stories," Edward said. "Then we went across the street to this shop that sold ice cream in cones you could eat. There were 31 flavors to choose from!"

"It does sound like a wonderful day," Eleanor said. "Thank you so much, Edward."

"You are welcome, I have quite enjoyed it," Edward said. "I almost am sad that we…" He reached into the small white bag he was carrying with him and handed Fly some books on elephants, as if he expected Eleanor to forget he had even started the sentence. "I had better check on Cassy."

"I finished my hat!" Isabella cried excitedly as her sisters, Edward, and Fly walked through the door.

"Ant-Man will love it," Riley said. Isabella huffed and rolled her eyes.

"We actually did something useful," Jane said. "Where's the ball?"

Eleanor looked embarrassed. "I couldn't get it. Anna kept getting in the way."

"One more day," Isabella sighed. Jane struggled not to simper too hard.

CASSANDRA WAS ABSENTMINDEDLY TWISTING her yarn around her fingers when Edward came in to check on her. He kissed her hand.

"How are you feeling?" he asked.

"Fine. I will feel better when we are back at Woodvale. Did you find what you wanted?"

"I think I did." He pulled the Sherlock Holmes books out of the plastic bag the library had given him when he checked out the books. "I even found some moving pictures with the same character. Riley said he would show me how to play them for us tonight."

"That is wonderful." Was Edward getting too fascinated by the future? *No, of course he is not,* Cassandra insisted to herself. *He will forget all this nonsense once we are home.*

Cassandra never asked about the other book in the bag, so Edward left it by the door. He would show her the GED study guide later, when she was less tired.

Chapter Ten

JANE LOOKED AT THE curtains in Mrs. Milner's living room the next morning, half expecting Alice to rip them open. It was 8:30 a.m., according to the clock on the nearby table. Jane tried to get some more sleep, but the urge to explore was returning to her.

She shook Isabella. "I'm going for a walk."

"Mmm, fine," Isabella muttered. "Harry, dearest, ring the bell for Chapman, I must talk to her about the fish..."

Jane grabbed the phone off the windowsill and walked out the door into the beautiful clear morning. She reached the end of the street, and then decided to see the next one. She kept walking down streets, wondering what she could find at the end of each. She walked until she found another village of shops. She went into another large store, this one belonging to a Mr. Target. Jane saw some dresses past some purses and walked toward them to find the most beautiful purple dress hanging on a display. Maybe it was a sign.

One of the ladies who worked at the shop showed Jane to a small "dressing room." Jane couldn't believe how easily the dress went on her. It was lighter than the Chameleon Cloth and much lighter than her dresses in 1815. Jane twirled around a few times, feeling like Princess Lily.

Jane bought the purple dress with the money Riley gave her, as well as a few more dresses she had found next to it, a few shirts, a pair of jeans, some undergarments, two new pairs of shoes, and a purse.

According to the phone, it was 10 a.m. by the time Jane was done. As she walked to find some place to eat, she saw women styling other people's hair in the window of the store next to Mr. Target's. Maybe one of the women could fix her hair for the party that night. Jane looked at a picture of a lady with hair that hugged her face. Riley had said she could have whatever she wanted in the future. She picked up her hair, looking at it in the glass. The woman at the front counter noticed her and beckoned her to come in.

"Can I help you, sweetie?" she asked.

Jane pointed to the picture. "Can I have hair like her?"

The woman laughed. "Of course." She led Jane to a chair.

The hairdresser wrapped a long black shawl around Jane. "Sweetie, who has been doing your hair?"

"My maid, Alice."

"Well, with all due respect to Alice, maybe you should get a new maid. She is not flattering your beautiful face at all." The hairdresser sprayed cold water over Jane's hair and started to cut it away in little snips. *Beautiful face?* Jane gazed in the mirror. She had never really paid attention to her eyes before, but now she had to admit they were quite fine.

CASSANDRA WATCHED THE BIRDS in the front garden from Mrs. Milner's bedroom window. She could almost fool herself into thinking she was back in the English countryside. She stretched out on the bed, patting her stomach and trying to focus on the little girl or boy she would be holding in her arms in another month instead of her aching back. Please let it be born at Woodvale instead of this horrid Texas, she prayed.

"REMEMBER MR. BUNNY!" Fly sang from the kitchen.

"Quiet, darling, Aunt Cassy is trying to rest," Eleanor said.

Edward knocked on the edge of the door. "Would you like some tea? It's made of a kind of berry called blueberries."

Cassandra sniffed the violet drink. It did smell sweet, but too overpoweringly so like the dough-nuts. She took a sip. It started calming Cassandra's nerves. "What are you doing?"

"Playing a game called 'Candyland' with Fly and Eleanor. Isabella is resting on the sofa."

"Where is Jane?"

"I do not know. I think she went for a walk."

"You do not know where she is?" Cassandra said.

"She's fine, I'm sure. She has that phone; she would have called us if there were any problems."

"She is out there all by herself!"

"It's not 1815 anymore, Cassandra!"

"It is not Utopia either, Edward!"

The red in Edward's face faded. "You are right, darling. I'm sorry. I'll go ask Mr. Granger to help me use the phone."

Isabella screamed. Was it those horrible drones again? Cassandra jumped off the bed, regretting ever complaining about an evening with Edward's sisters.

"Jane's butchered herself!" Isabella cried. Cassandra raced to the living room. All the hair below the top of Jane's neck was gone.

"Do... do you like it?" Jane asked nervously.

"It's quite... different..." Cassandra said.

"I think it's fantastic," Edward spoke up. "You got new spectacles too!"

Jane smiled and straightened her bright blue oval glasses. "Yes, these are much more attractive, don't you think?"

"Aunt and Uncle Jennings will never let you out of Reddings Hall again when they see you!" Isabella said.

"Well, I fail to see how that is a problem, considering I'm not going back to Reddings Hall!" Jane said.

"Yes you are!" Isabella said.

"Jane, dear, you really want to leave your family?" Cassandra said.

"What family? You're the ones with families." Jane stormed out of the house.

JANE SAT DOWN ON the front steps, stretching her legs. Anything to let go of the tension gripping her. Were Cassandra's own children not enough for her?

A cool breeze calmed her angry spirits. Jane looked up at the overcast sky and then across the street past the playground to the lake and the tall buildings.

She didn't hear the door open, or Phillips sitting down next to her. "She means well," he said. "She just can't stop being a mother, no matter what."

"I know." Jane sighed.

Phillips wrung his hands. "There's something I need you to keep in strictest confidence. I am close to financial ruin."

"What?" Jane cried softly.

"I was too trusting of an old family friend who asked me to invest in his shipbuilding business and he lost nearly all of my family's fortune when the boat sank. I don't know what kind of life awaits us back home."

"Oh Phillips... I'm so sorry. What are you going to do?"

"I think I would like to start a school."

"You would? That's wonderful!"

"I was thinking about starting it here."

"Here? As in... here?"

"Why not? My sisters would be mortified if I had to

lower myself to working for a living back home."

Jane hugged Phillips exuberantly. "You want to stay too!"

Phillips hushed her. "Please let me discuss it with Cassandra before you say anything."

"Of course I will, Phillips."

"You know you may call me Edward. We did not even have to come two hundred years into the future for that to be so. You are my family." Edward took her hand and Jane felt a sense of warmth.

Jane watched Edward go back inside, admiring her hair once more in the glass door of Mrs. Milner's house. Her old life with Aunt and Uncle Jennings was as gone as most of her hair and her old glasses. She hoped Edward would soon know the same feeling, if only she could keep a secret this time.

Chapter Eleven

ONCE JANE HERSELF RETURNED inside, she pulled out her notebook. It wasn't long, however, until thoughts of Brittany's party and dancing with Riley into the early hours of the morning drowned out her ideas, much like the rain outside was drowning everything. Most of the afternoon ended up being spent drawing abstract shapes in her notebook.

Eleanor gently tapped her on the shoulder. "It's 5:30, darling. Are you ready to go?"

"Yes! No, wait, I want to wear my new dress. May I change in your room?"

"Of course. You... have a new dress?"

Less than five minutes later, Jane was showing the purple party dress to Eleanor and Cassandra. "Oh, Jane," Eleanor said. "This century really suits you." Cassandra stood there, opening her mouth a few times like she wanted to say something only to close it again.

"Do you think Riley will like it?" Jane said.

"Jane, dearest... do you admire Riley?" Eleanor said.

"I don't know... he just makes me feel... well, the same way I'm sure Edward makes Cassy, and Frank made you."

Eleanor smiled wistfully. "Yes, I am sure he does. Just be careful, darling. You have no idea whether he returns your feelings or not."

"You don't think I deserve to be happy, do you?" Jane

said.

"I never said that."

"Isabella certainly thinks so."

"When are you going to learn you are not beholden to everything Isabella says?"

"You look amazing, Jane." Riley was at the door, still wearing a t-shirt and ragged jeans.

Jane's face fell. "You don't look very dressed up."

"Sorry, I've got to clean some things up in my apartment if I'm getting the machine back. I'll make it up to you by taking you out to the best ninety-nine cent bacon cheeseburger Dallas 1995 has to offer."

"Are we ready?" Isabella asked.

"Isabella, have you seen Jane?" Eleanor said.

"Yes, your dress is much too short, Jane," Isabella said.

Jane beamed. "Thank you."

"Can you two just be civilized for one night?" Eleanor said. "Let's go."

"I hope you have a great time," Cassandra said.

"So, up for a game of whist?" Edward asked her. He and Jane exchanged nervous glances. Jane wondered if Edward was trying to cushion Cassandra for the big announcement.

"That is all right, you should go and have a wonderful time, darling. I'll look after Fly and finish my knitting."

THE RAIN STOPPED IN time for Jane and her family to walk to Darcy House once again. Jane plotted new scenes of how the night could go in her head all the way there. If she spent the entire night in the corner again, Isabella would never let her forget it. On the other hand, Brittany seemed so much kinder than the Basingstoke society. Perhaps her friends would be as well, once Jane could be more at ease with their rambunctious spirits.

Jane didn't even have to use the box to call Brittany

when they arrived. Brittany raced out the door as soon as she saw them.

"Happy early birthday, Brittany," Jane said.

"Hey Jane, so glad you could make it!" Brittany gave her a hug and pulled back. "Hey, did you get your hair cut?" Jane nodded. "It looks great!"

"Thank you," Jane said. "May I present my brother Edward."

"You're Colin's friend, right?" Brittany said. Edward nodded. "Great to meet you!"

A small light flickered on Jane's shoulder as she walked into the living room. Strings of paper birds and small mirrors— reflecting the white lights strung across the wall— hung from the ceiling. "This is wonderful!"

"Yeah, I at least can't deny Anna's a great decorator."

"When will the dancing start?" Isabella asked.

"When I decide I haven't embarrassed myself enough," Brittany said. "We're just about to start a game of 'Apples to Apples'."

Instead of dancing or playing cards, three ladies and one gentleman were gathered around the television screen watching a ball knock down white pins. "Oh, they are controlling the ball with those white sticks," Jane murmured to Edward and Isabella.

Edward and Isabella, however, were at the fireplace, looking at some pictures of Brittany as a little girl. She was ballet dancing, playing the piano, and holding up pictures she had drawn. "You are so accomplished!" Edward said.

"Thanks, you have be the first person who's ever said that to me," Brittany said. "Come get some wings while they're hot." Brittany showed them to the kitchen table, where two ladies were talking and supping off plates filled with small wings of chicken, triangular slices of a large flat disc of bread topped with ground sausage and cheese, and yellow triangles topped with a bright orange sauce.

"Hey Jane, you met Kate at the auditions," Brittany said. "This is Marisa, she's playing the vicar's wife."

"You're from Hampshire?" Marisa asked. "That's where they film *Downton Abbey*, isn't it? Do you watch *Downton Abbey*?"

Someone tapped Jane from behind the shoulder before she could formulate some sort of response. "Happy Fake Birthday. Faker!" Jane nearly jumped a foot in the air.

"Oh, sorry, I thought you were Brittany," Scott said.

"Doesn't Jane look great, Scott?" Brittany asked.

"She kind of looks like Harry Potter," Scott said.

"No she doesn't!" Brittany said. "Ignore him, Jane."

"Want to go play some Quidditch, Potter?" Scott asked in a fake British accent. He was acting so stupid, but Jane laughed anyway. There was this rather charming manner about him. Brittany gave him a playful shove.

Jane took a thin, triangular slice of the cheese disc, as well as a few wings and a handful of the triangles. "Can I get you something to drink?" Brittany asked.

Jane had the feeling Brittany had no negus. "A little glass of wine would be great."

"Sure, white or red?"

"White." Jane followed Brittany to the refrigerator. "Are you and Scott...?" Jane asked, trying to determine what people called *courting* in the 21st century.

Brittany laughed. "Oh no. We went out once, and we agreed never to talk about it again. He's going out with some country star now, I think."

ELEANOR WATCHED JANE AND Edward play cards with Brittany and her friends. Isabella, who had walked away from the game the moment she could, was sitting with Anna and two other young women on the couch, looking at pictures of the castle where the wedding would be. Eleanor pulled out the flashlight and made it into the dining room without anyone seeing her.

Eleanor looked around until she finally assured herself she had some privacy. She waved her flashlight into every corner she could find. *I probably should check the pianoforte as well,* she thought. She ran her fingers across it. Surely there would be no harm in playing it. She forgot how good playing made her feel.

"Is that Pleyel?"

Eleanor stopped playing and looked up to face Colin. "Yes it is. I am sorry. I am just..."

"Not a huge fan of hysterical college students either?" Colin said. Eleanor laughed. "I told Brittany my present to her would be to make her a CD for her play."

Colin took a seat next to Eleanor on the piano bench and began to play a beautiful balled. "This was one of my mom's favorite songs when she was growing up in Ecuador. Do you like Willie Nelson?"

He must have been talking about a later composer. "I... my interests mostly lie in the 18th century."

"Ah, yes. I went to a performance of a Mozart piano concerto in Vienna last fall. It's amazing to see and hear." He played a few measures.

"I am pretty sure that is actually Boccherini."

"Really? I'm pretty sure it's Mozart."

"No, I practiced that piece enough to know."

"Wow, this must be what it's like for non-nerds talking about rock bands," Dr. Darcy said.

"Indeed." Eleanor laughed again, though she wasn't sure what a nerd was, let alone if she wanted to be identified as one. "You have been to Vienna?"

"Between Brit and I, we've been to every continent, actually. Well, we're still working on Antarctica."

Eleanor sighed. "I always wanted to go to Vienna, but the war always got in the way."

Colin stared at her. "What war?"

"Oh...."

The sound of whooshing came from Colin's pocket. He grabbed his phone and looked at the screen. "No, Sydney, the syllabus said I can't accept late work!" Colin muttered. He turned to Eleanor. "I just got this frantic e-mail from one of my students. I've got to go upstairs." He raced upstairs like a frantic penguin, muttering something to the effect of "Smooth, Darcy, smooth!"

Eleanor picked up the flashlight. "Eleanor, may I speak to you for a moment?" Now it was Anna.

Eleanor froze. Had Anna seen her alone with Colin? "Of course."

"I saw your sister Jane the other day in the emergency room with Riley Granger. Are they close?"

"I do not know."

"Well, I just wanted to let you know you should probably watch out. Riley Granger used to date Brittany, you know. I don't know all the details exactly of how it ended, but Brittany was extremely heartbroken."

"Thank you."

"Anything for a friend," Anna said oily.

"A friend who thinks my hair looks like a ragged dog?" Eleanor almost said before restraining herself.

"Oh excuse me, the chancellor's daughter just showed up, I must go say hello," Anna said.

JANE HAD NO IDEA who most of the people or places on the red cards were that she was supposed to match adjectives with, but the more random answers she gave, the more Brittany's friends laughed, in a playful, accepting way. She ended up winning two green adjective cards by the game's end.

Scott looked over at Brittany's green cards. "Congratulations, Brit, you are surly, strange, and presumptive."

"You're hilarious," Brittany said. "Well, it's your turn to be teased." She handed him a microphone and switched on the TV. After pressing the screen on her phone several times, words came on the TV and music started playing. Brittany and her friends roared with laughter as Scott sang about a truck and some beer.

"Come on, Jane, now it's your turn!" Brittany said.

"That's all right," Jane said, pushing stray hairs out of her eyes.

"Please!"

"I must tell you, I'm really a bad singer."

"That's okay! The whole point of karaoke is just to have fun."

Brittany showed Jane a list of songs on her phone. Jane only recognized one.

"'Watch Me Soar', please."

Jane's stomach tightened. The first verse was almost over before Jane realized she was supposed to start singing. "I'm so afraid..." Jane sang softly.

"You can do it, Jane!" Kate cried.

"But I'm gonna do it anyway!" Jane sang louder. She held the microphone closer to her. This was so much fun! Another song came on. Even though she had no idea what she was singing, she went along with it. It was wonderful to finally be accomplished at something people admired.

Another song started. Eleanor wrung her hands. How could she tell her sister discreetly that she should let someone else sing? She looked at Edward frantically, who was fixated in a conversation about cravats with Brittany, and then to Isabella.

"Let someone decent have a turn!" Isabella cried, snatching the microphone from Jane. Jane ran into the kitchen. Eleanor turned to the entrance from the stairs. Colin was there, shaking his head.

Edward looked up. "Maybe it is time to go home," Eleanor

said. Edward nodded.

"YOU ARE HOME SO early," Cassandra said. "How did the party go?"

"I'm really tired," Jane said. "I think I will get a drink of water and go to bed."

Riley was in the kitchen, colorful papers scattered all over the table. "Look what I found going through my comic book collection." He handed Jane a piece of paper with a picture of silver vines shooting upward from a rounded silver base.

"Is that the time machine?" Jane asked.

Riley grinned. "Sure is."

"It's the most beautiful thing I've ever seen," Jane said. "Did you design it?"

"I sure did."

"I wish I had had the patience to be better at art or music or singing... or anything besides making a great idiot of myself with Isabella."

"What in the world happened between you and Isabella?"

"When Isabella was sixteen, a regiment was quartered in town. A week after Cassandra's wedding, Isabella confided in me that she was going to run away to Scotland to marry one of the officers, a very untrustworthy man named Whitaker. I told my uncle and he stopped them just in time. Isabella's hated me ever since."

"For saving your family from disgrace and her from a bad marriage?"

Jane sighed. "I... I didn't exactly do it in the most tactful way. My aunt and Isabella were laughing at dinner that night how I had spent the entire of the last assembly sitting and reading in the corner again, and so I informed everyone of her plans right there in front of them... with the vicar and his gossipy wife present."

"Ouch."

"Eleanor and Isabella got married soon after that and Isabella sold the writing desk my papa bought me after my aunt gave it to her to write letters... and I was all alone at Reddings Hall, useless and unwanted."

Riley handed her a box of paper handkerchiefs. "I don't know why anyone wouldn't want you."

"Thank you... you are very kind." Jane rested her head on his shoulders. Riley gently picked her head up and kissed her. Jane pulled back in disbelief.

"I'm sorry," Riley said.

"No, that was actually..." Jane once more was at a loss for the best word, so she kissed him back instead.

Chapter Twelve

JANE SPENT THE WHOLE night and the morning as she awoke imagining the look on her aunt and uncle's faces when she presented Riley to them.

"Oh Jane, how wrong I was to undervalue you!" Aunt Jennings would say. "You truly attracted the handsomest and richest husband of all of your sisters."

"Well done," Uncle Jennings would add, finally looking up from his paper.

"You excited about finishing the play?" Riley asked, noticing Jane's stupid grin.

"Oh... yes, of course that's it- I mean, I am," Jane said.

"THIS IS WONDERFUL!" BRITTANY clicked the button to save Jane's script. "Thank you so much for all your great suggestions!"

"Thank you so much for giving me this opportunity," Jane said.

Brittany smiled sheepishly. "I wasn't lying when I told you all how good you were, but I actually had another motive in getting you guys involved."

"What's that?"

"I want my brother to be around Eleanor enough that he leaves lemon-face Anna for her. Eleanor brings out all his good qualities. Lemon-Face just brings out his grouchiness and nastiness."

Colin her brother-in-law? There were worse gentlemen, Jane supposed. She looked out the window and down to the backyard. Colin was throwing a ball to Bingley while Eleanor watched. He barely made eye contact with her sister at all. "He doesn't seem to like Eleanor very much. Or anyone."

"He's just really shy, that's all. Get him going about art or composers or really obscure fantasy novels— all the stuff Anna thinks is stupid— and you'll be talking for hours."

"GOOD DOGGIE!" COLIN TOOK the ball from Bingley's mouth. He looked in Eleanor's direction. "Thanks for doing this for Brittany. This play means so much to her."

"Of course," Eleanor said. She caressed Bingley's head. "Yes, you are a lovely dog."

"Yeah, when we got him at the shelter, the poor guy had been there for almost four months. I supposed the three of us were destined for each other."

Before Eleanor could ask Colin what he meant, Brittany and Jane raced out the door. "We finished the play!" Brittany said. She pulled them inside to the living room and thrust some paper in Colin and Eleanor's hands. "Colin, you read Mr. Dawson's part and Eleanor, you can read Elizabeth."

"I really need to grade some papers," Colin said.

"Oh come on!" Brittany cried. "I'll help you grade the papers if you help me with this."

Colin sighed. "I only desire… I only desire that you know how deeply sorry I am."

"You presume you can apologize after you exposed me to censure?" Eleanor cried. "You are the most conceited man I have ever met!"

Brittany pressed some buttons on her phone until an arrangement of Purcell's rondeau from *Abdelazer* came out of the tiny speakers. Colin mouthed no. "Come on!" Brittany said. "We need to see what it looks like when they're dancing!"

Eleanor sighed and led Colin up to the front of the room. Colin put his hand on her waist. "What are you doing?" Eleanor said. She took Colin's arm and twirled him around. "Now we dance in a circle. Jane, Brittany, come on. Now we clap our hands."

"And now we dosido again?" Colin asked. Colin twirled her around, twisting his ankle again in the process.

"I'm so sorry!" Eleanor cried.

Colin looked flustered. "That's okay." Eleanor helped him to the couch. "How exactly do people manage to talk through this?"

"There is actually a lot of standing and watching other people dance," Eleanor said.

Colin pulled out his phone. "Well, I'd be good at that part at least."

"You actually dance much better than my late husband."

"I'm so sorry."

"It is all right, I enjoy dancing."

"I meant about your husband."

"Oh, that is all right too. He and Mr. Dawson would have found much in..."

Bingley nearly knocked Eleanor down as he scrambled to the dining room window to bark at a squirrel in the front yard. In the sunlight, it almost looked like fairy dust was coming out of the floor. Eleanor looked at Colin, who was now entranced with his phone again. *It is worth a try,* she thought.

She shone the flashlight where a floorboard had come loose. Of course, the floorboard, just like in Edward's book! There was a blue package with "Spencer's Gum" written on it on the ground underneath, surrounded by at least a pound of reddish-gold dust. Eleanor bent down and took as much dust as she could before Bingley started sniffing her and whining.

Eleanor put the ball in her pocket and went back to the living room. "Jane, we should probably be going."

"I suppose we must," Jane said.

"Want to go get coffee sometime?" Brittany asked.

Jane wanted so much to say yes. She had never had a best friend, other than perhaps Isabella once. She wondered if she could leave Brittany. Then, she realized, she didn't have to. She could visit her anytime.

"That would be great," Jane said. "I'll give you a call."

"Okie dokie!" Brittany gave Jane and Eleanor more hugs.

Riley was waiting for them at the gate. "Did you get it?" he asked. Jane proudly showed him the ball.

"All right!" Riley gave her a fist bump. They both made exploding noises, then laughed and kissed. Jane looked over at Eleanor.

"Jane, is there something you need to tell me?" Eleanor said. "Or Uncle Jennings, for that matter?"

"Catch him!" Colin cried. Bingley charged toward Riley. Riley fell down on the ground and caught Bingley as the dog approached him.

"Hey buddy," Riley said.

Colin hobbled over to Riley. "Thanks..." He and Riley stared at each other awkwardly.

"Colin, this is Riley Granger, our host," Eleanor said. "Riley, this is Colin Darcy."

"We've met," Colin said tersely.

"Say hi to Brit for me," Riley said.

"You could yourself, you know," Colin said.

"Sorry, got to be heading out of town," Riley said. He hastened Jane and Eleanor into his truck.

"What was that all about?" Jane asked Riley.

"Oh... um, Brittany and I used to date," Riley said. "Colin made us break up because he didn't think I was good enough for her."

"That's terrible!" Jane said. "You're not the one who

treated her so uncouthly, were you?"

Riley frowned. "I see Brit's been trying to poison the well on me. What can I say? She just adores her brother too much."

A stinging feeling filled Jane's heart. She couldn't imagine anyone hurting sweet Brittany, but no one had been sweeter than her dearest Riley. She took Riley's hand. Colin must have lied to her about him, she decided.

ISABELLA HIT A PILLOW. "I need to get home now!"

"What is the problem?" Edward asked.

"The television is taking another stupid break to sell things! I'll never find out how this play ends."

The door opened. "Surprise!" Riley showed everyone the ball.

"At last!" Isabella cried. She wondered if she should tell Mrs. Chapman to make chicken or non-pulled pork roast for her and Harry once they were back home at Avondale.

"When will you be ready to go?" Riley said.

"Could we... have a few more hours?" Edward said. Isabella moaned. "Don't you want to know if the count gets his revenge?"

"Yes, and someone needs to tell Brittany we cannot be in the play anymore," Eleanor said, taking Isabella's hand.

"Okay," Riley said. "I guess we have all the time in the world."

CASSANDRA STRUGGLED TO MAKE Mrs. Milner's bed. "Here, let me do that," Edward said. He gazed at Cassandra. "Are you sure there's nowhere you'd like to see before we go back?"

"The only place I want to see is Woodvale Park," Cassandra said.

"Could we stay just one more night? Riley was just telling me at breakfast this morning about this place where people can ice skate inside a building."

"Edward, I am beginning to think you do not want to go back." Edward adjusted some books on Mrs. Milner's shelf, only for them to topple at Cassandra's *go back.* "You... you do not? Edward... our children, our friends, our lives!"

"We can bring the children back here and we can get new friends and new lives. You really want to go back to no plumbing, all that disease, no opportunities for either of us?"

"Yes!"

"Well, I don't!"

"Are you going to order me to stay here with you?"

"I don't want to do that! I just wish you would consider the possibility." The books toppled over again.

Jane raced into the room. "Is everything all right?"

"Yes, thank you," Edward said.

"No it is not!" Cassandra snapped. "Jane, did you convince Edward to stay?"

"Of course not," Jane said. "He told you he lost all your money, right?"

"You lost all our *what?*" Cassandra tried to make it onto the bed.

Edward reached out his hand. "I'm sorry, I meant to tell you..."

"Just give me some time to myself, please."

Edward turned to Jane. "I'm going on a walk."

EDWARD STORMED OUT THE door before Eleanor could stop him. "What just happened?" Eleanor thought out loud.

She turned to Isabella, who was sitting crossly on the couch watching the list of names at the end of her movie.

"How should I know? Nobody keeps me informed of anything." Eleanor sighed and followed Jane's loud sobs to Cassandra and Edward's room.

"Edward is broke and wants to stay here in the future," Jane explained. "I tried to apologize to Cassy. He should have known I can't keep a secret."

Eleanor hugged her. "Darling, she would have found out eventually." Eleanor found Cassandra on the front porch.

"What is he thinking?" Cassandra asked. "It's just like him, to change his mind in five minutes."

Eleanor gave her a hug as well. "I know, and you know, you always have. That is why you need to talk about it."

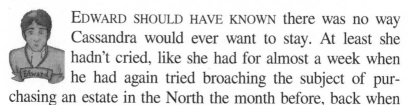 EDWARD SHOULD HAVE KNOWN there was no way Cassandra would ever want to stay. At least she hadn't cried, like she had for almost a week when he had again tried broaching the subject of purchasing an estate in the North the month before, back when it was still 1814.

It was useless. Augusta and Susan were right, Cassandra would never do anything that she thought would separate her from her sisters. He was tired of being told what to do, first by his father and sisters and now by Cassandra.

If only Cassandra hadn't kept herself housebound so much, she might know what she would be missing. Maybe if she couldn't or wouldn't go out into the world, some books from the library would bring the world to her.

He thought he heard a familiar voice in the library. He walked up the spiral staircase to find Brittany talking to a man at the desk.

"How weird, I was just thinking about you!" Brittany said. "What is that author you and Colin like?"

"David Andrews."

"David Andrews!" Brittany cried. The man typed into a computer and printed out a list of books for her. "He's read most of these… Oh, this looks like a good one." Brittany and Edward went to a shelf called "graphic novels."

Edward pulled out one book. The description on the back

cover talked of alien pirates. "He might like this one, too."

"Thanks!" Brittany said. "Is there anything I can help you find?"

"Some books about... things you like," Edward said. "For my wife."

Brittany smiled. "Follow me." She led him to the fiction section and handed him six books. Edward recognized *Mansfield Park*, which had been published only the year before, back in 1815 anyway. The other five were also written by the same Jane Austen, who had become no longer anonymous in the past 200 years.

Brittany noticed the look on Edward's face. "Oh, has she read these already?"

"No, this is... exactly what I was looking for," Edward said. "Thank you." They headed down the staircase to check out the books.

"So how did you become an actress?" Edward asked.

"I played Gretl in my mom's friend's production of *The Sound of Music* when I was six," Brittany said. "I knew even then I had found my function in the big clock of the world. Like Hugo Cabret, you know? How about you?"

"Me?" Edward kept forgetting his supposed job. "My father..." He thought again about his family and Mr. Hartnell, and his own part in the clock. "I really want to quit acting and start my own school." He stepped back, hoping he had just not offended her. "I want to teach literature."

"Really?" Brittany said. "You would make an awesome teacher! I have some old classics— the kind with all the essays in the back— you could use. We can run over to my house real quick if it's okay with your wife."

Edward wondered if he should go home... back to tedious afternoons at his brothers-in-law's clubs, calling on insipid neighbors only because they had a title, getting out of debt... He didn't know what to do, but for the first time in his life, he had to do *something* worthwhile. "It's okay."

It started to mizzle as they left the library. "It's a good thing I learned to carry an umbrella everywhere in England," Brittany said, reaching into her bag. She opened it and motioned for Edward to join her.

"No, I am all right, thank you."

"You're going to catch cold!" Brittany laughed. Edward edged his way under her umbrella.

 CASSANDRA TAPPED HER FINGERS on the passenger seat door as Riley drove her, Jane, and Eleanor down the street. "Where do you think he could have gone?" Riley asked.

"I do not know!" Cassandra snapped. "Maybe I never knew him."

One of the buildings said "31 Flavors". Jane remembered the ice cream Edward and Fly had gotten and looked across the street. "He might have gone back to the library to get more books on starting a school," Jane said.

Cassandra clutched her stomach. "Edward wanted to start a school?" Eleanor took her hand and they got out of the car to walk through the most beautiful courtyard Cassandra had ever seen. It seemed so peaceful, like something from home. Two little girls not much older than her little Cassy were drawing on the pavement with chalk. On the street, an older couple were walking a small dog, laughing and holding hands. Perhaps not everything about the future was so horrid...

"Eleanor!" A woman in a pink outfit that looked like undergarments waved from the front door.

"Oh, hello Anna."

"I was just about to mail these 'Save the Date' cards." Anna thrust a picture of her and Colin smiling at each other by the lake into Eleanor's hands.

"How nice. I hope you are very happy together."

"Thanks. I know we will. I've always been there for him."

Anna looked over at Cassandra. "You haven't met my older sister Cassandra yet, have you?" Eleanor asked.

"Pleased to meet you darling," Anna said. "What are you staring at?"

"Oh nothing," Cassandra said, deciding not to tell anyone she was wondering if she had met a descendant of one of Edward's sisters.

"Are you heading out?" Eleanor asked.

"Yes, I was supposed to meet Brittany here so we could start looking for bridesmaid dresses, but she just texted me saying she was taking Edward back to her house. I suppose I should just be happy she's found a real gentleman this time."

The courtyard became as ugly as the horrid gray hallway in the movie with those ghost-like figures. She had lost Edward forever, because Jane couldn't handle being an old maid. Cassandra raced back to the car, resisting the urge to curse her husband and poor sister.

Meanwhile, Anna turned to Eleanor. "What's her problem?" Anna asked.

"She's Edward's wife," Eleanor said.

"Wife?" Anna said. "Oh, I'm so sorry, I thought he was your brother..." Eleanor raced after her sister.

Anna looked down at the cards. Colin didn't seem very happy. No, she couldn't stand another Christmas with obnoxious engagement ring ads or certain relatives who didn't care about her job and only wanted to know when she was going to settle down like her little sister. A sick feeling came over Anna; her smile was rather forced as well.

Anna picked up the phone. Brittany's phone went straight to voice mail. "Brittany, don't rush back. I need to think over some things."

SOMEONE WHO LOOKED LIKE Edward walked down the street. It couldn't be him, Cassandra thought, because he was with another woman.

 A feeling like a coach was running over Cassandra's heart seized her chest. It was Edward, laughing with Brittany. That would have been her with him, back in the days after their engagement when they would steal away for little walks in the park around Reddings Hall. Cassandra yanked open the car door.

"At least let me stop!" Riley cried. He pulled over and let Cassandra get out.

"What is going on here?" Cassandra said. She looked at Brittany and then back at Edward. "So *she* is what you want to stay here for?"

"What?" Brittany asked.

"It's not like that," Edward said. "She wants to support me." Of all the explanations Edward could have given, why did that had to be the one that slipped out?

Cassandra slapped him and raced into Riley's car. Edward couldn't motivate his feet. Chasing them would mean giving up everything. He remembered their wedding day, when Cassandra had worn that beautiful muslin gown with pink lace, and the promises he had made to her and her family. A tear came down his cheek. He had to do something worthwhile, but he wanted to do it with Cassandra. "I'm sorry, I have to go!" he told Brittany.

"Take my umbrella at least!" Brittany called after him, but Edward was almost to the traffic light already.

 ELEANOR HAD NO IDEA what uncouth thing Frank had boasted of when the men had gathered after dinner that night at Woodvale, but it was enough for Edward to take her aside before she and Frank left, telling her "I am always here for you."

She couldn't believe as Cassandra sobbed in her arms on the way back to Riley's car that Edward— of all men!— had now given in to similar temptation. She couldn't imagine what Jane and Isabella would think, either. One of the few things they could agree on anymore was their adoration of him.

"Did you find Edward?" Jane asked when they opened the car door.

"She did," Eleanor said. "Let's get Isabella."

"What about Edward?" Riley asked.

"He has made his choice," Eleanor said. "I only hope he comes to regret what he has lost." Eleanor was about to get in the car when Riley pushed her and Cassandra to the ground. "What in the world was that about?" Cassandra screamed.

"Stay down!" Riley cried. It was another one of the drones!

"Not this again!" Cassandra cried. She grabbed Eleanor's flashlight that had fallen out of her pocket and threw it at the drone. The drone shot dust at her as it fell.

Edward made it back to witness the scene. "Cassandra!" he cried. The dust completely engulfed Cassandra before Edward could grab her.

Chapter Thirteen

"MA'AM, ARE YOU ALL right?"

A man was shaking Cassandra. Except perhaps it was actually a woman. Her hair was even shorter than Jane's, and every strand was a different vibrant color. The woman helped Cassandra up. Cassandra looked around in a daze. She was in a white room with translucent silver cases of dust-filled glass balls. In the reflection of one of the cases, Cassandra realized her Chameleon Cloth looked merely like the pink fabric she had covered her body with.

A balding man ran into the room. "It's not him!" the woman told him.

"Unauthorized time traveler!" the balding man cried.

"Oh, get off it, Roberts," the woman said. "I'm Agent Keller. This is the Central Time Service offices. We service registered time travelers with anything they need. Chameleon Cloths to blend in, any documentation and such. What century did you come from?"

"The ninetee– the twenty-first century," Cassandra said. "Why? Where am I now?"

Agent Keller gave her a reassuring glance. "It's 2215."

Cassandra nearly collapsed again. "2215? I have traveled *another* 200 years..." Cassandra's mouth became too numb to finish.

"We meant to get Riley Granger," Roberts said unapologetically. "Been giving us quite the slip. He just stole some passports and Chameleon Cloths from us."

That kindly Mr. Granger stole from them? Cassandra tried to protest, but she was still too overwhelmed.

"Come now, let's get you calmed down," Agent Keller said. "Roberts will explain everything, I'm sure."

JANE AND ISABELLA HELPED Eleanor get Fly in the truck back at Mrs. Milner's. The silence was so unnerving; Eleanor almost wished her sisters would start sniping at each other again. She had always known she could lose her dearest Cassandra in an instant, but she never imagined it would be like this.

"Eleanor, please wait." Eleanor turned around to find Edward racing toward the truck.

"I have made the biggest mistake of my life," he said. "I need to at least make it right for my children... my other children."

Eleanor looked at his contrite face. She wondered if Edward was trying to trace a resemblance to Cassandra's face in hers. Eleanor took his hand. "We'll always be there for you."

"Can I just take one thing from the house before we leave?" Edward asked.

"I suppose," Eleanor said.

Edward hastened into Mrs. Milner's room and grabbed his copy of *The Gate of the Year* close. The 21st century wasn't meant to be, but at least he could take a small reminder of it back.

THE WALK THROUGH THE clear-walled Time Service hallways only made Cassandra want to shake and cry more.

Roberts held her back. "Careful." A coughing woman materialized in front of them.

"Sorry I'm late, Roberts, this cold is throwing everything off," the woman said.

"No problem, MacDonald," Roberts said in a detached accent. "Modern medicine. We can regenerate body parts, but we still can't cure the common cold, eh Perez?" he asked a man staring at the wall and scowling.

"You watching the news?" Mr. Perez asked. "The drasted Luddites control the government *again*. We can expect another round of cutbacks by New Year's, I'm sure."

"We'll just do the best we can with what we have," Roberts said. "Why don't you re-watch last night's Cowboys game instead?" Mr. Perez blinked twice.

"He's wearing something like your 21st century contact lenses that projects three-dimensional reconstructions," Roberts explained. Cassandra nodded.

Cassandra looked out the window. That one building in Dallas— the tower with the large ball— was still there, but now behind it were even taller buildings, made of the same translucent silver, with bridges between them and advertisements projecting from the glass like Mr. Granger's television. Between them and the skyline was much forest and a field where Cassandra could see large rodents that barked like small dogs running around.

"Why are there so few people?" Cassandra finally worked up the nerve to ask. Her mouth immediately froze again. She didn't know if she wanted to hear that answer.

"The more old-fashioned of us stayed here instead of moving to the lunar communities or the space stations." Roberts beckoned Cassandra to a large room filled with beautiful furniture and art. "Everything in this room was brought here by a time traveler. It can be a pain to move it all in, once you get so used to compressible furniture." Cassandra took a seat on a sofa that reminded her of her favorite in the drawing room at Woodvale Park.

"Mrs. Phillips?" a familiar voice said.

Cassandra turned around in disbelief. "Colonel Finster?" The drone had gotten him too, she remembered. Mr. Granger had lied about what the drones did, she realized, feeling nauseated. What else had he lied about?

"Colonel, why don't we and Mrs. Phillips have some tea?" Roberts asked.

"Blueberry?" Cassandra said.

"Of course," Colonel Finster said. He spoke into a red ring, "Could you send us up some blueberry tea? And maybe some of those cinnamon scones." He waved his hand and a tea set and a plate of scones materialized in a swirl of that dust.

"This must all seem like magic to you," Roberts said in the same detached accent.

Colonel Finster handed Cassandra a cup. "How long have you been here?" Cassandra asked him.

"Almost four weeks," the colonel said.

"Why didn't you go back to 1815?" Cassandra asked.

Roberts snorted. "That's the problem with you novice time travelers. You think time pockets are some kind of Flux Capacitor that can take you whenever you want."

"What Roberts means is that there are currently no pockets available to take me back to then and no time travelers with the pockets I need have come along yet either."

Cassandra tried to collect her thoughts. "So you cannot take me back?"

"Most of the dust has been confiscated in the attempt to capture Mr. Granger. We have some pockets in that storage room, but probably none to where you're interested."

"So what exactly has Mr. Granger done?" Cassandra asked.

"You're suddenly asking a lot of questions," Roberts said. "You remind me of my granddaughter." His face became sad for a moment, then quickly became a frown, a deeper one at least, and he blinked rapidly several times.

"Another Red Scarf breach!" Roberts cried. "I told Keller we needed to change the drasted pass codes on the entry ports!" He grabbed a gun and raced out of the room.

"What is going on?" Cassandra cried.

Colonel Finster grabbed Cassandra's hand. "We need to get you out of here." Two men wearing bright red scarves appeared in a swirl of dust. A shot rang out even before the dust completely cleared. The Colonel stumbled and slumped down on the floor.

Cassandra cradled him. "Please tell Miss Farnsworth she looked so handsome that night," he said as he stiffened.

Cassandra threw the scones at the men and raced through the halls. "Where is a door in this place?" she screamed. She raced back into the storage room to hide behind the pockets. By now the men had caught up with her.

The men aimed their guns at Cassandra. "Let us take the time pockets and we'll spare you, sweets," one of the men said.

"No, she'll just find some more," the other said.

Numbness was seizing Cassandra again. She thought of her sisters and Edward and the children. *No,* she told the numbness. She grabbed a ball and threw it at the red-scarved men. The ball missed and shattered on the floor, but reddish-gold came out, causing them to disappear. More footsteps were coming.

Cassandra rifled through the balls. What year were her sisters and Edward heading towards again? It ended with a *five*... Edward had said it was twenty years before them... The footsteps were coming closer. She found a ball that said *1995* and tapped on it furiously. Another man in the red scarf was about to fire when the dust finally came out, causing Cassandra to disappear.

ELEANOR WAS ABLE TO finish a letter to Brittany by the time Riley found a parking space at the university. It would probably be much more articulate in explaining matters to Brittany, and Eleanor wouldn't have to face her if she gave it to Colin. Riley helped everyone out of the car and they walked to the lawn in front of the Egerton, stopping at a metal sculpture of the Greek muses.

"Okay, anyone who wants to say their good-byes to anyone or anything, get it done in an hour," Riley said. "We'll all go back at noon."

"I am fine," Isabella said, planting herself on a bench.

"I'll take a walk with Fly if you want to find Colin," Jane told Eleanor.

Eleanor realized she had no idea where to start looking as she walked past the gift shop. Around the corner, an older man was showing a portrait of irises to a group of students.

"Why do you think one of the irises is white?" the older man asked.

"Because Van Gogh ran out of blue paint?" one of the students said. A few of the other students laughed.

"Because he felt like he did not belong?" Eleanor spoke up. She shirked back, realizing she wasn't part of the class.

The older man gave her a comforting smile. "I've always thought so myself."

"Dr. Williamson, do we have to double-space the paper?" a girl asked as the students walked away. Eleanor admired the irises some more, wondering what it would be like to travel around time and maybe ask some of the artists what they were thinking. No, if she got Fly home, then perhaps she could work to prevent Reddings Hall from being torn down. Her window to adventures, as small as it had been to start with, was closed for good.

Eleanor approached Dr. Williamson. "I am so sorry, sir. Where is Dr. Darcy's office?"

"Room 208," Dr. Williamson said. Realizing Eleanor

still looked lost, Dr. Williamson gave her another comforting smile and said, "The stairs are around the corner."

The door to the office was open, but Eleanor could not see or hear people inside. She gingerly made it in, looking around her for a piece of paper. The walls were plastered with artwork from all through the centuries. On the desk was a blue rectangular box, with something about the police written on it. It made screeching noises when Eleanor touched it. Eleanor jumped back almost two feet. Colin raced in from behind her and tapped it, stopping the screeching.

"Hi Eleanor," Colin said. He reached into the blue box. "Want a caramel?"

"Thank you."

"Oh, and you were right. It was Boccherini." Eleanor walked back and forth past the desk in agitation. "Is everything okay?" Colin asked.

Eleanor took a deep breath and handed him the letter. "Please tell Brittany I'm so sorry, we must go back to Hampshire tonight."

"Did someone die or something?" Colin shook his head.

"No, nothing like that."

Colin looked as if he was physically restraining himself from asking any further questions. "Oh, well, I'm sorry. I wi- I'm sure Brit will miss you. Can I pass along an e-mail address? Or you're on Facebook, I'm sure."

"What are..." For once, Eleanor had had enough of repressing the truth. "Colin, I am from Hampshire, but I was born in 1790. My family and I were taken 200 years into the future. I will never be able to reach you or Brittany when I get back."

Colin's eyes grew wide in anger. "You've got to be kidding me."

"I am telling you the truth! We really traveled through time."

"Of course, and I'm the king of England. Riley Granger put you up to this, didn't he? What more does that creep want?"

"Riley Granger is a good man!"

"Oh yes, a good man who treated my sister's heart worse than the mess on a shoe!"

What could Colin be talking about? "Well, maybe if Brittany wasn't such a shameless flirt, she would have never gotten into trouble!"

"What?" Colin slammed the door so hard the desk shook. "What makes you so sure you know Riley Granger?"

"I know he has extended every kindness to me since I met him, unlike you!"

"Who are you to lecture me on kindness, when you just keep insulting everything about me?"

Eleanor wished to say something cutting, but didn't know how. Why did the thought of getting the last word with Colin hurt deeper than with Frank? "This was obviously a mistake. I should go now."

"Well, fine. I'll let Brittany know."

"Good day to you." Eleanor made it all the way to the stairs before the tears started. There was no way she was going to let Darcy see her cry.

Chapter Fourteen

ISABELLA WAVED TO ELEANOR from the gift shop when Eleanor opened the door to the stairs. Eleanor managed to clear her tears before rejoining her.

"I thought you were staying on the lawn," Eleanor said.

"I saw this in the shop!" Isabella cried. She showed Eleanor a gold necklace with a large green stone. "Harry will adore it!"

Eleanor managed a smile. "I'm sure he will, darling."

Fly was climbing on the statue of the muses when Eleanor and Isabella arrived. Jane was standing a few feet away with Riley. Riley whispered something in her ear and they laughed and kissed.

"Jane, you cannot kiss someone you are not married to!" Isabella said.

"Mind your own affairs, Isabella," Eleanor said. Colin and Anna's warnings came back to her. How did she know they knew Riley any better than her? Cassandra would want to give Riley a chance, she told herself. She grabbed Fly before he fell off the statue. "No more emergency rooms."

"Is everyone ready?" Riley asked.

Eleanor nodded. "Let us go home."

Jane looked at her family and tapped the ball. "Just think, tonight you and I will be feasting with Henry the-" Reddish gold dust swirled all over her, Riley, Eleanor, and her family, knocking her out again.

"WHAT IS GOING ON here?" a police officer asked, shaking Jane. Jane was still lying on the grass.

"It's all right, they're with me," Riley said. He was dressed in a purple collared shirt with a purple tie and wearing a flat white wide-brimmed hat.

"Well, tell them to take whatever they're protesting now somewhere else!" the police officer said.

"You're adjusting fast," Riley said, helping Jane up. "You were only out about five minutes this time."

Jane looked around her. She was still on the university campus, but instead of the Egerton, there was a large parking lot in front of her. Her family wasn't dressed too differently than they had in 2015, except their sleeves were longer— it was supposed to be fall where they were going, Jane remembered. Eleanor was wearing a green denim jacket over her sweater and Isabella wore a white checkered skirt.

Riley placed his hat on Edward's head and handed Jane a copy of *The Dallas Morning News*. "It's October 27th. We hit our target."

"What time is it?" Eleanor asked.

Riley looked across the lawn to a clock tower. "It's two-thirty. We've got to get that machine before Dr. Bennet comes to meet you for your little tea-time."

Jane tried to keep up with him while examining even more new surroundings. The phones (or whatever all the students were carrying around) and the cars were much bulkier. Three ladies they passed on the street were wearing extremely short skirts even though there was a cold wind. Jane realized she had never saw what she was wearing and stopped to take a look at herself in a fountain. She was wearing a beautiful short yellow dress with long sleeves and tight yellow stockings. She tousled her hair. It was the perfect touch.

Riley led them into Willis Hall and down the stairs into a small room he called a "laboratory" in the basement. Jane looked around the room, waiting for the beautiful time machine. Riley picked what looked like a small silver plate off the floor.

"How in the world are we all going to fit in that?" Isabella asked.

"It's compressed right now," Riley said. "I built it out of 23rd century materials. This thing would attract a lot of unwanted attention on travels otherwise, not to mention someone might unknowingly use it if it was left unlocked. It must have gotten stuck like this, because Dr. Bennet didn't have a cord to talk to it."

"A machine can understand her?" Eleanor asked.

Riley pulled out his phone. "It can understand Ziggy." Riley stuck one end of the cord into Ziggy and the other end with the stick into the machine. The silver plate expanded into a pad large enough for several people to stand on. Clear tube came out of three points on the edge of the pad and spiraled around Riley.

Jane held her hand over her mouth to keep her breath. It was even more beautiful than Riley's sketchings. It was about the size of his truck, except taller where Riley's truck was long. Sparkling balls that must have contained time pockets filled the spiral.

"How does it work?" Jane asked.

"Well, first, we have to get in," Riley said. "Look into that screen." A bright light flashed. Jane shrieked and stumbled backwards. Riley squeezed her hand. "It's okay, it just needs to take a scan of your eyes. You can do it." Jane looked into the screen again. The machine flashed a few times and then the spirals spread out far enough so someone could enter.

Riley grinned. "Now give me the ball." Jane handed it

to him and he opened the top of one of the tubes, letting the machine suck up the dust. "Now we tell Ziggy to retrieve the 1815 ball." He frowned. "Except Dr. Bennet put another password on top of this."

"What are we going to do?" Jane said.

"I'm sorry, but you're going to have to go find Dr. Bennett and sweet-talk her into telling you the password," Riley said.

"Very well," Eleanor said, picking up Fly. "I am rather curious to finally meet her."

"Where are we going?" Fly asked.

"You're going to leave Dallas and go home," Riley said.

 "But I want to stay!" Fly burst into loud tears. Edward and Eleanor tried to comfort him. Eleanor beckoned for Jane and Isabella to go ahead.

Remembering the caramel, Eleanor reached in her pocket. Eleanor looked at it for a moment, imagining what Colin would think if he could see her now. She quickly handed the caramel to Fly.

"I THINK YOU SHOULD let me talk to my descendant," Isabella told Jane as they took the elevator to the third floor.

"Do whatever you please," Jane said.

The door opened. "Not *her*," Isabella moaned.

"Who?" Jane asked.

"That awful old receptionist Cassy and I met in 2015," Isabella said. "Well, she is not so old now, but she still looks irritable. I think I will buy Fly some ice cream."

"You're not being so helpful for someone who wants-" Jane stopped herself in time. She looked over to the receptionist.

"Can I help you?"

"I need to see Dr. Bennet."

"There's no Dr. Bennet in this department."

"I'm Jane Farnsworth. She told me to meet her here. Are you sure there's no Gillian Bennet?"

"*Gillian* Bennet?" The receptionist looked perplexed.

"Jane?" she heard a voice from behind her say. Jane turned around. An older woman in an orange dress ran toward her, tears streaming down her cheeks.

"Are you Gillian Bennet?" Jane asked. The woman nodded. She had Isabella's eyes, and her cheekbones were in the same place. Jane looked away in sadness, remembering all too vividly Isabella's boast about descendants. "You're a receptionist?"

Dr. Bennet pulled her close to her. "People don't readily accept Ph.D.s that won't be issued another two years from now, I'm afraid," she whispered. "I do make the best pot of Lady Grey in Willis Hall, though." She turned to the receptionist and spoke up. "It's all right, Connie, she's family from out of town."

Dr. Bennet took Jane's hand and led her behind the desk. "What are you doing here?"

"I'm here to meet you, just like you asked us in your notes." Jane handed her the papers.

Dr. Bennet's eyebrows furrowed. "I didn't write these." Her face fell. "Riley Granger found you first, didn't he?"

"What is it to you if he did?"

Dr. Bennet grabbed her hand. "Miss Bennet, have you made those copies yet?" a professor asked.

"I don't have time, make them yourself!" Dr. Bennet cried. She pressed the elevator button, but when the elevator didn't come fast enough, she turned to the stairs.

"Where are we going?" Jane asked.

"To get to the time machine before he leaves us stranded again!" Dr. Bennet said.

"Leaves *us*? *You* left *him* stranded!"

"Let me guess. He told you all these fantastic stories about he was going to escort you through time, didn't he?"

"How do I know I can trust you?"

Dr. Bennet's face sunk into a sad smile. "Yes, I suppose you're right. Please believe me, I've been trying to protect you and your sisters your whole lives."

"My whole life?"

"You don't even know who I am, do you?"

"You're Isabella's great-great-great-great-great-great granddaughter."

"Isabella's great-great... oh dear, I do have so much to explain."

"Jane, did you find her?" Eleanor was at the bottom of the staircase. "Isabella wandered off with Fly..." Eleanor stared at Dr. Bennet in shock.

"I suppose the resemblance is uncanny, isn't it?" Jane said. Eleanor and Dr. Bennet kept staring at each other, both looking as if they wanted to cry.

"Mamma?" Eleanor finally managed.

"Eleanor?" Eleanor nodded. Dr. Bennet embraced her and they both burst into tears. "My little girl! Oh, look at you! Look at you!"

Jane studied Dr. Bennet in shock. All of a sudden, she could see Cassandra and Eleanor and even herself in the doctor's face as well. "But my mother was Cassandra Farnsworth."

Dr. Bennet smiled. "Cassandra Gillian Bennet Farnsworth, to be precise. I started going by my middle name in primary school because there was another Cassandra."

"You're... you're my mother? You didn't die in that carriage accident?"

Dr. Bennet grabbed Jane and Eleanor's hands. "No, baby, I'm so sorry. I meant for you and your sisters and your father to come much sooner than this." She hastened to the laboratory, opening the door to find Edward slumped down on the floor. Riley was in the time machine, dust swirling all over him.

"Riley Granger!" Dr. Bennet cried.

"Sorry Gill, maybe you should have stayed in the 18th century long enough to raise your daughters to have some common sense!" Riley said. He pulled a gun from the floor of the machine and aimed it at Dr. Bennet. Jane jumped in front of her and got hit with a force in the right shoulder that caused it to go numb. Eleanor almost made it to the door of the machine, but Riley pressed a button emitting a force that pushed her back as the machine disappeared.

Jane staggered over to Edward and Eleanor. "I'm sorry. I'm so, so sorry." Dr. Bennet bent down and massaged her shoulder. For the first time in her life, Jane finally did what she had longed to do after all those balls when no one asked her to dance and all those days Isabella had demanded everyone's congratulations on her engagement. She collapsed into her mother's arms, sobbing.

"It's going to be okay, baby," Dr. Bennet said. "We'll find Riley and kick his behind to the Stone Age."

"I don't understand," Eleanor said. "Who exactly stranded who here?"

Dr. Bennet sighed. "I've better put on that pot."

Chapter Fifteen

IT WAS VERY EASY to be taken in by Riley Granger. He had that old-fashioned Texan charm. Riley had made fast friends with the equally charming Nathan Arnold while he and his cousin Audrey were studying abroad for a year at Oxford for their master's degrees. Nate and Riley's potential caught the attention of the head of their college, who introduced them to Gillian right away.

The three of them may have been the punch line of the scientific community, but that didn't stop the excitement when they found a new time pocket, especially one that took the three of them— plus Audrey, now Nate's fiancée— more than two hundred years into the future. It was there they found a community for other travelers like them. It was also where they found the Luddites.

The Luddite movement had come together as society rebuilt from the devastation of the great solar flare of 2106. They believed the energy from the time pockets could be used for more widely beneficial purposes, such as replacing other dwindling energy sources. To them, time travel was a fringe hobby with little to no benefit to society.

Gillian admired their principles, though she gladly argued that time travel had its benefits, and the majority of the Luddites were harmless. There was just one radical faction, the Red Scarves, who wanted to kill every time traveler they could find before they wasted the pockets.

One night, while Nate and Audrey were dining on the Mars satellite space station, the Red Scarves ambushed and kidnapped them. By the time Gillian, Riley, and the law enforcement could come to the rescue, Audrey was dead and Nate was nearly so from the torture. It took him almost three weeks in a 23rd century hospital to recover, but Nate insisted they keep time traveling to honor Audrey's memory and to defy the Red Scarves.

When the drones started coming after them to take Riley and Nate back to 2215, Riley confessed to Gillian that he and Nate had killed Jennifer Foreman, an aspiring Luddite politician. He insisted they had done it in self-defense, but then Tom Perez from the Time Agency showed Gillian a three-dimensional reconstruction from Jennifer's lens camera that proved it had been done in cold blood. When she tried to return Nate and Riley to be prosecuted, they left her stranded outside Oxford in 1786.

With the help of a kind curate named James Farnsworth, Cassandra— she had started going by her first name again to blend in better— got a job as a governess in a small village outside of Basingstoke in Hampshire. She hoped it would be quiet enough to continue her research. James's sister had gotten her husband, a baronet, to give James the recently vacated living there. Gillian knew at thirty-one, she was well past a marriageable age by 18th century standards, so she figured love was the last thing on his mind. It was definitely the last thing on hers.

However, it wasn't long until James's kind heart and progressive ideas struck Gillian, while her tenacity and caring soul struck James. Gillian hadn't been in Hampshire two months when James rode over to the estate where Gillian worked to express his deepest admiration and his hopes for their union in marriage.

Gillian tried to blink back her tears. "James, I came

from nearly two hundred years in the future."

James frowned. "A simple *no* would have sufficed."

It was when James read one of the stories he had heard her tell her charges in a book that had only recently been published that he believed her. He asked her once again, and this time Gillian accepted. Within a month of their marriage, Gillian was pregnant.

She spent the next eleven years working to find other time pockets, in between giving birth to and caring for four daughters. Each of them spurred on her quest. She wanted them to grow up to have all the same opportunities her parents had worked so hard for her to have.

Then one night, after drinking tea with Sir Francis and Lady Jennings, Gillian took a walk and found high levels on time dust in the conservatory. She collected the dust and tapped the ball. It took her to 2004!

She hurried back to 1798 to get her family and her research. She was taking the Jennings's carriage home when drones from the 23rd century came and scared the horses. The coachman escaped, but the carriage went off Honeysuckle Bridge.

Gillian woke up in a Basingstoke hospital in 2004. "Where is the ball?" she asked the nurses. Nobody knew what she was even talking about. It must have broken in her hands. She was stranded again, this time in her original century, without her family or the machine.

She got a job at a university in the States— in Dallas, Texas, where the pockets seemed to be centered— and spent every waking moment tracking down another pocket that would allow her to get back to her family. After almost ten years, she found another to 2215 outside of Waco.

Gillian's first object was to go to the Time Service library. She found through a letter from Mrs. Parker written in 1814 that Cassandra and Eleanor were married. Gillian secured the necessary Chameleon Cloths, and Phyllis Mac-

Donald from the Agency helped her make passports for her family.

Now the only thing she needed was a time pocket to 1814, or the closest she could get. What she found instead in the storage room was Riley.

"How long has it been since you last saw me?" Riley asked.

"Nearly fifteen years," Gillian stared at his still-youthful face. "Goodness, how long has it been for you, a week? Where's Nate? Did you leave him stranded too?"

"He's gone insane since losing Audrey," Riley said. "I feel terrible for what we did to you. The only thing that's been keeping me going was the distant idea that you might be able to give me a second chance. The machine got decompressed and I need a way for Ziggy to talk to it. I promise I'll help you with whatever you need if you help me."

Something about Riley's words seemed insincere, but Gillian's thoughts of Cassandra and Eleanor having complications in childbirth; or of shy, sensitive Jane on the marriage market; or of Isabella being sick yet again overwhelmed her doubts. "You give me the machine to start with," Gillian said. Riley complied with that stupid grin of his.

"Red Scarf breach!" Phyllis cried. Gillian looked for the Chameleon Cloths and the passports. They were in Riley's hands. She turned to face Phyllis, who aimed a phaser at her.

"Thanks for believing me, MacDonald," Riley said. MacDonald fired at Gillian, stunning her in the head. Riley threw a time pocket at her, sending her back to 1995 with a useless, decompressed machine.

Chapter Sixteen

JANE TRIED TO WRAP her head around two different versions of history. Everything seemed to make sense with Dr. Bennet— her mother's— explanation. Had she really been so desperate to believe Riley loved her to disregard every hole in his explanations?

It wasn't just Riley's story that made sense. All of a sudden, it seemed like Jane's entire life made sense for the first time: why she had always tired easily of needlework, piano lessons, and balls, as if her heart always knew it didn't belong in the 19th century. Jane took her mother's hand as Dr. Bennet finished her story.

"Where are your father and Cassandra and Isabella?" Gillian asked.

Jane and Eleanor looked at each other. "Cassandra was taken by the drones, and Papa... he..." Jane couldn't bring herself to finish.

"I'm so sorry, Mamma, it was so sudden," Eleanor said. "He went out during a rainstorm to visit a sick parishioner and a week later he was gone."

"Drasted fool," Gillian said, wiping a tear from her eye. "I told him over and over that compromised his immunity. Just please tell me he didn't leave you girls to be cared for by that horrid sister of his." Jane and Eleanor gave each other more awkward looks. "Drasted *fool*! That was always his one weak spot, thinking everyone deep down had good intentions. I loved him so much for it, though. Where is Isabella?"

"She's taking care of Francis, my son... your grandson."

Gillian's eyes misted. "I have a grandson?"

"You have five grandchildren actually," Jane said. "Eleanor has another son, and Cassandra and Edward, her husband, have three children. You'll have a sixth soon... and a seventh, Isabella's expecting as well." Jane tried to withhold her selfish despair telling her mother all this, but the look on her face obviously betrayed her again.

Gillian gave Jane a hug. "I was the last of my sisters to get married. My father always used to tell me there's no point trying to get out of the starting gate first if you're not focused on finishing well."

"A woman has fainted!" Connie, the secretary, cried from down the hall. Jane ran to where people were crowding around a young woman in a light pink blouse and a long pink skirt with roses printed on it. Eleanor pushed her way through and shook Cassandra. Another of the clear pocket-collecting balls slipped out of Cassandra's hands.

"Eleanor?" Cassandra murmured. Eleanor helped her sister up and hugged her. Upon seeing Jane, Cassandra pulled her in as well. "What happened?"

"Riley left us stranded," Jane said. "And we found Dr. Bennet, only she's not Isabella's great-great... you know." Cassandra looked at Gillian with disbelief.

"Mamma?"

"My dearest Cassy!" Gillian gave her a hug and pulled back to admire her stomach. "Oh, we have so much to catch up on."

"How are you... here?"

"I'll explain everything to you and Isabella once we get her."

Cassandra turned to Jane and Eleanor. "Is Edward here?" They looked at each other. Jane led Cassandra to the lab, but Cassandra raced past her and to Edward's side.

"No... please..." Cassandra cried, stroking his face.

"It looks like he was just stunned," Gillian said.

Edward woke up slowly. "Riley... Granger... where is he?"

"Don't worry about him."

"Darling!" Edward fell into Cassandra's arms and then pulled back. "Look at you!"

Cassandra admired Edward's blue knitted coat. "Look at you, you're so handsome. Oh dearest Edward, I'm so sorry."

"For what? I'm the one who should be sorry." Edward kissed her hand and then Cassandra kissed him on the lips.

"This is your husband, I presume," Gillian said.

"Yes, may I present my husband, Edward Phillips. Edward, this is my mother, Cassandra Farnsworth- I mean, Gillian Bennet."

"I answer to both," Gillian said, giving a shocked Edward a hug.

"So where were you?" Jane asked Cassandra.

"I went another two hundred years into the future!" Cassandra said. "I saw Colonel Finster... he said you were so handsome that night at the ball, Jane."

"You saw him?" Jane asked. She saw the sad look in Cassandra's eyes.

"I'm so sorry, darling." Cassandra wiped the tears streaming down Jane's face.

"No, I'm so sorry," Jane said. "I was so focused on myself that night... the poor man..." Cassandra hugged Jane, and Jane, for once, didn't resent it.

"You went to the 23rd century?" Gillian asked Cassandra. "Do you still have the ball?" Cassandra handed it to Gillian, who then examined it with a flashlight. "There might be enough 2215 dust to extract."

"I am sorry, but what is 2215 dust?" Eleanor asked.

"They put a little dust that can travel back to 2215 in case people get stranded and need to return," Gillian said.

"Dust?"

"I guess I have a lot to explain. Let's go get Isabella first."

ISABELLA HANDED FLY a small chocolate ice cream cone. "Eat this darling, you will feel much better."

"Why do we have to go home, Aunt Bella?"

"Because that's where your brother and Uncle Harry are."

"Why can't they come here?"

Isabella took a bite of her own cone, nearly freezing her front teeth. Could Harry come to the future? There was no Royal Navy, at least not one with a grand ship, and no way to bring his immense fortune. No, she had to go back to him.

"Isabella!"

"Cassandra?" Isabella raced to her sister. "Where have you been?"

"The 23rd century!" Cassandra admired Isabella's dress. "You look so beautiful."

"Where is Riley?" Isabella asked. She looked at the older woman standing next to Eleanor, looking as if being in the presence of Isabella was about to make her cry. "Who is she?"

"Riley left us," Eleanor said. "The machine is gone."

"We did not get the time machine?" Isabella cried angrily.

"Well, it's not like you helped," Jane snapped.

"Jane!" the older woman said.

"Are you Dr. Bennet?" Isabella said.

The woman nodded. "Isabella?"

"Yes, that is me," Isabella said. "Hello, my darling descendant... why are you staring at me like that?"

"My little baby." Dr. Bennet... was she choking upon her tears? "I can't believe it."

"Isabella, Dr. Bennet is our mother," Eleanor said.

"I do not understand," Isabella said. "How can you be both my mother and my great-great-great-great-great-great granddaughter?"

"She's not your great-great-great-great-great-great granddaughter, you fool!" Jane said. "That was another one of Riley's lies to us."

"Jane, don't talk to your sister that way!" Dr. Bennet and Cassandra both said.

Fly slipped under the table to hide from his shouting aunt and the stranger. Eleanor and Gillian bent down. "It is all right, dear," Eleanor said. "This is your grandmamma."

"Do you like elephants?" Fly asked.

"I love elephants," Dr. Bennet said. She crawled under the table and let Fly hug her. "I'll love them even more when I'm showing them to you at the lunar wildlife preserve in 2215."

JANE WAS READY TO leave 1995 behind, and the awful memory of Riley jilting her— jilting all of them— with it. She and her family drank their tea as Gillian extracted and examined the dust with her scientific equipment.

"There's not too much dust left, but I was able to extract a few 2215 particles," Dr. Bennet said. "If we had a time machine, it may be able to concentrate it enough to get us back."

"There's nothing else we can do?" Jane asked.

"I do have an experimental serum that can multiply the dust, but it's back in my lab in 2015."

"How are we going to get back to 2015?" Eleanor asked. "Just sit here and wait?" Jane would be forty-three, she realized, even older than Colonel Finster. She wondered if she and Isabella would still be squabbling in their middle age.

"What about the pocket at Darcy House?" Isabella asked.

"What pocket from Darcy House?" Gillian asked.

"We took dust from the dining room at Darcy House to get here," Eleanor said. "I only took half of it. Could it also be here in the 1990's? Could there be 2015 dust in it?"

Gillian took another ball from a drawer. "We could try."

CASSANDRA AND GILLIAN TOOK turns filling in the remaining holes for everyone as they took a cab to Darcy House.

"So how did a time pocket end up at Reddings House?" Eleanor asked.

"Riley must have found one in 2215 and left it for you to find," Gillian said. "The dust feeds off sugar. He must have left it behind on something sweet."

"Like chewing gum?" Edward asked. "Just like in this book." Edward showed Gillian *The Gate of the Year*.

Gillian beamed. "David will be so glad to hear you're such a fan. He was complaining to me the last time I saw him how he still hasn't had a major motion picture like Jack or Ronald."

"You've met David Andrews?" Edward asked.

"Met him? We've done quite a bit of time traveling together. You never noticed how well-researched his books are?"

"If you know other time travelers, why didn't you use one of their machines to go back to us?" Isabella asked.

"You just can't take time pockets to wherever you want," Cassandra said.

"I see you met Connor Roberts," Gillian said. "The only pocket I know of that goes back to 1815 is with my old machine. We just need to figure out where Riley is and get the pocket from him, willingly or not."

The car pulled up to Darcy House. All Gillian had to do to get in was to open the gate; the Darcys had apparently not secured their house yet. "Do you think Colin's family is at home?" Eleanor asked. "I mean, Dr. Darcy's."

Gillian's face brightened with interest. "You've met Colin Darcy?"

"It's a long story." Eleanor knocked on the door, trying to keep the redness from filling her face. "How do you know him?"

"Bill and Anita, his parents, were major supporters of my research, before that terrible plane crash."

"Colin's parents died in a plane crash?" Eleanor asked.

"Yes, their private plane went down outside of Fort Worth," Gillian said. "No one survived."

"Oh, no wonder he was so nervous on the plane." Eleanor said. What other horrible assumptions had she made?

"Can you call on them so we can get into their house?" Cassandra asked.

"Not for another nine years," Gillian said. "We'll tell them we got locked out of our house and need to call a locksmith."

"All of us?" Isabella said.

"Probably only one of us actually needs to go in," Gillian said. "The rest of us will wait in the yard."

"You should go, Eleanor," Jane said. "You know where to look."

Eleanor didn't want to argue in front of Gillian. "Very well."

"I'll go with you," Jane said. "It's my fault we're all stranded here, so I'll help get us back."

Eleanor took a deep breath and rung the bell. Mrs. Darcy— nearly identical to the picture Eleanor had seen over the fireplace, only her hair was slightly longer— opened the door. "Bill, the baby-sitter's here!" she cried.

Eleanor assumed her different accent was Ecuadorian.

"Oh, I am not here to sit on any babies...." Eleanor said.

"Mom, Tim and Josh stopped my *Doctor Who* tape to play their stupid video game!" a little boy cried. Eleanor shivered. It was Colin, only about nine or ten years old. He didn't have a beard, but his hair was almost the same length and just as wild.

Colin's father, nearly identical to his portrait, came in, followed by a girl Colin's age with brown hair. "Colin, please don't ruin this," Mr. Darcy said. "This is your mom's first chance to go out since the baby."

"The baby?" Eleanor said. "Brittany?"

"No, my name is Anna," the brown-haired girl said. Of course, her voice was just as oily as her older self, if perhaps a little higher-pitched.

"Well, you've met Colin, and this is the Kelly's oldest daughter Anna," Mrs. Darcy said, leading them into the living room. The furniture was nearly the same, but the carpet was green. Two boys Colin and Anna's age were playing a video game on a bulky television screen, while a girl who looked about five or six sat on the couch pretending to feed a blond-haired doll that looked like a small child.

"These are my nephews, Tim and Josh, and Anna's sister Samantha," Mrs. Darcy said. "Their parents are at the restaurant already. Kids, say hi to..."

"El-" Eleanor looked at Colin. "Nelly."

"Jenny," Jane said.

"Hi," the three children said, not even looking up from their games. Eleanor realized Mrs. Darcy was asking her to watch these children!

"Colin, are you slowing down your mother?" an elderly lady with Colin's eyes who smelled strongly of lavender said.

"He's fine, Cathy," Mrs. Darcy said. "This is Cathy Darcy, Bill's mother."

The elder Mrs. Darcy— Cathy— must have noticed the uneasiness on Eleanor's face, for she glared at her with much suspicion. "Where did you meet these girls?"

"I told you, Debbie from the school of education said she would send some students," the younger Mrs. Darcy— Anita— said. She turned back to Eleanor and Jane. "Okay, the tater tot casserole is in the oven. I rented a few movies from Blockbuster for them. Make sure Colin doesn't get into the Halloween candy. Brittany's formula is in the fridge..." Eleanor glanced over at the floorboard as Anita kept prattling on instructions.

Anita picked up a baby who looked to be seven or eight months from a padded enclosure in the corner. "And here is Brittany." She placed her in Eleanor's arms.

"Hello, darling," Eleanor said, stroking her curly light-brown hair. Brittany made some sort of babbling noise that for a moment Eleanor was sure sounded like "Okie Dokie." Cathy saw how comfortable Eleanor was with Brittany and seemed to relax.

Anita gave Colin a kiss. "Please be good."

"Okay," Colin said, trying hard to smile. He pulled a huge book off the shelf as his parents went through the kitchen to a room where the car was.

"What are you reading?" Jane asked. Colin held up the cover. It had Michaelangelo's sculpture of David on the cover. "Oh, is that about art?"

"No, it's about Paul," Colin said sarcastically.

Cathy slapped him on the back of the head. "*This* is why you still need a baby-sitter, you smart-mouthed brat!"

"Cathy, are you ready?" Anita called from the car room.

"I just need to grab my purse," Cathy said. She glanced at Eleanor and Jane once more and grabbed Colin's face. "Be good to the baby-sitters. Remember, you never, ever have a second chance..."

"To make a first impression," Colin finished over her.

She gave him another slap before heading out to the car.

Jane hugged Colin. "I'm so sorry. I have an aunt just as horrible as her."

"It's okay," Colin mumbled, covering his face with the book.

Eleanor looked at Colin, trying to figure out something to say. She realized she needed to say it to the man, not the boy. Eleanor handed Brittany to Jane. "Stay here with the children. I'll go get the time pocket."

"What if I drop her?" Jane said. She didn't want to kill her best friend before she even had a chance to be her best friend.

"Dearest, you managed not to drop Fly or James, or Cassandra's children," Eleanor said.

Jane sat down with Brittany next to Samantha and watched Tim and Josh play their game. Eleanor walked into the dining room, trying to remember which floorboard was the loose one. She tried to imagine for a moment she was Mr. Bingley, which as ridiculous as it seemed, helped her remember it was by the window. The floorboard was more secure than it would be in twenty years, but she was able to take it off. *Please let there still be dust...* Eleanor prayed. Something was being sucked up into the ball.

"What are you doing?" It was Colin. Eleanor yanked her arm away, scraping the top side of it against the floorboard. She waved her arm around, trying not to scream.

"Is your arm hurt?" Colin asked.

"Just a little scrape," Eleanor said.

"Here, have an *Animaniacs* bandage." Colin reached into his pocket and handed Eleanor a strip of blue paper decorated with strange creatures that looked like a cross between dogs and monkeys.

"Thank you, you are so kind." Eleanor shivered. "Why do you keep these things in your pocket?"

"If you knew my cousins, you would too," Colin said.

"Your cousins really are not that violent against you, are they?"

"They punched me in the nose last week because I wouldn't give them my last piece of Fruit Stripe gum," Colin said. "My parents don't notice because of the stupid baby."

"Nelly, I think we have a problem!" Jane cried. Eleanor and Colin raced into the living room. Tim and Josh were playing with her phone.

"Look at this camera!" Tim said. "I've never seen anything like it!"

"Give it back to Jenny!" Colin said.

"Hey, let's get a picture of him with his girlfriend!" Josh said.

"She is *not* my girlfriend!" Colin screeched.

"Yeah, that would require people liking you!" Tim said. Josh kicked Colin in the groin. Colin let out a cry of pain.

"Don't cry, baby!" Josh said. "Or we'll put you in the playpen!" Tim tried to pick Colin up.

"Stop it now!" Eleanor cried, pulling them away. She looked at Anna on the couch, engrossed in a bright purple book called *Kristy's Big Day*. "Always been there for him, Anna?" Eleanor said quietly to herself. She realized, perhaps too late, that maybe teasing Frank never made her feel as bad as teasing Colin did because she had never cared about Frank the way she cared about Colin.

There was a knock from the front door. "Sit here!" Eleanor told the boys. Eleanor opened the door; two young ladies were standing on the front porch.

"I'm so sorry," the taller lady said. "I tried to call to tell you we were running late, but I kept getting a busy signal."

"That is all right," Eleanor said. "Jenny, are you ready?"

"Ready!" Jane said.

"Where are you going?" Colin asked.

Jane handed him Brittany. "I'm sorry, but I must go

now. Just please take care of your sister. She may be all you have some day."

Eleanor and Jane hastened to rejoin their family back out in the front yard. Eleanor handed Gillian the ball.

"I wonder if I should have told Mr. and Mrs. Darcy to be careful on airplanes," Eleanor said.

Gillian looked sad. "I'm under strict orders by my project's funders to not tell anyone, past or present, what I do. Something about the potential for catastrophic effects to the time line, though I've found I have yet to change anything during my travels."

"So we cannot tell anyone?" Eleanor asked.

"Not outside the project or my family, and even for my family I had to pull a lot of strings. You haven't told anyone, have you?"

Eleanor looked back at the house. "Not… yet."

Colin ran toward them. "I got your camera back from my cousins, Jenny."

Jane took the phone from him. "Thank you."

"You showed the children your *smartphone*?" Gillian asked.

"I'm sorry, they were fighting and I thought it would be a distraction," Jane said.

Colin looked at Eleanor and her family. "Are you like Mary Poppins or something?"

"No, I am not," Eleanor said. "I must be... going home now."

"Can I go with you, please?" Colin said. "I've got to get away from those people!"

Edward bent down to Colin. "No, not this time. You can give this back to me the next time you see me, though." He handed Colin his copy of *The Gate of the Year*.

Colin examined the book. "Hey, it's about time travel, just like *Doctor Who*! Thanks!"

Eleanor looked over at Cassandra. "He would make a

wonderful teacher, " Cassandra said quietly.

"What are you doing?" Now it was Cathy, with Colin's parents, the two real baby-sitters, and the children. She looked at the baby-sitters. "So, thought you could use Darcy House to party with your friends, is that it?"

"No, it is not their fault," Eleanor said. "I have never even met them."

"Then what are you doing here?" Cathy demanded.

"They were taking something from the floorboard!" Anna said, pointing at Eleanor. "I saw her!"

"What in the world were you doing poking around our floorboards?" Cathy asked. "Bill, call the police!"

Cassandra slipped down on the floor. "I think the baby's coming!" She motioned at Eleanor to tap the ball.

Edward took Cassandra's hand. "This can't happen now, you still have another month!"

"Edward, you can't help her if you're not calm," Gillian said. "Just do what you did the last three times."

"I was in town on business all those times," Edward admitted.

Eleanor tapped the ball, and dust started swirling around her. Cassandra straightened up. "Oh dear, I do so hate these false alarms." Cassandra grabbed onto Jane and Eleanor and hastily grabbed on to Edward and her mother as Isabella grabbed her.

THE NEXT THING JANE knew, something wet pressed on her nose. Bingley was sniffing her face. She blinked a few times; there was daylight again. She was still in the front yard of Darcy House.

"Mr. Bingley, what on earth-" Brittany yanked Bingley away. "What are all of you doing here? Colin told me you were going back to England."

"They got stranded at the airport." Gillian and Edward helped Cassandra up. "Passport snafu. I picked them up."

"Dr. Bennet?" Brittany said. "I thought you were on sabbatical. What exactly is going on here?" Cassandra groaned and grabbed under her dress.

"The baby's coming!" Cassandra said.

Isabella grabbed Cassandra's shoulder. "You'll be all right, darling!" she said like she was reading a poem for the hundredth time.

"No, please… something feels wrong…." Cassandra fainted in Isabella's frozen arms.

"Call the hospital, please!" Gillian said. Brittany pulled out her phone. Jane held on to Cassandra, desperately hoping her sisters' luck in childbirth hadn't just run out.

Chapter Seventeen

"So Riley Granger left you stranded at the airport?" Brittany asked as they waited at a Whataburger across the street from the hospital.

Jane looked over at Gillian, who sadly nodded. "Yes," Jane said.

Brittany took Jane's hand. "Oh Jane... I'm so sorry. I wish I would have known. I could have saved you a lot of trouble and punched him in the face for you."

"So he tried to court you?"

"Oh yeah, he did that whole Prince Charming act on me, promising me he would take me around in his 'time machine' if I helped him find your mom. He told me to meet him on the White Rock Trail, but he left me waiting on a freezing November night, like Linus waiting for the Great Pumpkin. Colin figured out what was going on and picked me up at 3 a.m." The fact that Riley had been as cruel to Brittany as Jane once had been to Isabella gave Jane a sick headache.

Edward came in. Jane couldn't tell what the look on his face meant. She swallowed her French fry whole.

"How is she?" Jane said, holding on to her mother.

"There was some hemorrhaging," Edward said. "We're incredibly fortunate. The doctor said if she came in any later than she did, both she and the baby might be gone now."

Jane sighed with relief. "So she's all right?"

"She's not completely out of danger yet," Edward said.

"But she and the baby are resting comfortably now." He turned to Gillian. "You have another beautiful granddaughter." Gillian collapsed into Edward's arm, sobbing.

Eleanor wiped a few tears from her face. "You probably want something to eat, don't you?"

"I would love something to eat," Edward said. "I can see if we can see the baby at least afterwards."

CASSANDRA WOKE UP SLOWLY, trying to grab a sense of where she was. She was in a beautiful white room with portraits of various flowers. She realized she wasn't wearing the pink Chameleon Cloth for the first time in days; she was wearing a light pink gown with no back instead. She reminded herself she was in the hospital in 2015, like the last few times she had woken.

She looked up to see Edward, stubble on his cheeks, reading out loud from a green book. "Nothing more alarming occurred than a fear on Mrs. Allen's side, of having once left her clogs behind her at an inn..." He stopped when he noticed she was awake. Tears came down his cheeks as he took her hand.

"Is she all right?" Cassandra asked.

"The baby?" Edward asked. Cassandra nodded. "She still needs a little help breathing, so she's in something called a nick-you— but the doctor said she should be fine. He said we can visit her now if you'd like." He helped Cassandra up and into a chair with two large wheels, one on each side, and pushed her down a hallway.

That awful numbness returned momentarily when Cassandra saw all the wires attached to the clear box. *They're keeping her alive,* Cassandra reminded herself. *I'm alive too. I'm alive for all of my children.*

The nurse showed Cassandra where to place her hands so she could touch the baby. Cassandra rested her hand against her daughter's face, her numbness transferring into tears.

"She's beautiful."

"Of course she is, she looks just like her mother."

"May we come in?" Gillian asked. Edward looked over at Cassandra.

"Of course," Cassandra said.

Gillian looked at the small pink bundle. "She looks just like Cassandra when she was born." Gillian pulled a tissue of her pocket. It seemed like yesterday that she had placed little Cassy in James's arms. James was gone, but her heart's dearest desire since that day, to see their daughters in the 21st century, had finally come true.

"I'm so glad you're both all right," Eleanor said.

"Thank you," Cassandra said.

"What's her name?" Jane asked.

Cassandra and Edward looked at each other. "We'll get back to you on that," Edward said.

"What a beautiful darling!" Isabella said. "She and my baby will be such friends!" Isabella had apparently decided to make up for how silent she had been most of the evening. Jane took a deep breath, smiled, and ignored her.

"I'm sorry about all the trouble I caused," Jane said.

"It's all right, darling," Cassandra said. "You made no trouble that wasn't already there." She and Edward took each other's hands. Gillian looked toward the clock and cleared her throat.

"Is something in your throat, Mamma?" Jane asked.

"It's almost nine o'clock. Let's give Cassy and Edward some time to say goodnight."

Edward turned to Cassandra as soon as everyone left. "So what is her name going to be?"

"I was thinking Gillian."

"Lovely. Though it's rather modern, isn't it?"

"Well, she'll fit in quite nicely here then."

"Are you sure? Your mother said she can help me with

my debts."

"I heard what the doctor said. Can you even imagine where Gilly and I would be now if I gave birth at Woodvale Park? We'll figure out a way to bring the other children here."

"I don't care when or where we live, as long as we and the children are always together."

"Are we having another fight?"

Edward laughed. "I think we are." He bent down to Cassandra in her chair and they kissed each other on the lips. It was like Edward had cut his business in London short and called on her at Reddings Hall to ask for her hand all over again. No, Cassandra decided, it was much better.

"Mr. Phillips, I'm sorry, but visiting hours are over," the nurse said.

Edward looked over at Cassandra. "It's all right," she said. "I'm not afraid anymore."

 JANE NOTICED A BLOND man in purple scrubs in the parking lot while looking for her mother's car. *That looks like Riley.* Jane tried to cry quietly so Isabella wouldn't laugh at her.

Eleanor took Jane's hand. "I am so sorry, darling. This could have all been avoided if not for my pride. I just accepted Riley's intentions were good because forgiving Colin would be harder if he was wrong about... everything."

"I guess I'll never know love like you and Frank."

Eleanor frowned. "Jane, darling, Frank only married me because he thought if I provided Uncle Jennings with heirs, he'd be less inclined to remarry if Aunt Jennings died." The relief on Eleanor's face suggested she had been withholding this information from everyone, even Cassandra. "After he died, I learned he had massive gambling debts and two mistresses. I still have my suspicions about a third."

"Do you mean all this time you never fell in love with

him?"

"I was visiting Cassandra at Woodvale Park, back when she was first pregnant with little Cassy, shortly after Isabella had nearly ran away with Mr. Whitaker. I overheard Edward's sisters telling him none of us should ever be welcomed at Woodvale again because of the scandal. I pretended I had seen Frank's good qualities after I broke my foot so that you and Isabella could always have a home at Reddings Hall, no matter what."

"I'm so sorry I caused so much misery for you," Jane said. "You must despise me so much."

"It was entirely my choice," Eleanor said. "I was scared and I allowed that fear to influence my foolishness. There is nothing worse on earth than marrying without affection."

Gillian pulled up with Isabella in the front seat. Brittany looked upon them and Jane and Eleanor with curiosity. "So how exactly did you end up at my house from the airport? And how come you just met your mother now?"

Jane looked over at Gillian again. "Because Riley didn't make up the time machine," Gillian said. "I was stranded in the 18th century, when the girls were born."

"And lived up until last week," Eleanor said.

Brittany's face lit up. "You're all time travelers? Really?"

"You think we could make a thing like that up?" Jane said.

Brittany burst into joyful laughter. "So that's how you know so much about Regency times! I can't believe it! Oh no, no wonder Cassandra had the wrong idea about Edward and me. If I had known you guys were so... um, traditional... anyway, I would never steal someone's husband, especially not the husband of someone just about to give birth. My parents raised me much better than that."

"I'm sure she'll be glad to hear that when you see her," Gillian said.

"Does Colin know?" Brittany asked.

Eleanor frowned. "I told him, but he didn't believe me and got quite angry."

"Yeah, Colin's had problems with anxiety and awkwardness even before I was born— thanks largely to our stupid toxic extended family— but he's had so much more trouble regulating them in the last year, with his new dream job that he's afraid he could lose at any moment for hurting someone's feelings. Then Riley came and now he's afraid I'm going to do something stupid again on top of that, though I've told the blockhead over and over again I'm doing background checks on all future boyfriends. It's the worst he's been since our parents died."

"Brit!"

Jane, Brittany, and Eleanor turned around. Colin rushed up to Brittany and embraced her. "The only thing I could make out of all the static in your message was 'Presbyterian Hospital'! Is everything okay?"

"Sorry, I'm fine, it was Cassandra." Colin looked over at Eleanor and then to Gillian in her car.

"Hello, Colin," Gillian said.

"Oh, hey Gill," Colin said. "What are you doing here?"

"Cassandra is my daughter."

Colin looked at Gillian and Eleanor in disbelief. "I thought you said your mother had died."

"That fault lies entirely with me, I'm afraid," Gillian said. "I had to leave them and their father quite abruptly. I've regretted it ever since."

Colin looked at Eleanor, looking like he wanted to say something he couldn't formulate. "I'm sorry about what I said about your family," he finally said.

"That is all right," Eleanor said. "I am sorry about what I said about Brittany. She is a sweet…"

The arrival of Edward interrupted Eleanor's sentence. Jane saw the look in his eyes and knew, somehow, Cassandra had decided to stay as well. Her lips quivered, this time to avoid shrieking with delight.

"Hey, is your wife okay?" Colin asked.

"Yes she is, thank you," Edward said. "She's going to have to stay overnight, though."

Colin turned to his sister. "Well, ready to go Brit?"

"Sure," Brittany said. "Keep me posted about Cassandra, okay?"

"Of course we will," Eleanor said.

Brittany was half-way to her car with Colin when she raced back. "Oh, if you're still interested, rehearsals for the play start Monday! I mean, you all have to stay now and be my historical advisers! Sorry, your secret's safe with me, if it's supposed to be a secret, that is."

"The higher-ups haven't exactly taken the project off classified status, so don't go around telling all your social media friends or anything."

Brittany turned to hug Jane. "You really have the best mom in the world, by the way."

Jane let Isabella have the front seat, while she, Edward, Eleanor, and Fly managed to all fit in the back . "I thought you could only tell your family," Jane said to Gillian.

"Brittany was like my daughter when I didn't have you. I couldn't hurt her with covering the truth. If my funders don't like that, I'll just tell them they've been recruited. I've been looking for a new historian, and an actress would be a pretty good asset as well." She looked at her watch. "We've best be getting home too."

"Home?" Jane asked in confusion. "I presume you don't mean back to Mrs. Milner's."

Gillian took her hand from the driver's seat. "No. You and your sisters are really going home."

Chapter Eighteen

JANE GAPED AT GILLIAN'S enormous house. "You live there all by yourself?"

"I've been setting up rooms for all of you for a while," Gillian said.

"How much do you have?" Eleanor asked.

"Oh yes, I've missed the 18th century's lack of discreetness when it comes to money. I have about ten million dollars."

"That is even more than Mr. Granger!" Isabella said. "So you actually have servants and lots of cars?"

"Just because Riley's an unscrupulous so-and-so doesn't mean he's not right about some things," Gillian said. "I merely prefer to buy what I need and save the rest for friends in need and rainy days."

The house may have been plain compared to Reddings Hall, but a sense of welcome Jane hadn't felt since the vicarage filled her as she walked past the vestibule into the living room. She only caught a slight glimpse of the green couches or the cabinets filled with various books and heirlooms before she caught up with Gillian, who was heading up some stairs to a hallway with several doors.

Gillian opened the first door on the left. "You can put your things in here, Jane."

Jane looked around in disbelief. "Is this my room?" Gillian nodded.

There was a bookshelf full of books she had never heard of, with titles such as *Little Women*, *Anne of Green Gables*, and *My First Book of Quantum Physics*. She laid on her bed, touching the pink silk sheets. On the pillow was a stuffed bear wearing a blue coat and large red hat.

"I'm so sorry, I was planning for little girls..." Gillian said. She wiped a tear from her cheek.

Jane gave her mother a hug. "It's all right. It's wonderful."

The family went to the room next to Jane's. "Here's yours, Eleanor," Gillian said. "I'll get a cot for Fly."

"Elephant!" Fly cried, racing to the giant elephant-shaped chair in the corner.

Gillian's face brightened. "I guess somehow I knew."

"Thank you, Mamma," Eleanor said.

Gillian turned to the room across from Eleanor's. "And here is yours, Isabella."

"Thank you, but I hope I will not need it very long," Isabella said.

"Me neither," Gillian said with a wistful sigh.

Isabella looked to the corner in disbelief. "That looks just like the vicarage..." She opened the small dollhouse. Inside were a mother, a father, and four little girls.

"Your uncle Gary made that for you girls based on my descriptions."

"I have an uncle Gary?" Isabella asked.

"Yes, you have three uncles on my side: my brother and my two sisters' husbands. That reminds me, I must tell my family you're here. They'll all be so anxious to meet you."

"Is Uncle Gary a time traveler too?" Jane asked.

"No, he sells life insurance." Gillian showed everyone to the last bedroom. "Here's Cassandra's, Edward. Again, I'm so sorry I didn't think to make accommodations for a husband."

Edward smiled. "That's quite all right, I'll sleep on the

couch until we find our own house."

"Why in the world do you need your own house?" Isabella asked. "You are not..."

"Both of you wish to stay in 2015 now?" Eleanor asked in disbelief.

Edward nodded. Jane nearly jumped on him. Eleanor and Isabella stared, Eleanor sad, Isabella almost angry. Jane felt sorry for both of them, especially Eleanor, realizing Cassandra staying would mean that she would be separated from her dearest friend.

"What about that serum?" Eleanor finally asked.

"I'll try to find it in the morning," Gillian said. "I think we all need some sleep for now."

JANE LAY IN BED, holding Paddington, the bear, close to her. Her mother had said she had never been able to change anything. Riley's words about her dying an old maid stung in her ears. He had known and never even cared. Out of all those horrible things he had said and done, that was probably the most horrible.

Jane went downstairs to find her mother watching a man telling jokes on the television. Eleanor was there as well, looking at the *My First Book of Quantum Physics* she had borrowed from Jane.

"It's hard to adjust physically to time travel," Gillian said. Jane nodded, not ready to tell her mother the full details. "Come watch the late show with me, darling, it's been a stressful day."

Despite her dire future, Jane felt a peace she hadn't felt in a long time, certainly not at Reddings and not even with Riley. She fell asleep on the couch, not even waking up when someone draped a blanket over her.

Chapter Nineteen

"MR. DAWSON IS DEAD."

"Isabella, could you sound a little less detached?" Brittany asked. Play rehearsals were going to go all day at this rate, Jane thought. "Your lover just died."

"Mr. Dawson is *dead*!" Isabella said.

"Nice!" Brittany said.

"Oof, I'm getting kind of stiff here," Scott said. "Get it? Stiff?"

"Yes, you're hilarious," Brittany said. "Okie dokie, I'm getting hungry, why don't we call it a day?" She turned to Jane. "So, Ms. Assistant Director, what did you think?"

"It's getting better," Jane said. Some sleep, services at her mother's church, a visit to Cassandra and Gilly at the hospital, and shopping at a farmer's market in downtown Dallas had put some distance from Riley's betrayal two days before. "What are you smiling so stupidly about?"

"The wedding's off."

"What?"

"Lemon-Face came over last night. She and my brother talked for almost three hours, and they agreed they couldn't go through with it anymore."

"Oh, dear, I hope she is all right."

"She'll be fine, I'm sure. Want to get some Slurpees and celebrate?"

"Thank you, but Cassandra's coming home from the hospital in a few hours."

"Okie dokie! Give Cassandra a hug for me."

 ISABELLA'S THROAT WAS DRY from saying those same stupid lines over and over. She went off-stage to a water fountain. "Pay no heed to Jane," she could imagine her Harry saying. "You are wonderful."

"I miss you," Isabella said.

"Are you all right?" It was Dr. Darcy.

"Yes, thank you." Isabella walked off in a huff past Eleanor.

Eleanor looked over to Colin. "Hello," she said.

"Oh, hi, it's- um- good to see you. I brought Brittany her CD for the play." He put on the CD and bowed to her. "May I have this dance?"

"Yes, thank you." Eleanor gave him her arm and they "dosidoed." Brittany came in for water, and ran to bring back Jane, both grinning as wide as the cat in the *Alice in Wonderland* book Eleanor had read to Fly the night before.

"What happened to your arm?" Colin asked.

"Oh, the bandages? I scraped it... on a floor... I fell."

"How weird. I used to have these *Animaniacs* band-aids when I was a kid."

"How weird indeed."

Brittany's grin crumpled. "You... you went to my house when Colin was a kid?" she asked Eleanor.

"Oh no, I'm so sorry, Brittany."

"No, it's okay... I just wish that rat Riley would have told me there was dust in my own house that could take me to see my parents again." Brittany wiped a tear from her face.

"What's going on here?" Colin asked.

"Nothing!" Brittany snapped.

"It's time for… to be somewhere," Colin told Eleanor. He bowed to her before hurrying away.

COLIN GLANCED AT THE university library on his way to the car. He had always suspected Dr. Bennet had found a way to travel in time, but he needed some evidence.

Samina, one of the library assistants, waved at him as she took inventory of some books on a shelving cart. "Need some art books, Dr. Darcy?"

"Actually, I need some books about time travel," Colin said.

"Oh, working on another *Doctor Who* fan-fic?"

"Something like that." Was he being too much of a grouch? Two students were watching him and Samina; they might tell their friends not to sign up for rude and grouchy Dr. Darcy's class. If class figures went down, so did he. He rushed to grab every book about time travel and string theory he could find and took them home.

He tried reading some, only to find he couldn't understand anything any of the authors were talking about. He tried doing some more research on time travel on the Internet that evening, but then he noticed Mr. Bingley chewing up the couch cushions.

Colin's sinuses started hurting, so he lay on the chair. In his dreams, Eleanor was wearing that beautiful lilac Regency dress and fighting Cybermen with Maggie, Peter and Winston Churchill.

"What do you have to lose if you're wrong, Colin?" Maggie asked, just like her friend Bill had asked her in *The Gate of the Year* when she didn't know whether to believe Peter was writing to her from the future.

Colin raced to Eleanor. "You really are a time traveler! I'm so sorry."

Eleanor sneered. "What difference does it make now?"

Eleanor sounded just like his grandmother. "You think you deserve a second chance?" Colin slowly woke up, having to assure himself over and over it didn't really happen. Maybe it was better to work on his paper on the Egerton exhibit for the conference in June instead.

ELEANOR AND EDWARD HELPED Cassandra up the stairs and showed her to her bedroom.

"It's beautiful," Cassandra said. She sat on the yellow sheets and picked up the Minnie Mouse lamp.

"Yes, I am sorry it was all meant for an eleven-year-old," Eleanor said.

"I can save it for my girls," Cassandra said.

"Would you like some tea?" Edward asked.

"Yes, please." Cassandra sat down on the bed. She and Eleanor exchanged uneasy smiles.

Eleanor took a deep breath and finally addressed what she had never worked up the nerve to address at the hospital the day before. "So you and Edward are really not going to return to Woodvale?"

"Only to get the other children and make sure our affairs are settled," Cassandra said. "Edward has already started applying to the university."

"So you really think there's nothing to be afraid of here?"

"There will be something to be afraid of in any time, Eleanor. I can just choose to live my life in spite of it."

"What are you going to do?"

"I will take care of the children, of course, perhaps finally learn to knit... but I think I would like to be a teacher as well."

"You should be a teacher! Or even a headmistress. No one could be a better mother figure to all those pupils than you."

Edward brought Cassandra a cup of blueberry tea and a small phone. "Look, darling, we can see Gilly in her room at the hospital!"

"She's looking so much stronger," Cassandra said. "Where is the application to the university?"

"It's on the computer," Edward said. "Why?"

"Because I am going to school too," Cassandra said. "I want to be a teacher as well."

"That is wonderful!" Edward said. "If you're sure. I want this to be *our* dream." Cassandra nodded. Eleanor turned aside with a smile as they kissed.

Cassandra gave Eleanor a hug. "Oh, Eleanor, if only you could be as happy as I am right now!"

"Darling, when I can have half your goodness, then perhaps I can have half your happiness," Eleanor said. "Until then, I will go home to manage Reddings House. If I am fortunate, perhaps I will meet another Frank eventually."

Cassandra frowned. "I do so wish you would not say those things, Eleanor, even in jest. You deserve to marry for love as well."

Gillian knocked on the door. "Cassandra, would you like some of the professors to hold a baby shower for Gilly?" she asked.

"Why, is she dirty?" Cassandra asked.

"I mean, would you like to have a small party for Gilly so they can give her clothes and other things you'll need?" Gillian asked.

"That would be great," Cassandra said.

"I had better wake up Fly from his nap, he'll be so happy to see you," Eleanor said. She crossed the hall, so grateful that her marriage to Frank had brought Fly and James into her life. She couldn't help imagining what it would be like to marry someone who made her smile as Edward made Cassandra, though.

ELEANOR KEPT IMAGINING INTO the next day as she, Jane, and Isabella went with Brittany and the other cast members to a city half an hour away to try on costumes for the play.

"You might not want to sew this up so tight, with the baby," Isabella told the dressing room attendant.

"You're pregnant?" Brittany asked.

"Yes, will that be a problem?" Isabella asked.

"No, I guess we'll work around it." Brittany said. "They worked around it with my friend when she did *Wicked*. At least you're not flying on a broom."

Kate stepped out of the dressing room with a frown. "I don't think this one is going to work either, Eleanor. Any ideas?"

Eleanor looked through the shelves. There was one that looked like the lilac dress she had worn the night she came to 2015. Eleanor had often wondered what Riley had ever done with it.

KATE TWIRLED AROUND IN the lilac dress. "I love it!"

The cast and crew went next door to a shop that served cold milk tea with chewy tapioca-like bubbles at the bottom. Jane, Brittany and Marisa helped Kate as she played a crossword game with Scott on her phone. Jane had never had a more enjoyable time out, certainly not at an assembly or supper party.

"Can Marisa give you guys a ride back to your mom's?" Brittany said. "I need to go ahead and get home. Colin's not feeling well."

"Of course," Jane said. "Did you say anything more to him about the... traveling?"

Brittany sighed. "No, I didn't want to get your mom in anymore trouble. Anyway, my word probably wouldn't do a thing, not after Scott and I spent all of last summer pretending we switched bodies after touching one of the old

Egyptian artifacts at the museum."

"Well, I suppose at least we know he won't go running to all the newspapers this way."

"Ha, ha, you really are from another century, aren't you?" Brittany asked. Jane gave her a playful shove.

Jane looked over at Scott and tried to imagine him acting like Brittany. She noticed Scott smiled back at her and shirked back into her chair.

"It's good to see you smiling again, Potter," Scott said. "I like the way you smile when you write. I feel the exact same way when I act."

"Thank you," Jane said, for once deciding to leave it at that. Anyway, she and Gillian had researched the country star Scott was dating on the computer the other night and she seemed really kind and funny.

"You should apply for the creative writing program at the university," Scott said. "That's where the head writer for my show got started. I can't guarantee anything, but she might be able to get you a job when you're done."

CASSANDRA AND EDWARD WERE filling out application forms for the university when Jane, Isabella, and Eleanor came home.

"It says we need a high school transcript," Cassandra said.

"Just tell them you were home-schooled," Gillian, who was playing Legos with Fly on the floor, said. "I'll take care of it."

"Can I see what the application looks like?" Jane asked Cassandra.

"Of course, darling," Cassandra said. Cassandra patted the back of Jane's hair as Jane sat down.

Gillian got up and turned to Eleanor and Isabella. "Want to see the serum?" Gillian said. Eleanor picked up Fly and followed her mother and sister to the garage.

"Isabella, dear, could you hand me that box on the top shelf?" Gillian asked.

"I do not know if that is wise," Isabella said. "You do not want anything happening to me or the baby, do you?"

"By picking up a nearly empty box? Darling, when I was pregnant with Jane, I was handling scientific equipment ten times as heavy as that little box up until the last few weeks."

"Yes, but then you had Jane," Isabella said.

"I will not have you talk about anyone, let alone your own sister, that way, Isabella."

"Very *well*." Isabella sighed and handed Gillian the box. Gillian pulled Cassandra's 2215 pocket out of the box and a small clear bottle out of the drawer.

"Careful, Fly!" Eleanor cried. Fly was about to knock over the box of empty dust-collecting balls.

"Just like his mother, endlessly fascinated with my equipment," Gillian said. She bent down to Fly's eye level. "How would you like your own dust-locating torch?" She handed Fly the flashlight.

"Tell Grandmamma thank you," Eleanor said.

"Thank you, Grandmamma!" Fly cried. He shined the flashlight in Gillian's face.

"On the ball, darling," Gillian said. She inserted the serum into the ball.

The dust remained a small swirl. "It does not look like it's working!" Isabella said.

"It works very slowly," Gillian said. "It could be a few months."

"What are we going to do in two months?" Isabella said.

"Well, you've got the play, and I'll make arrangements to visit my family in London once Gilly's cleared to travel."

ELEANOR THOUGHT THE WAIT would be tedious, but the weeks actually flew by. Mornings were filled with play rehearsals, and then the afternoons were filled with all sorts of new places to shop, to explore, or to eat. Gillian doted on her daughters, son-in-law, grandson, and granddaughter— once Gilly came home from the hospital the first week of March— and took them anywhere in which they expressed even the slightest interest. At night, she would tell them about her various travels in time as they played cards or chess.

Eleanor saw Colin from time to time but he always seemed to have somewhere he needed to be at that instant. She did the best she could not to think about him by advising Brittany with the play.

Fly was forgetting more and more about the 19th century as his grandmother took him to feed the ducks on the lake or to the zoo to see elephants or to Dairy Queen for ice cream cones to make up for getting vaccinations. Eleanor tried to tell him stories of their life at Reddings Hall to help him remember, but she was starting to forget the size of the drawing room or her favorite spot in the park herself.

Isabella was starting to forget details about her former life as well, much to her horror. She spent every moment she wasn't rehearsing the play or being dragged somewhere else by her mother painting a picture of Harry with the art supplies her mother had bought her.

"Isn't Harry's nose larger?" Jane asked one day.

"I think I know how my own husband's nose looks," Isabella snapped. She looked at Harry, and redid her sketch just in case.

Jane tried to write in her spare moments, but it was hard when every glance at her story reminded her of Riley. Instead, she would take copious notes as she and her sisters caught up on the last 200 years of books and movies on what she would do differently.

Eleanor watched Jane and Cassandra learn to cook, drive, and buy things with interest. She was grateful for all Fly and her sisters were getting to experience, but she missed James and knew she couldn't keep cheating Reddings Hall of its heir, even if was only presumptive. The thought of Augusta as the future Lady Jennings made her sick.

THE WINTER TURNED INTO a rainy spring. Edward and Cassandra got jobs as a page at the public library and a clerk in the university's financial services, respectively. A recommendation from one of Cassandra's co-workers brought them to a house on the same street as Mrs. Milner's, right across from the playground. They signed the paperwork a week before the mystery night play and moved in a few days later.

Edward and Cassandra set up their new kitchen table to eat lunch. "I will be so glad when they invent compressible furniture," Cassandra said. She and Edward sat down and dished out the Pad Thai they had ordered from the restaurant down the street.

"I never realized chicken could taste this fantastic!" Edward said.

"Just wait until I make the tikka masala recipe Mamma gave me."

"You're so adventurous now."

"After facing down a Red Scarf, spicy food is nothing." Cassandra looked into the living room. "Your sisters should be happy, we finally own a home. Even if it's not Chatsworth."

Edward took her hand. "I like this one better."

A sound which Cassandra realized was their new doorbell reverberated throughout the house. An older lady was at the door, with a plate of chocolate chip muffins.

"I'm so glad someone has finally taken the old

Middleton place," she said. "I'm Judy Milner, I live three doors down. Please drop by anytime you'd like and make yourselves at home."

Edward and Cassandra exchanged glances. "Thanks, I'm sure we will," Edward said.

Mrs. Milner walked away at almost the same time Brittany came by with a large blue bag. "Hi neighbor!" Brittany gave Cassandra a hug. "I'm so glad you're just going to be on the other side of the lake."

Cassandra hugged her back. "Me too." Brittany smiled at Edward. Edward looked over at Cassandra. Cassandra nodded and Edward shook Brittany's hand.

"I thought your daughters might like some of my old Barbies," Brittany said. "Or your son. Colin would play with me sometimes. I'd get so frustrated with him because most of his story lines ended up with them on a distant planet fighting aliens."

"Thank you, that is very kind."

Brittany admired the beautiful silver frame Jane had given Cassandra as a housewarming gift. "Let me know if you need any pictures to fill that with."

Cassandra looked at the bride and groom whose black-and-white picture currently was in the frame. "I do wish we had a picture of our wedding."

"Maybe you could renew your vows," Brittany said.

Cassandra looked at Edward. "I do like the sound of that." Edward said. "New vows for a new century."

"And a new marriage license, since no one would believe one from 1811," Cassandra said.

"That's true as well," Edward said.

"Well, I'll let you guys finish your lunch," Brittany said. "Let me know if you need anything else!"

"Thank you, Brittany," Cassandra said. She went upstairs and placed the dolls on Cassy's *Winging It* bed sheets. She stared at the light pink walls and out the window to the playground where three girls kicked a soccer ball around and a woman pushed two boys on the swing set. She wished so desperately that Cassy, Neddy, and Charlotte could be in a world with antibiotics and central heating, and tried not to entertain the possibility that she would end up like her own poor mother.

Chapter Twenty

THE MORNING BEFORE THE big performance began with a visit to the doctor for Isabella. After the close call with Cassandra, Isabella had agreed with her mother without much reservation that she would see an obstetrician for as long as she was here. Isabella couldn't believe she had been pregnant for almost four months. She tried to imagine Harry standing beside her as the doctor rubbed her belly with a large warm white object.

"Everything is going beautifully normal," Dr. Li said. "Would you like to know if you're having a boy or a girl?"

"We can know while the baby is still in the womb?" Isabella imagined Harry saying. She looked over at Gillian.

"It's completely up to you, darling," Gillian said.

"I suppose," Isabella said.

"From what I can see, it looks like a beautiful baby girl."

A girl! Visions of Harry twirling their daughter around made her wild. "She will be named Henrietta, of course," Isabella said.

"I'm sure Harry will be so thrilled," Gillian said.

"THIS IS TOO FAR for the university," Edward said as Cassandra led him off the light rail. "Where are we going?"

"Keep your eyes shut!" Cassandra said. Edward laughed. "All right, now."

Edward looked in confusion at the desolate building, all covered in cardboard and graffiti.

"It's an old school building," Cassandra said. "Mamma helped me buy the property. We can fix it up while we take classes at the university."

Edward bent down on one knee and kissed her hand. "I love it." He reached into his pocket and pulled out a small box containing a ring with garnet, Cassandra's birthstone. "This seems like just as good of an occasion as any. I'm not much better at speeches than I was in 1810, but you are the one I want to spend every century with. Please marry me again." Cassandra wiped her tears away as she nodded her affirmation.

ELEANOR WAS HELPING ISABELLA with her hair for the play when Brittany charged into the dressing room.

"No, no, *no!*" Brittany cried.

"What is the matter, Brittany?" Eleanor asked.

"Scott's flight from New York is delayed and Kate has strep! Eleanor, you need to play Elizabeth, please!"

"Are you sure you want me? I'm not the best actress."

"Eleanor, *please*? Just do stuff like how you normally did stuff in 1815 and I'm sure you'll do great."

There was no way the play could fall apart now. "Okie… dokie!" Eleanor said.

IT WAS FORTUNATE SHE and Kate were nearly the same size, Eleanor thought as Gillian and Jane helped her into the lilac dress. Eleanor looked in the mirror. It was discombobulating to see herself dressed in Regency clothes again.

Brittany smiled widely as she met Eleanor outside the dressing room. "You look amazing, Eleanor! You're so lucky you got to dress like this all the time, at least."

"Thank you, but you can dress like this whenever you want and still attend university and have toothpaste." Trying not to think too much on that, Eleanor added: "So who did you find to play Mr. Dawson?"

Brittany simpered. "I promised him a steak dinner." Eleanor looked down the hall at the man in the blue coat and breeches in disbelief.

"Colin?" Colin had shaved and put his contacts on, and his hair had been cut and curled.

"Oh, hello, Eleanor," Colin said. "Please tell me you're not going to post this all over Facebook."

"Fortunately for you, I still don't have one." Eleanor helped Colin adjust his cravat. Her hand brushed across his and, for a moment, Eleanor wondered what it might have been like had she met Colin at one of the assemblies back in Basingstoke. Would he be too attached to his phone— or a newspaper, like Uncle Jennings— to even look at her?

"YOU MEAN TO RUN away with my sister?" Eleanor cried.

"You mean you could never tell?" Isabella asked, playfully nudging Colin.

"I would do anything to spare you the humiliation, but I cannot make you happy!" Colin insisted.

Jane tried to restrain her giddiness as she watched her sisters and the other actors recite her lines. "I'm so proud of you, darling," Gillian whispered, as she took her hand.

"This is quite melodramatic," Edward said.

"Don't listen to him, it's wonderful, darling," Cassandra said.

"Well, if people did the things they were supposed to do, half of fiction wouldn't exist," Jane said. Edward laughed and patted her shoulder.

"YOU KNEW ABOUT MR. DAWSON's plan?" Eleanor asked

the actor playing her father for the tenth time that night. The guests were now moving around the museum watching Eleanor and the other actors perform their scenes.

"Yes, I heard it from John," her fictional father said. "I would have done anything to avoid him ruining you-- ruining us." He turned to the audience. "Do you have any questions?"

Eleanor took advantage of the pause to take a quick breath. This was getting rather tiresome.

"Yes, I have one for Elizabeth," one of the audience members said. "Did you really love him?"

Eleanor paused. Brittany had told her to answer the way she thought her character would. "Mr. Darcy- Mr. Dawson?" A couple of the ladies in the group snickered. "He's so exasperating, but I think I did."

 COLIN WATCHED ELEANOR, ENRAPTURED. She did seem like she had stepped out of the 19th century.

"Congratulations, you're a regular Laurence Olivier," Gillian said. Jane handed him some meatballs and a glass of champagne from the snack tables.

Colin smiled. "Thanks, but I think I won't give up my day job for now."

"I heard back from my funders this morning," Gillian said. "You and Brittany passed the screening. You are now part of the project."

Colin tried to piece Gillian's words together. "What project?"

Jane handed him her phone. There was a picture of him and his cousins, when he was only ten, with Eleanor and Jane.

Colin's head lightened. He wouldn't be surprised at that moment if Pablo Picasso came in, wondering if there were more cheese sticks.

"I... I'm sorry, I can't do this," Colin said.

"Why not?" Jane said.

"I can't work with Eleanor," Colin said. "I've burned too many bridges with her."

"All she has been talking about for the last month is how worried she is that she hurt your feelings," Jane said.

"Really?" Colin asked. Gillian nodded.

"Don't listen to your grandmother," Jane said. "Eleanor wants to give you a second chance."

Colin looked back at Eleanor. Eleanor had always been willing to forgive him. Only his pride had kept him from believing it.

"Okay, Maggie, what do I have to lose?" he said to himself.

COLIN TRIED TO CATCH up with the cast as they assembled for the final act. "Eleanor..."

"Okie dokie, everyone to the drawing room, let's do some summation!" Brittany said.

Something seemed off about Colin's face. Eleanor tried not to glance at him as the rest of the cast went through why they couldn't have murdered Mr. Dawson. Finally, it was Eleanor and Isabella's turn.

Isabella fell into Eleanor's arms. "I am so sorry I tricked Mr. Dawson into leaving you. I did not want to lose you to such a horrible man. I never wanted you to murder him."

"I did not," Eleanor said. "I made it to the drawing room with the knife, but I did not want you and Papa to be disgraced."

"And then I picked up the knife!" Kevin, the actor playing the younger Mr. Dawson, said.

"Why ever did you do that?" Marisa said.

"I had so many debts!" Kevin said. "I asked him over and over again for the money, but he would not help me. Only his inheritance from my father would save me."

Everyone clapped, the two teams that had selected Kevin as the murderer the loudest. Colin took Eleanor's hand and they went for their curtain call. "Call me 'Your majesty,'" he whispered in her ear. Once she remembered what Colin had told her in his office, she grinned even wider than Riley and bowed to the audience.

Eleanor heard the sounds of giggling as she looked for her sisters. Two college girls were getting a picture with Colin.

"Ooh, can you be in the picture too, Elizabeth?" one of the girls said.

"Of course," Eleanor said.

"I suppose I should do this for a living," Colin said.

Jane and Isabella were with Gillian by the picture of Princess Charlotte. Jane gave Eleanor a hug. "You were great!"

"Thank you, I had good lines," Eleanor said.

Isabella yawned, even louder than the first two times. "Ready to go home, Eleanor?" Gillian asked. Eleanor nodded.

"Eleanor, please wait."

"Mamma, why are you squeezing my hand?" Jane asked. She looked at Colin and Eleanor. "Oh, yes... I'll see you in the car, Eleanor."

"I've been such a jerk," Colin said.

"No you have not, not entirely," Eleanor said. "I'm sorry about all those things I said about you. Please never force yourself to be someone else's definition of polite. You are thoughtful enough the way you are."

Colin looked taken aback. "Thank you. All the same, I have a surprise for you and Fly if you'd like to see my more friendly side."

Eleanor looked into his face. Something she had always thought she should feel around Frank came over her. "I would love to."

"Fantastic!' Colin said. "I'll pick you guys up tomorrow at noon."

For the first time since she had arrived in 2015, the following morning could not move slower for Eleanor. She tried knitting, building Elephant World with Fly and Gillian, and watching Star Wars, which Cassandra had brought over to show Jane and Isabella, but ended up walking back and forth up Gillian's street.

Colin's car was parked in front when Eleanor passed Gillian's house for the fourth time. Eleanor gathered her courage and walked inside. Colin was talking to her mother in the living room. His glasses were back on, but his hair was still in the same style as from the play.

"I might keep this look for a while," he said.

"I like it," Eleanor said. Colin was wearing a blue-gray sleeveless doublet over a white shirt and gray jeans. "Why are you dressed as if you're going to the Renaissance?"

Colin had a look that Gillian would call a "bad poker face." "You'll see," he said.

Eleanor looked out the window at the Texas countryside. After almost a month of continuous rain, that Saturday was beautiful and clear. She checked on Fly in the back seat.

"Don't eat too many of Dr. Darcy's cheese crackers, darling," Eleanor said. She looked back over at Colin. She tried to think of something to say to him so they both wouldn't be so nervous.

Eleanor remembered what Jane had told her Brittany said. "I just started reading *The Gate of the Year*."

"Really?" Colin said. "There's three more books about Maggie and Peter traveling in time together." Colin squirmed in his seat, as if he was embarrassed for being so eager about the books.

"You mean they travel together, like David and my-" Eleanor hoped she hadn't given away some classified information.

Colin's eyes widened. "David Andrews is a *time traveler*?" he asked. Eleanor nodded. "Wow, that explains so much."

"Have you ever thought about where you'd like to travel in time?"

"Your mom said I probably can't save my parents, right?"

"Yes, or I would go tell my father to not delay calling for a physician."

Colin thought for a long time. "Back to college, to do a better job on my papers."

"All of time at your disposal and you want to go back to school?" Eleanor laughed, until she realized she might have hurt his feelings. Colin just laughed too.

"Well, how about you?" he asked.

"My mamma was telling Jane and I the other night about a monastery in the 900's in the Outer Hebrides where she used to visit." This was exactly the lively conversation she could never have with Frank. "It had the most wonderful library."

"That sounds amazing. Maybe we— you can visit someday." Colin looked down at the radio. "I'm so sorry I didn't believe you."

"That's all right. A few months before, I wouldn't have believed myself either."

"I was so afraid Brittany would be abandoned in the middle of Dallas at 2 a.m. again, or worse. She's pretty much my only family."

"You have no other family?"

"My mom's family is all in Ecuador, and my dad's... well, you met my cousins and my grandmother. They're older. That's about the only thing that's changed. You know?"

Eleanor sighed. "I know all too well. Is there anyone you can talk to?"

"What, you mean like a psychologist? My friend Matt at the school's counseling center always says I can come by whenever, but I don't know."

"Don't know what?"

"I talked to him a couple of times, but it didn't help."

"Did you tell him everything?"

"No, I can't do that."

"Well, you can't get too far without telling the truth... I am so sorry."

"No, you should never be sorry for speaking your mind."

Eleanor was reminded of Frank, even more unpleasantly so. "Yes, thank you."

Colin exited the highway and drove past some rows of corn into a field full of cars. He found a spot on the grass and they walked up to a castle where a lady who was also dressed like she was from the Renaissance took their tickets.

Colin led them through the gates into a wooded area. Eleanor could see small shops that looked like houses to her right and left. Some of the men and women walking around were dressed like Colin, while others wore T-shirts and shorts. One young woman even wore a hat and colorful scarf like Colin's.

"We want to go to the right, past the bridge," Colin told Eleanor. Colin and Eleanor tried to keep up with Fly as he raced toward a young woman playing a harp, and then a man holding a large staff with branches of pretzels.

"He's a fast little kid," Colin said. "My friend coaches a soccer team. Maybe you should sign him up."

"Thank you."

"Elephant!" Fly screamed as Colin finally brought them to their destination. Behind a fence, a man was leading a young girl as she rode atop an elephant's back.

"Yeah, would you like to ride it?" Colin asked.

"I ride it?" Fly asked. He turned to Eleanor. "May I ride it?"

"Yes, of course you may," Eleanor said.

Eleanor, Colin, and Fly all got on the elephant's back. Eleanor imagined she was with Colonel Finster in India, on one of his more appealing-sounding adventures, anyway. "So are you going to stay... here with your mother or go back to... Basingstoke?" Colin asked.

"I need to return to Reddings Hall."

"Why?"

"James, my youngest son, is there."

"Can't you bring him here like Fly?"

"Of course."

"Then what else is making you want to go back?" Colin added a few quiet "sorries."

"It's my role, I suppose."

Colin patted the elephant. "Well, there have been twelve Doctors on *Doctor Who*. If they can all leave when they knew it was time to and let someone else have their role, why can't you?"

Eleanor thought of Augusta again. What did it matter who was mistress of Reddings Hall when, no matter what, it would most likely be gone in a little over a hundred years? "No, I suppose it doesn't make a difference."

"What do you want to do?"

"I've been thinking about university."

"You want to study music?"

"Actually, I am becoming increasingly interested in physics."

Colin nodded with a smile. "Your mother's daughter. Well, the deadline to apply for next fall is in a few weeks. I can help you with your application."

Colin helped Eleanor and Fly off the elephant and down the stairs. "Tell Dr. Darcy thank..." Fly raced into Colin's open arms before she could finish. Eleanor wiped a tear from her eye. She did want to apply to the university. And sign up Fly for the team. And let Richard and Augusta have Reddings all to themselves.

"JUST FOR YOU." COLIN slipped a Pleyel CD in the car's player as he started on the way home.

Eleanor looked out the window, straightening the floral hair wreath Colin had bought her for beating him in archery. "Are you okay?" Colin asked.

"It is quite loud," Eleanor said. "May I turn it down?"

"I can do it."

"No. please focus on your driving." Eleanor struggled with the knob.

"Good grief, you'd think you were born in the eighteenth century or something." Eleanor laughed. Colin reached over to help her. "Like this." They touched hands and smiled.

Fly started to gag. "Hurts."

Eleanor looked over at the empty box of cheese crackers. "Oh no…"

Colin pulled over at the first gas station and hastened him over to a bush. "It's going to be okay," he said gently as Fly threw up. "Better out than in."

"I'll go get some water," Eleanor said.

Eleanor had a bad feeling about the brown-haired lady talking to the man at the cash register. "The pump took my credit card," she said in a familiar oily voice. Eleanor's own stomach sank.

Why, of all places, did Anna have to be in this drasted— she was starting to sound like her mother— gas station now? Eleanor would have walked out the door, but she ridiculed herself for putting a petty conflict before her sick son. She attempted a casual walk to the water bottles, hoping Anna would be finished by the time she had to pay.

"Hello Eleanor." Eleanor forced herself to turn around and face Anna. "I thought you went back to England."

Eleanor, realizing she was still wearing the hair wreath, hastily took it off. "I decided to stay."

"Really?" Anna asked. "What made you change your mind?" Anna's face sunk. "Of course," she muttered. Eleanor turned around to see Colin coming in.

"Fly's back in the car," Colin said. He noticed Anna. "Oh, hey. You doing okay?"

A resigned smile came across Anna's face. "Yes, thank you. I was offered a job with an interior design firm in Los Angeles. I'm leaving in a week."

"That's great!"

Anna grabbed her purse. "I've better go, I've got to meet with my landlord."

Colin squeezed Eleanor's hand. "She'll be all right. Let's get Fly home."

COLIN HOPED ELEANOR WOULDN'T notice that he took a longer way back to Gillian's house. Fly was asleep in the back seat, so it seemed okay.

Eleanor mouth bent into a slight smile at the sight of her mother's house. "Thank you so much. I hope to see you again."

"Me too," Colin said. "Are you available after finals? Instead of cheese crackers, I can take you to Uptown for the best sushi you ever tasted."

"That sounds delightful," Eleanor said, deciding not to tell Colin she had never tasted sushi before.

Colin helped Eleanor get Fly inside the house and into Gillian's arms. "See you soon," Colin said.

"Yes, I'm really looking forward to seeing you again soon," Eleanor said. Eleanor watched Colin get in the car. She laughed and did a small dance of joy. She was embarrassed until she looked to the car and realized he was doing the same thing.

Chapter Twenty-One

ELEANOR BARELY MADE IT through the door when her sisters accosted her.

"How was it?" Cassandra asked.

"We went to a lovely Renaissance fair," Eleanor said. "We rode an elephant, then we saw an acrobat, then Colin took Fly on some rides so I could do some shopping, then we ate turkey legs…"

"That is not what we meant and you know it," Isabella said with a devious smile, as if she was expecting Colin to dine with her and Harry someday soon.

"Girls, let Eleanor sit down," Gillian said. "Would you like to tell us more over some tea?"

ELEANOR TOOK A SLICE of Victoria sponge cake from Gillian. "I do seem to have misjudged Colin. He is very kind and very encouraging."

Jane's eyes brightened. "Are you going to marry him?"

Eleanor laughed. "I'm nowhere near there, Jane. But it might be worth it to stay and find out."

Cassandra hugged her sister. "You're staying here too!"

Eleanor nodded. "I have an appointment with an admissions adviser at the university on Tuesday. Colin helped me set it up on the way home."

"No, you cannot!" Isabella stormed out of the dining room. Eleanor got up. "I'll talk to her," Jane said. Cassandra grabbed Eleanor's arm and finally encouraged her to sit down.

JANE RAN TO ISABELLA'S room, while Gillian lingered in the hall as her back-up. Isabella was looking at the doll house.

"Isabella, it will be all right," Jane said.

"Please wipe that stupid smirk off your face, Jane. You are right again, you and Mamma won everyone else over."

"You could stay too, you know," Jane said. "I would miss you."

"Yes you would, because there is no Colonel Finster or Riley Granger, no one to take pity or advantage of you," Isabella said. "Stay in the stupid 21st century! You will still end up an old maid, no matter what."

Unpleasant memories of Riley filled Jane's mind. "Please don't call me that ever again."

"What, *old maid*?" Isabella simpered. "Old maid, old maid, ooooolldd maaaaiii-"

"Isabella Farnsworth Pym, this stops now," Gillian cried. "I will not allow my own daughter to become a bully, especially when she's about to have her own daughter to set an example for."

Isabella had no retort for the first time Jane could remember. She slammed the door in Jane and Gillian's faces.

ISABELLA SAT ON HER bed all night, staring at the dollhouse and crying. She imagined Harry holding her hand.

"Who does that woman think she is, only now wanting to be my mother?" she asked him quietly.

"You do not need her and you do not need any of your sisters," Harry said. Isabella threw the rest of the family in the dollhouse.

JANE STARED AT THE door, wondering if an hour was long enough for Isabella to have calmed down, or if Isabella would still backhandedly snipe at any of her attempts at an apology. It was best to give her the night. At this point, it was probably best to give her a week.

Jane grabbed her notebook and went downstairs, where Gillian was pointing out all the historical inaccuracies in the 1930s-set television drama she and Eleanor were watching.

"I'm going to go find someplace to write, Mamma," Jane said.

"That's fine." Gillian seemed to understand. She pulled Jane aside before Jane left. "Jane, don't think you have nothing to apologize for. You did force Isabella away from her husband, at one of the most crucial times in their marriage to boot."

"I did." Jane sighed. "I really don't deserve anything my sisters have."

Gillian frowned. "Did that creature Aunt Jennings tell you that?"

"No... I suppose I just always thought... I'm not sure why."

"Take it from someone who's seen a lot of history firsthand, darling. Bad and good things don't necessarily happen to punish or reward us, but they always happen to guide us."

"Thank you."

"Of course. And do try to make things up with Isabella. She desperately loves you. She just lets her anger get mixed up in things too much."

Jane had been the proud owner of a driver's license for almost a week, but walking still felt so natural. Even though frozen yogurt would forever be linked in her mind with Riley, it was also linked with the moment her story took shape.

None other than Anna was there, eating a bowl that seemed to be full of nothing but sweets, looking as if she had been crying. *Her face looks just like mine when Riley...* Even in her mind, she couldn't abide using the *j* word again.

Jane approached her nervously. "Hello there."

"Oh, great, it's not enough that your sister stole my fiancé, she sent you to rub it in," Anna said bitterly.

"I just came to make sure you were all right. I know what it's like."

"How could *you* possibly know? You're what, 21?"

"23."

"I'm 29! That would be spinster age in Jane Austen's time."

Jane took her hand. "But you don't live in that time. You have an amazing job! You don't need anyone's permission to live your life the way you wish."

Jane stayed with Anna as they finished their yogurt. Anna told her about her new job in another state called California and her new apartment which overlooked the mountains, and then Jane told Anna about her writing. She could not imagine ever being friends with Anna, but Jane did quite enjoy talking with her.

Anna took Jane's hand before she left. "Regardless of anything else, you're a good kid. Good luck on your book. It sounds wonderful."

Jane couldn't believe she had made Anna feel better. Her mother had been right. Everything that had led up to this moment was to guide her, so she could guide others in similar situations in turn.

The girl on the radio overhead her sang about a book beginning. Jane took out her notebook and wrote furiously.

Julia tried going to one of Shakespeare's plays, but she couldn't forget the plays she used to put on with her sisters. Nothing would give her more pleasure than seeing her sisters enjoying the benefits of time travel as well.

She took the machine back to 1815. Anne and Louisa were stunned to see the time machine and even more stunned when Julia told them about all the places she had been. They got lost in Ancient Sparta....

Jane stayed at the shop until it closed.

Chapter Twenty-Two

JANE WROTE EVERY SPARE moment she could in the week that followed. What looked to be a tranquil week, however, was pleasantly interrupted that Monday afternoon by acceptance letters to the university for her, Edward, and Cassandra. Tuesday, Wednesday, Thursday, and Friday became filled with much celebration and arrangements for orientation and classes.

The celebrations went into Saturday, the day of Edward and Cassandra's vow renewal ceremony. Cassandra came over to Gillian's house early, as did Jane's friend Ashley from the theater department.

"Why did you ever talk me into this, Jane?" Cassandra cried as Ashley clipped the first piece of her hair.

Jane took her hand. "You're going to look great," she said. "It will be perfect for the ceremony."

Cassandra couldn't stop admiring what Ashley called her "pixie" hair in the mirror of what had been her bedroom for almost two months. She stopped long enough so her sisters and Gillian could help her into the long white dress with lace sleeves, a light pink bow in front, and light pink silk roses across the skirt.

Gillian wiped tears from her face. "You look beautiful, darling."

"Thank you, Mamma," Cassandra said. "Hopefully this

makes up for missing our wedding somewhat."

They got in the car and drove down the road to Gillian's church. Cassandra told herself she wasn't going to cry this time, but as soon as she saw Edward in his new suit at the altar, the tears poured out.

He stroked her hair when she arrived. "I like your hair," he mouthed.

"Thank you," Cassandra mouthed back. There was no desire to travel forwards or backwards now, in her head. She wanted to savor the moment as much as possible. She took his hands as soon as she could grasp them and they proceeded to renew the wedding vows they had made a little more than two hundred and three years before.

A small wedding breakfast followed the ceremony in the church hall. Cassandra looked for Gilly. Jane was holding her while talking and laughing with Brittany and Amara, Cassandra's friend from the accounting office. Relief washed over Cassandra. Jane had never looked so happy in years.

Isabella was a few tables over, sitting by herself. Cassandra headed over toward her, but was distracted by Dr. Williamson and his wife. From the other side of the room, Colin noticed Isabella as well, and made it to the table.

"Yes, my gown was much lovelier," Isabella murmured.

"Who are you talking to?" Colin said. He immediately shirked back.

"Oh, just to…"

"Yourself?" Colin tried to redeem the conversation. "You keep doing whatever makes you comfortable, Is. I'm not one to judge."

Isabella cracked a smile. Colin took a seat next to her. "Are you drawing something?" he asked. She nodded. "May I see it?"

Isabella looked at him with some apprehension, but handed him her pad. It was a picture of Cassandra in her dress.

"That looks amazing."

"Thank you."

"Eleanor showed me some of your pictures. You should go to the university with your sisters and Edward and study art."

"But what would Harry think?" Isabella said, with some frustration. Colin sensed he was not the first person to bring up the idea. "What would he do in the future?"

"Yeah, I definitely know I couldn't be separated from anyone I cared about that much. Well, maybe once we have your mom's machine, you can visit. Or we can visit you. Or meet halfway. Have a picnic in the Wild West or something."

Isabella managed a small laugh. Jane and Eleanor joined them at the table. "Ready to get some dinner, Belle?" Jane asked.

"I suppose," Isabella said.

Colin took Eleanor's hand. "Want to get that sushi?" he asked. "Eddie said go for it."

"Well, if Edward said to go for it, then why not?"

"YOU'RE DOING FINE," COLIN said.

Eleanor sighed. "Half of my rice is in the soy sauce."

"Here, don't cross the chopsticks for starters," Colin said. He helped her with the chopsticks. "I talked to Matt last week."

"That's wonderful! Do you feel more comfortable opening up to him?"

"Yeah, I told him everything. Well, not the part about my girlfriend from the 19th century and her Time Lady mother." Eleanor flicked her chopsticks at him playfully. "He said there might be some new medicine that can help me manage the anxiety attacks better than the stuff I was on before. The trials start after my trip."

"Trip?"

"Oh, I'm going to London next month to present a paper and, um, not get married."

"Of course you are."

"What is that supposed to mean?"

"I'm going to London next month to visit my mother's family."

"Of course you are. Hey, if you want to marry me, I'll have been there long enough and everything..." Colin tore up a napkin.

"Do you by rule propose marriage on the second date?"

"Sometimes, if I have a castle." Eleanor and Colin both laughed. "Well, if marriage doesn't sound good yet, we could take the train down to Vienna for a long weekend instead."

"That would be wonderful!" Eleanor heard a screeching noise, the same screeching that the blue caramel box had made, coming from his pocket.

"Is that your phone?" Eleanor asked.

"Just an e-mail," Colin said. "It can wait."

COLIN VISITED GILLIAN'S HOUSE almost every day, when Eleanor wasn't over at Darcy House. He and Eleanor would visit the Arboretum or go for walks around the White Rock Lake Trail, sometimes with Fly, sometimes with Mr. Bingley, and sometimes by themselves. At nights, they went to the movies, the opera, or to a kind of assembly where people danced a lively dance called "swing." Eleanor had never enjoyed another man's company so much. Colin had never enjoyed anyone's company so much.

Jane, in the meantime, had finished with the arrangements for the university when the doctor okayed Gilly and Isabella for travel, and it was time to make arrangements for her family's trip to London. All the time she could ask for to write finally came on the overnight flight from DFW to Heathrow.

"How is it going?" Eleanor asked her when Jane took a break.

"I'm almost done with the first draft," Jane said. She closed the notebook and stretched.

"That's wonderful." Eleanor checked on Fly, who was sleeping on her chest, and went back to her SAT study guide.

In the row ahead of her, Isabella and Gillian were sleeping, Isabella muttering something about Harry and the draperies. Jane looked over to Cassandra and Edward, who were sitting in the aisle next to her. Cassandra was waking up and stroking Edward's chin.

"You still haven't shaved," Cassandra said.

"I'll do it tomorrow."

"No, I like it." She pulled the blanket over Gilly, who after a long struggle, was sleeping peacefully in the carry-cot.

Jane plugged her headphones into the small TV and selected some relaxation music. She finally fell asleep when Eleanor nudged her. "We're getting ready to land."

Jane looked out the window, where the morning sun illuminated the British countryside. She couldn't believe she was now back in England, almost six months from making the reverse trip with Riley. How much had changed since then! She wondered what her mother's family would think of her.

Outside of customs, a balding man with a beard waited with a Chinese woman and three preteens holding a huge sign that said, "Aunt Gill."

"Look at all of you!" Gillian cried. "You haven't been time traveling on me, have you?"

"Jane?" the balding man asked. "Hi, I'm your Uncle Gary! This is your Aunt Linda and your cousins Jeffrey,

Kaitlyn, and Clara." Aunt Linda gave Jane a hug and a kiss on the cheek.

Jane turned to her cousins. "Do you remember me?" Kaitlyn asked. Jane stared at her, wondering what she could be talking about. "I helped you in the toilets!" Jane smiled as she remembered the motorway service station all those months ago. She gave Kaitlyn a hug.

Uncle Gary loaded everyone's suitcases into the back of a gray minivan. "Okay, no naps for any of you. We're going to keep you awake until bedtime tonight." Isabella responded with a loud yawn.

Edward, Cassandra with Gilly, Eleanor, Fly and Isabella got into the back of the van with their aunt and uncle. Jane crowded in the back of a cab with her mother and cousins.

"Have you ever been to London before?" Clara asked Jane.

"No, Eleanor and Cassandra stayed with one of my father's sisters for a few months and Isabella and her husband visited London when they first married, but I have never been."

"We should go to Earl's Court and get her picture taken with a TARDIS!" Jeffrey said.

"And go on the London Eye!" Kaitlyn said. "And to the Tower!"

"But where does *Jane* want to go?" Clara asked.

Jane laughed. "I would love anywhere you take me. I am just so excited to finally be able to visit."

The cab followed the van to Victoria Station. They got some breakfast from McDonald's and then boarded the next double-decker bus.

"Let us know if you see anything interesting," Uncle Gary said.

Cassandra hadn't been to London since before Neddy was born, when she helped Edward's sister Augusta buy wedding clothes. London looked so different and yet was still as noisy and busy and endlessly fascinating as it had been then. Cassandra looked down Grosvenor Street in amazement. "Is that your sister Susan's husband's house?" she asked Edward.

"I think it is," Edward said.

"Should we..."

Edward smiled. "Knock on the door and see if any descendants answer?" Cassandra laughed. Edward took her hand and they got off the bus.

"Mamma, I need to use the toilets," Fly said.

"I thought you took care of that at the station," Eleanor said with a sigh. "Oh well, let's go find a shop or something. I could use a walk myself."

"I'll get off with you," Aunt Linda said. "We can meet everyone else back at Westminster Abbey."

A familiar figure walked out the door of Edward's sister's house as they walked down Grosvenor Street. Fly raced into Colin's arms.

"How wonderfully odd to see you!" Edward said.

"Wonderful, yes. Odd, I hope not. My friends live in these apartments."

"Of course they do," Eleanor said. Colin gave her a friendly pat on the back. "Is Brittany here too?"

Brittany darted out of the house. "I sure am!" Brittany hugged Eleanor, Cassandra, and Edward.

"May I present my Mrs. Linda Bennet, my aunt," Eleanor said. "Aunt Linda, these are my dearest friends Colin and Brittany Darcy."

Aunt Linda shook their hands. "Well, any dearest friends of Eleanor's are dearest friends of mine."

"I'm so glad I ran into you all," Colin said. "I'm about to go crazy preparing this whole presentation. Want to walk down to the park?"

"That's very kind of you, but I'm spending the day with

my family." Eleanor motioned to Aunt Linda.

"Oh, yes of course," Colin said.

Aunt Linda grinned even worse than Brittany. "Your friends can come along us."

"Are you sure?" Eleanor asked.

"Have you been on a double-decker bus before?" Aunt Linda asked.

"Not since I was in high school, but that sounds like fun if you really don't mind," Colin said.

 IT TOOK FLY ALMOST ten minutes to stop being distracted and finally use Colin's friend's toilet, but they made the next bus. Jane saw Colin and Brittany getting off the bus at Westminster Abbey and raced to give them hugs.

Gary handed them maps. "All right, everyone meet back at Victoria Station at four. Your aunts and grandparents are meeting us for dinner tonight."

"Was the British Museum around when you lived, Elle?" Brittany asked.

"I don't remember," Eleanor said. "I don't even know where to begin, not even taking 200 years into account."

"I can show you where all the good shopping is," Linda said.

Isabella perked up. "Shopping?"

"I saw on the news last night that some letters from David Andrews were just donated to the British Library," Gary said.

Gillian blushed. "I wouldn't mind a little shopping."

"Where are the birdies?" Fly asked.

"What happened to elephants?" Colin asked.

"Jane found *Winging It* on one of those movie streaming Web sites the other week and now he can't stop talking about birds," Eleanor said.

"You could take him down to St. James's Park to see the

ducks," Brittany said.

Edward turned to Cassandra. "I'll go to the library if that's all right with you."

"Of course, darling," Cassandra said. "You took care of Gilly on the plane so I could sleep. I'll take her to the park." She turned to Jane and Brittany. "Don't get him in too much trouble."

"We'll do our best," Jane said. Cassandra smiled and gave her a hug.

Edward gave his wife and daughter a kiss. He got in a cab with Jane, Brittany, and Gary to the British Library. Cassandra— with Gilly in tow— Eleanor, Fly, Colin, Jeffrey, and Clara headed toward St. James's Park, while Gillian, Isabella, Linda, and Kaitlyn walked to Oxford Street.

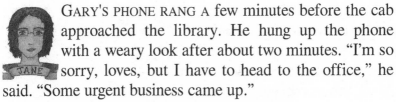

GARY'S PHONE RANG A few minutes before the cab approached the library. He hung up the phone with a weary look after about two minutes. "I'm so sorry, loves, but I have to head to the office," he said. "Some urgent business came up."

"No, of course, that's all right," Jane said.

Gary handed her his phone. "My office phone is this button. I'll be over on Gracechurch Street. If you need anything, give me a ring. Otherwise, I'll see you back at the house for dinner."

"Follow me," Brittany said. "I've been to the Treasures Gallery several times."

"This must be what the library at the Times Services is like," Jane whispered to Edward as they stopped to see another old manuscript in search of the letters. Edward nodded. "The Andrews letters are over here, by the sheet music," Brittany said.

David Andrews's handwriting seemed so austere. "Wow," Edward said. "To think your mother's actually met him."

"Do you think he ever mentioned her?" Brittany asked.

Jane looked closer. For an odd moment, Jane thought her name was underlined. Her whole chest fluttered. It was! Riley's name was in the letter too, also underlined, as was 2015. She pulled her notebook out of her backpack, only to realize she must have left her pen on the plane. Jane pulled out Uncle Gary's phone and took a picture, hoping she wasn't flouting some rule about photography.

Jane, Brittany, and Edward bought a new pen and some sandwiches from the shop across the street and unscrambled the underlined words on the cab ride back to St. James's Park.

"Jane," Brittany read. "Machine in Outer Hebrides, 915. David will pick you up at Eagle and Child, 16-6-2015. Riley."

"What's the Eagle and Child?" Jane asked.

"It's a pub in Oxford," Edward said. "That's where Andrews and Tolkien and Lewis and all their other writer friends used to meet to listen to each other's stories."

"Is it still around?" Jane asked.

"Yeah, Colin and I went there last summer," Brittany said. "We sat right where the Inklings used to sit. I got the most amazing lamb shank pie with mint jelly and a puff pastry crust... um, short version: yes."

They found Eleanor on a bench near the entrance reading an alphabet book to Gilly. Colin and Cassandra were playing freeze tag with Fly, Jeffrey, and Clara.

"Exterminate!" Jeffrey cried as he tagged Colin.

Colin sat down next to Eleanor. "You're it." Eleanor smiled and handed him Gilly.

Jane showed them the picture of David's letter. "The Outer Hebrides... didn't you say there was some monastery there, Eleanor?" Colin asked.

"Yes, but what would Riley want with us there?" Eleanor asked.

"Maybe Mamma knows," Jane said.

JANE &c HEADED BACK to Victoria Station and joined Gillian, Linda, Kaitlyn, and Isabella for coffee. Jane kept glancing at the phone, but between Linda and Isabella, she could hardly get a word in. Jane sent the picture to Eleanor's phone, hoping she'd have better luck, but Eleanor and Colin were fixed in conversation with Cassandra and Edward.

"I'd better get back to my friends' house to do some more work on that presentation," Colin said. "Thanks again, Mrs. Bennet."

"I've better get back too," Brittany said. "I still need to Skype Kate and make sure Mr. Bingley's okay." She gave Jane a hug. "I was thinking about taking the train to Bath tomorrow. Want to come with me? We can run around town like Catherine Morland and Isabella Thorpe."

"Only if I'm not Isabella," Jane said. "Is that all right, Mamma?"

Gillian yawned. "If you can stay awake long enough, you can do whatever you want."

Jane tried again to show Gillian the picture when they both got into the van, but Kaitlyn blasted her new One Direction CD all the way back to Finchley. Cars packed the small driveway of Gary and Linda's terraced house. Jane barely got her suitcase through the door before two ladies who looked like older versions of Cassandra and Eleanor accosted her.

"Jane, these are my sisters, your Aunt Sophie and Aunt Beth," Gillian said. Jane freed herself long enough from her aunt's embraces to find herself in the arms of an older woman.

"This is your grandmother Jane," Aunt Sophie said. Jane forgot all about the letter, and the time machine and Riley for that matter, and embraced her grandmother and namesake.

Gran proceeded to introduce everyone else: Granddad, Aunt Beth's husband Uncle George and their twin boys Luke and Charlie, and Aunt Sophie's husband Uncle John and their daughter Miranda.

Isabella showed Miranda her new shoes. "So you're the artist?" Granddad asked Isabella. Isabella nodded. "I did a little drawing during the war."

"Really?" Isabella asked. "Which war?"

Granddad smiled. "You're my new favorite grandchild."

"Do you like cards?" Kaitlyn asked Cassandra.

"I love cards," Cassandra said. She played with Kaitlyn, Jeffrey, Luke, and Charlie.

Jane slipped into the kitchen, where Aunt Linda was stirring chili in a Crock-Pot. "Do you need help with dinner?" Jane asked.

"That's really sweet of you," Aunt Linda said. "You can grate the cheese while I check on the jacket potatoes."

"So how long have you known my mother was a time traveler?" Jane asked.

"Gary got a call when we were first married from a hospital in Basingstoke that Gill was found unconscious at the edge of a stream. She knew then she had to tell us all the truth, even though her funders didn't want her to."

"Is it very hard to know she could be gone so long?"

"It is, but I think it's harder to not have people you love to confide in. That's probably what drove those two research assistants of hers to rationalize all the terrible things they did."

Jane stopped grating, thinking of Riley. "Is everything all right?" Aunt Linda asked.

"Yes, thank you. It's just that Riley Granger... I thought he loved me."

"I know your family loves you. There's so many more love stories that have nothing to do with romance."

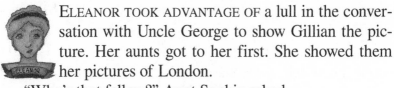

ELEANOR TOOK ADVANTAGE OF a lull in the conversation with Uncle George to show Gillian the picture. Her aunts got to her first. She showed them her pictures of London.

"Who's that fellow?" Aunt Sophie asked.

Eleanor blushed, realizing her picture of her and Colin at the play was still on her phone. "Oh... just... a friend," Eleanor said. Aunt Sophie and Aunt Beth laughed.

"Edward and I saw those letters from David Andrews today," Jane spoke up.

"Oh, yes, how is David?" Aunt Sophie asked Gillian. She and Aunt Beth laughed again.

"Honestly, you girls are worse than pre-teens," Gran said.

Jane and Isabella silently prompted each other to say something. "Eleanor, can we bother you for a little music?" Isabella asked.

"Why yes, I would so love to dance," Jane said.

"That would be lovely," Gran said. Eleanor gave Jane and Isabella a grateful smile and escaped to the piano. Edward took Isabella and Granddad took Jane and they danced a reel.

"How lovely!" Aunt Linda said, clapping. "All right, one more dance and dinner should be ready."

Isabella watched Cassandra and Edward dance, wondering what Harry would think of her family. "They are quite loud," she imagined him saying.

"Yes, but I like them," Isabella said. "I hope we can visit."

"Jane would never stop rubbing it if she knew she got her way again. It would be even worse than Whitaker. Are Henrietta and I not all you need?"

Humiliating memories of nights confined to Reddings Hall after the thwarted elopement playing quadrille with boring Mrs. Blake came back to Isabella. Even in her imagination, she struggled to argue back with Harry. "Of course you are," she finally said.

"Are you okay, darling?" It was Aunt Beth. Isabella shook her head, realizing to her embarrassment she had said those last four words out loud.

 GRAN AND GRANDAD WERE the last to head out that night. They gave all their granddaughters a hug, including an extra long one for Isabella.

"Take care of yourself, darling," Gran told Isabella.

"I will, thank you," Isabella said.

"Hopefully we'll get to meet this dashing naval hero someday," Granddad said.

"I hope so," Isabella said in a detached voice.

"We'll see the rest of you in Birmingham this weekend?" Gran asked.

"That sounds wonderful," Eleanor said.

"We'll pick you up at New Street at 10:30," Granddad said.

Jeffrey, Clara, and Kaitlyn hugged Jane as well and then went to the backyard, where they had set up a tent for themselves. Jane stretched and looked down at her phone. It was almost eleven o'clock. She remembered Mr. Andrews's letter and eagerly gathered everyone in Clara and Kaitlyn's room where she, Gillian, and Isabella were staying.

Eleanor showed Gillian David's letter. "So you think Riley told you to meet him at this monastery?" Cassandra asked.

"I think so," Jane said.

"And how do you know it's not another trap to strand us?" Isabella said.

"It's better than going to 2215 and hoping there is a pocket," Eleanor said. "What do you think, Mamma? Can we trust Mr. Andrews if Riley got him entangled in this?"

Gillian ran her index finger over the word *David* again. "I have never had a reason not to trust Mr. Andrews."

"It says the sixteenth," Jane said. "What's today?"

Gillian looked at the phone. "Today was the fifteenth. You better rest up, with a plane ride last night and a train tomorrow. I'll go talk to your uncle and buy the tickets to Oxford."

Cassandra turned to Eleanor. "Edward and I can watch Fly."

"You're not coming with us?" Eleanor asked.

"I don't want to leave Gilly just yet and I certainly don't want to take her back to all that disease."

Jane took Cassandra's hand. "I'm afraid too."

Cassandra looked over at Edward. "Then again, Aunt Linda does seem to dote on her so much."

"I'd better call Brittany and tell her I can't go to Bath with her tomorrow," Jane said. She remembered how Riley had disappointed her too. "Can we invite Brittany to come with us to the monastery, Mamma?"

"Of course," Gillian said. "She and her brother are part of the project now too."

"AAAAH, I'M ACTUALLY GOING to see the Regency period!" Brittany cried. "That's like ten thousand trips to Bath!"

Colin picked up the phone Brittany had dropped to dance around the room.

"Do you want to come too, Colin?" Jane asked.

"Um, that's okay, I need to get my presentation ready..." Colin looked at Brittany doing what looked like the Macarena on one of Mayah's couches. If Gillian was faking his sister out, it would be the end of Gillian. "You know, why not? How often do you get invited to go back in time?"

JANE WOKE AT 6:30 the next morning. She put on her contacts, even though she hated them. They would be better than any medieval glasses. She realized she was putting on the Chameleon Cloth for the first time since she and Riley had gone to 1995. She wondered what Riley had been doing for the last six weeks, or however long it had been for him this time.

UNCLE GARY DROPPED ELEANOR, her sisters, her mother, and Edward off at Paddington Station on the way to his office. Eleanor didn't see Colin or Brittany anywhere. Of course he did not believe her in the end.

The train was about to leave when two streaks, one of light purple and the other of blue and a rainbow, raced toward the train. Colin was wearing the same hat and scarf he had tried to wear for his engagement picture.

Eleanor opened the door for Colin and Brittany. "You look all suited up," she told Colin.

"Yeah, got my Sonic Screwdriver in my pocket too," Colin said. Brittany high-fived Jane and sat next to her. Gillian nodded toward Brittany as she joined Isabella in sleep. As the train pulled away, Jane went back to writing in her notebook while Brittany stared out of the window. Colin could hear her new Josh Groban album coming out her phone ear buds.

Colin put his ear buds in and tried to log on to the train's Wi-Fi with his phone. Was the phone out of charge already? He must have forgotten to switch the outlet on back at Paul and Mayah's house. Oh well, it wasn't like he'd have much use for a phone in the Middle Ages.

Edward pulled out a deck of cards from his pocket. "Come Darcy, I won't have you listening to your iTunes in that stupid matter."

Eleanor looked at Colin. "Oh no, we are fine, thank you."

"It's okay," Colin said. "I've always wondered how you play whist." Edward dealt the cards and he, Colin, Cassandra, and Eleanor played all the way to Oxford. It ended up being a lot like Hearts, his father's favorite game. Colin was pretty sure he would not enjoy most things about the 19th century, but it was fun to play and talk with his friends rather than be so attached to computers and phones like he and Brittany were most nights.

"Good thing we weren't playing for money," Colin said as they walked out onto the platform. "I had a great time, though."

"The Eagle and Child is about a mile away," Gillian said. "You think we can walk?"

"Eleanor should be used to walking," Colin said. His stomach wanted to punch his brain. He knew he should have gotten more sleep.

"Yes, well using the carriage is such a hassle," Eleanor said, taking his hand.

A LUNCH CROWD WAS already gathering at the Eagle and Child. It was hard for all eight of them to make their way through.

Colin took Eleanor's hand. "Let's look near the back."

"May I help you?" a server asked.

"We're looking for a friend," Eleanor said.

"I'm over here, Eleanor," a Welsh-accented voice said from the corner. A slightly pudgy man dressed in a light blue suit and who had thinning, fading brown hair waved to them. "How splendid, Colin's here too. Good to see you two again."

"Again?" Eleanor asked. "We've met before?"

"You visited me shortly after your... oh dear, it is quite hard to keep these things in order."

Colin stared into the face of the man that he had previously only seen on book covers. "I'm David Andrews, I mean, I'm Andrew Darcy, you're Colin David..." Colin shook his head.

David smiled. "It's always a pleasure to meet a fan."

Gillian noticed Colin and Eleanor. Within minutes, the entire group was centered around David's table. "Hello, David," Gillian said. "You look well."

"Hello, Gill. Goodness, how many children did you and James have?"

"Just these four girls are mine," Gillian said. "This is Cassandra's husband Edward, and Colin and Brittany Darcy, our friends."

"Hasn't anyone recognized you?" Edward asked.

"My Wikipedia article can't even get a decent picture," David said. "Want another round of J2Os?"

"I'd much rather get to the machine if you don't mind," Gillian said.

"Of course," David said. "Just let me take some of this butter. Haven't even had a decent piece of toast in two months, with the war on."

The nine of them waded their way out of the pub. "So James decided to sit this one out?" David asked Gillian.

"James... didn't make it," Gillian said.

"I'm so sorry, Gill. I know what that's like."

"Thanks David, that means a lot to me. I'm so grateful I have my girls here at least."

"How did Riley find you?" Cassandra asked.

"He found a small time pocket at the monastery," David said. "Not enough dust to take him back, but enough to get a letter to me back in 1940 to tell me to come here for you. He gave me quite a good idea for a novel."

Jane smiled. "A novel?"

"I figured I'd show the fellows at the Bird and Baby I can write fiction too," David said. "I still can't settle on a title."

"*The Gate of the Year*?" Edward said.

"The poem the King mentioned in last year's Christmas message?" David rubbed his chin. "Yes, I do see it."

"Jane's writing a novel too," Gillian said.

"You are?" David said. "I'll have to take a look at it sometime."

Jane blushed. "That would be wonderful, thank you."

They went about a block away from the Eagle and Child to a hotel across the street from the Ashmolean museum. David led the crowd up to his room.

Eleanor and Isabella admired an antique grandfather clock next to the bed. "Where's the time machine?" Isabella asked.

"You're looking at it," David said.

"That's the time machine?" Colin said.

David smiled. "You were expecting a blue police box?"

"I guess I was."

"Do you still have enough space-shifting dust from your last visit to the 23rd century to take us to the Outer Hebrides in 915?" Gillian asked.

"I think I have just enough." David turned the hands of the clock. "All right, everyone grab a hold of me." Once everyone did, he tapped the face of the clock. Reddish-gold dust came out of a small hole above the *12* and swirled around them.

Chapter Twenty-Three

JANE ONLY BLACKED OUT for a few seconds as they materialized in 915. Isabella's bloodcurdling screams were enough to rouse her. The two of them had materialized in a big mud puddle.

"Colin!" Eleanor cried, shaking him and Brittany, who were both unconscious on the ground.

"It's his first time, darling," Gillian said. "They could be out for a while."

All nine of them were on an extremely chilly beach. Jane tried to shake off her drowsiness by going to wash her feet off in the ocean. She could vaguely see that she was wearing a long yellow dress that covered her entire body. It was plain, but kind of beautiful in its own unique way.

David looked around the beach. "No sign of Vikings yet, but I should probably stay here and compress the machine all the same."

"I'll stay here with Colin and Brittany," Cassandra said.

"I'll stay here too," Edward said.

Gillian, Jane, Eleanor, and Isabella walked past the beach for about a mile until they saw what Jane assumed was the abbey. "Wait," Gillian said, holding Jane back. She took a rock and tossed it between two large metal poles. A high-pitched squeal sounded. Isabella screamed again as everyone covered their ears.

"Are you lost?" a voice asked. Jane turned around. An

elderly man, or at least one who looked as if he were elderly, dressed in monk's robes walked toward them. "Why, it is Lady Cassandra Bennet! It is so good to see you again."

Gillian's face lightened with recognition. "Hello, Brother Richard. It is so good to see you again as well."

"Are these your daughters?"

"Yes, three of them. May I present Eleanor, Jane, and Isabella. Girls, this is Brother Richard."

"Are you here to visit the library?" Brother Richard asked.

"No, I have a more serious matter, I'm afraid," Gillian said. "Has Riley Granger come by lately?"

"He has been staying here for a month, on the promise that he would help prepare the monastery for a Viking attack if we would give him refuge."

"Could you take us to him?" Jane asked.

"I gave him my word that we would protect him," Brother Richard said. "I will not tell you where he is, but I will not stop you from looking for him, either. You should know he does seem really penitent about something."

"Yes, he's a good actor," Jane said with a sigh.

COLIN WOKE UP ON a windy beach. Edward and Cassandra were shouting, or at least it sounded like shouting to him. *Oh yeah, I'm in the Middle Ages with Eleanor and David Andrews, because of course I am.* He turned to find Brittany stirring as well.

Cassandra helped him up. "I'm actually... we're actually...?" he asked.

Cassandra smiled. "Yes."

"Where's Eleanor?" Colin asked.

"In the monastery with her mother and other sisters, which is where we should be heading as well," David said. He examined Colin and Brittany's jeans and T-shirts. "After we get you into something more temporally appropriate." He opened a small drawer at the bottom of the clock and took out a red and an indigo bodysuit. "Take your pick."

Colin looked at the cloth. "This doesn't look very medieval."

"It will to others once you put it on," Edward said.

Colin could hear Cassandra and Edward talking to David while he and Brittany dressed in the forest.

"So how do you know my mother?" Cassandra asked David.

"She visited me shortly after she and her research assistants had built the time machine," David explained. "She read my biography of Richard III and thought I was a time traveler. The funny thing is, I wasn't until I met her."

Brittany tapped Colin on the shoulder. "Well, how do I look?" She twirled around.

Colin blinked several times. "You look incredible." Brittany was wearing, or appeared at least to Colin to be wearing, a shining red dress with those bell-like sleeves. "How about me?"

"Even better than your Scarborough Faire costume," Brittany said. "You just need a few more things." Brittany handed him the hat, the scarf, and the Sonic Screwdriver.

"Thanks."

David pulled what looked like a rounded gun out of the drawer. "Just in case." He turned the hands on the clock some more and the grandfather clock shrank into a pocket watch.

"SO BROTHER RICHARD DOESN'T know who you really are, does he?" Jane asked Gillian as soon as they were out of earshot.

"No, he and the rest of the monastery think I am an eccentric earl's daughter from outside of Birmingham," Gillian said.

"Do you think Colin has woken up yet?" Eleanor asked.

"I'm sure he'll be here soon, darling," Gillian said.

"He's not Frank, right?" Jane asked.

Eleanor smiled. "No, I think I finally know what love is like."

"How do you know?"

"I look into his eyes and I never want to look away."

"What's that light?" Isabella asked. It was like the light from the little mirrors at Brittany's party. Isabella &c followed it out to the garden. The sun was peeking out of the clouds and its light reflected off a small silver disc. The machine was compressed again. Jane picked the machine up as a hand touched her shoulder.

"Riley?" Jane nearly slapped him in her disbelief.

"Jane, I'm so glad you found me," Riley said. "How long has it been for you since you last saw me?"

"About four months. Why? How long has it been for you?"

"About two years, I think. I got stranded and I need you to unlock the machine again."

"That's it?" Jane stormed out of the garden and through the halls into the chapel.

"Jane, wait!" Riley cried. "I've been on the run a lot. Thinking of you is the only thing that's kept me sane."

"Riley, please *stop*. You don't have to keep pretending you love me."

Riley's face fell. "Jane, I lied about a lot of things, I know. But I really fell in love in with you. Why else would I tell you where to find me?"

"How do I know you're not taking advantage of me again?"

"Honestly, Jane, have you been listening to Isabella? People are perfectly capable of actually falling in love with you, you wonderfully fearless and sweet you." He took her hand. "I was about to ask you to come with me back in

1995 when the machine was leaving."

"When you fired at my mother?"

"I'm sorry, I couldn't let her turn me in again. I'll take your family home and then we can travel through time together like I promised. Please just say you love me too."

Jane tried to envision a life with Riley, always on the run. The fact he had murdered another woman, or at least been an accomplice to it, was not something to take lightly either. "I don't know."

"What's not to know?" Riley said. "My name is Riley Neil Granger and I was born December 24, 1968 outside of Houston, Texas. My dad was an engineer for NASA..."

"You're... 46 years old?" Eleanor walked through the door of the chapel, Gillian and Isabella behind her.

"We can subtract too, Eleanor," Isabella said.

"I don't even know how old I am actually. I think I'm about the same age as Colin."

"It's easy to lose count when you've been time traveling so long and in so many different places," Gillian explained. "Everyone in 2015 thinks I'm just an unnervingly well-preserved fifty-seven."

"I don't mean I don't know anything about you, though that's certainly true," Jane told Riley. "I meant that I don't know if I really fell in love with you or if I just felt lost and vulnerable because you said I would die an old maid."

Riley looked guilty. "I... actually made that up because I needed you to come with me to unlock the machine. Honestly, I have no idea what happens to you or your sisters."

"So you took advantage of my poor sister's desperation to help you elude justice?" Eleanor asked.

"I'm not desperate!" Jane insisted.

"I believe a certain Colonel would disagree," Isabella said.

"Isabella, is this really the proper time?" Eleanor said.

"What do you want, Riley?" Gillian said. "Do you want

to keep running from the 23rd century justice system all your life?"

"I'm not on the run from the justice system," Riley said. "I never have been. I'm on the run from the Red Scarves. The Luddites will just throw me in jail for the rest of my life. The Red Scarves will torture me to the point of insanity, like they did to Nate. I think Roberts at the Time Services is helping them track me down."

"Connor Roberts, Mr. 'Time Travel Will Solve Everything'?" Gillian sputtered. "How gullible do you think we are?"

"He almost killed my parents looking for me." Riley pulled out the cord and stuck it into the machine to decompress it. "That's why I settled twenty years in my future and stopped seeing them or anyone else in my family. I made them all a target too."

"So you're lonely and you want me as your companion now?" Jane said.

"Don't you still want to see those pyramids or eat a salad with Julius Caesar, Jane?"

"Not if I have to abandon my family in the process."

"Yes, your family. Isabella and her baby are going to go back to happily ever after with the Captain, and Eleanor and Cassandra will be wrapped up in Cub Scout meetings and parent/teacher conferences before you know it."

"That's not true!" Eleanor said.

Jane glared at Riley, partially because she had the suspicion he was right. At the very least, she could unlock the machine for everyone. She looked into the machine and let it scan her face. "Happy now?"

Riley took her hand. "Thank you." Jane tried to look into his eyes, only to see a man wearing a red scarf behind Riley, aiming a gun at them. Jane ducked as the man fired. The man fired again and, taking advantage of the confusion, ran to the machine.

Cassandra and the rest of the remaining party raced into the chapel. "Get out of there!"

"You!" the man said. "You're the reason we're here!" He aimed a gun at her and Brittany. David pulled out his gun and stunned him point-blank in the head.

"Where did you learn that?" Brittany asked.

"The Battle of Hastings," David said matter-of-factly.

Colin raced into Eleanor's arms. "You look nice," he said.

Eleanor smiled. "You look nice too."

"You look nice, Brittany," Riley said.

"Shut up, Granger," Brittany snapped.

"Who was that man?" Isabella asked.

"A Red Scarf from the 23rd century," Cassandra said. "They want to kill all time travelers."

"*Kill?*" Colin said. "There are people who try to *kill* time travelers?"

Another man in a red scarf burst through the door. David &c reached to grab a hold of the machine as Riley and Gillian turned it on.

"Why aren't we leaving?" Isabella asked.

"Ziggy's frozen!" Riley cried.

"I'm going to kill that drasted phone!" Gillian said. The Red Scarf grabbed her and threw her out of the machine, pinning her to the floor with his gun.

"There's room for all of us, you know!" Gillian said.

"I'm no longer taking chances," the Red Scarf said. "You're all dead." One of David's shots hit the Red Scarf in the arm.

"I really don't have to stun you!" David said. The man aimed the gun at David. Isabella grabbed Torch out of her pocket and shone it into the Red Scarf's eyes. The Red Scarf changed hands and aimed at Isabella. Riley pulled a lever and the machine shot out reddish-gold dust at Isabella. Isabella disappeared before the bullet reached her.

"Belle!" Jane cried.

"Don't worry, she's back in 1815," Riley said. The Red Scarf aimed once more at Riley. Riley pressed the button, emitting the force field and throwing him against the wall. Jane and everyone else raced to the machine, but Riley kept the force field up to hold him back.

David reached into his pocket, pulling out a watch. He twisted the hands and it expanded into his machine. "Everyone grab onto me!" he said. Jane looked over at the Red Scarf, who was stirring, and grabbed onto her family. David's machine disappeared the same time as Riley's.

Chapter Twenty-Four

EVERYONE WAS ACCOUNTED FOR when David's machine rematerialized across the street from the Oxford train station. Everyone except Isabella, that was, Eleanor reminded herself. She tried not to further remind herself how close she had come to holding James in her arms again. She could only hope Isabella had made it back to 1815, unharmed.

"Well, Jane, did you want me to take a look at your manuscript?" David said.

Jane looked at her mother. "Will you be upset if I stay in Oxford with David a little while longer, Mamma?"

"Of course not, darling," Gillian said.

Colin turned to Eleanor. "I think I'm going to take a later train. I need to think through some stuff."

"Is everything all right?" Eleanor asked.

"I don't think I can do this after all."

"Do what?"

"Time travel. Not if people always get hurt. Not if the people most precious to me get hurt. I'm sorry if I wasted your time." Colin and Eleanor held hands for a moment. Colin made a few noises like he was trying to determine something to say before making it to the elevator as fast as he could.

Eleanor managed to keep her smile the entire train ride home. Uncle Gary and Aunt Linda were waiting for them outside the platform, with Fly and Gilly. Fly raced into Eleanor's arms.

"Where's Jamey?" Fly asked. Eleanor couldn't take it anymore. She wondered why she always had to put on an act for her family. She collapsed into tears. "Colin... I think it's over."

"Darling, I'm so sorry," Gillian said, embracing her.

"No, it's okay." Eleanor wiped her tears. It wasn't like her life depended on marrying well anymore, she reminded herself. She could make a bright future on her own.

"We were going to the West End this evening to see *Charlie and the Chocolate Factory* with some friends, but I can cancel," Aunt Linda said.

"No, a play actually sounds good right now," Eleanor said.

A COLD BREEZE BLASTED Isabella as she material- ized. Once she realized no one was shooting at her, she got up.

Honeysuckle Bridge was less than a mile ahead of her. Strangers were on the bridge, with reddish-gold dust swirling around them. Isabella recognized her own face as her less-pregnant self disappeared along with Mr. Granger and her family.

"I have only been gone a few minutes!" Isabella tried to restrain her joyful tears. She raced to the bridge as Harry himself made it. His Royal Navy uniform looked even more beautiful and heroic.

"Harry!"

"Bella?" Harry said. "Oh my dearest darling, what happened?"

"That awful Mr. Granger took us to the future and I've been trying ever so hard for four months to get back to you. You believe me, don't you?"

"Of course I do, darling," Harry said. He stroked Isabella's stomach. "Bella? Are you...?"

Isabella smiled. "Yes, I am, Harry. It's a little girl. They can tell these things in the future." Harry beamed and squeezed her hand.

Isabella tried to smile back as Harry took her back to Reddings House in Edward's coach and back through the halls. This should have been the happiest moment of her life. Why did it feel so empty? She tried to imagine her sisters and Edward walking alongside the rooms with her.

"It is so wonderful to be home!" Eleanor cried.

"Yes, it is." Isabella said.

"Did you say something, darling?"

"Oh no, I'm sorry."

"You don't look very well," Harry said. He sat her down in their bedchamber and draped a blanket over her, like she had all those nights for Jane. She would probably never see her family again, and the last thing she had ever said to Jane was horrid, as usual. Isabella tried not to burst into tears.

"I'm fine, thank you," she said. "I'm just so happy to be home."

Harry rang the bell for the head housemaid. "Alice, please get Mrs. Pym something to eat."

"Yes, Captain," Alice said.

"You just relax, my dearest," Harry said. "Riley will never bother us again."

 COLIN WALKED AROUND OXFORD, looking for someplace to charge his phone. He tried to ignore the voice of Mrs. Reynolds, his father's old secretary, imaginary but so audible, telling him Eleanor or Brittany were gone, like when she had broken the news of his parent's plane crash the spring break of his junior year, on that ski trip in Aspen with his friends.

He found a small coffee shop close to the train station. As Colin waited for his espresso, he thought he heard someone talking about Maggie and Peter in the Cotswolds. David was sitting in the corner table, reading what had to be an early version of *The Gate of the Year* to Jane. Colin tried to get out of there, but David noticed him first.

"Have a seat, Colin," David said.

"Sure, it's been that kind of a day I guess." Colin turned to Jane awkwardly, wondering if she knew about what he had said to Eleanor yet. "How is your book coming?"

"Wonderful," Jane said. "David and I are reviewing each other's drafts. It's like a miniature Inklings meeting."

"That's great." Colin plugged his phone in and turned it on to check his e-mail. Suddenly looking at his phone made him sick for some reason. He put his phone in his pocket and listened to Jane read her story to David.

"Louisa held off the Vikings long enough so Julia could escape…" Jane's voice faltered.

"You're doing a great job, darling," David said.

"I just hope Isabella is all right."

"I'm sure she's fine," Colin said.

"I should have gone back to London with my family," Jane said. "I want to be there for them as I much as I can, even more so if they do all leave me."

"You still think your family would leave you, after all they've done?" David asked.

"Well… no, but Riley said they would."

"Riley Granger?" David said. "He tried to convince me to put all my money on West Germany in the 1966 World Cup final. I wouldn't rely too heavily on his persuasion." David nursed the ring his coffee left behind. "Your mother on the other hand… God sent her to me during one of my darkest times. Gwendolen, my wife, and our three-year-old son were killed in a car accident, and I didn't want to eat or sleep or teach, much less travel in time. She didn't hear a word of it, dragging me to the Battle of Hastings, like Princess Rose dragging Princess Myrtle on another adventure."

A jolt hit Colin's entire body. The espresso must have just kicked in. "So you're a *Winging It* fan?" Colin said.

"What in the world is 'Winging It'?" David said. "I was talking about my story, 'The Girl and the Golden Goose.' I wrote it for Gill to read to Jane and her sisters, since their father already told them two hundred years' worth of stories."

"You wrote *Winging It!*" Jane said, nearly crying. Colin went to an on-line movie database and showed David the trailer.

"Well, what do you know, I have gotten a movie after all!" David said. "I'll show Ronald and all his Academy Awards."

"I appreciate your help so much, David, but I should get probably be getting back to my uncle's," Jane said. "Otherwise the only one in my family who ever leaves is really me."

"Of course," David said. "Can you reach into my wallet and see if you can get the proper currency?" David asked. "I'm going to take some of this sugar."

There were some photos in the wallet. They looked like they had been taken with a modern camera, but they were from all sorts of historical eras. "Is that you and my mother?" she asked David, looking at the younger woman in a bright orange dress.

"Oh yes, that's when we and Riley and that other fellow— I think Riley used to call him Ant-Man because he was so short— went to one of the Queen's diamond jubilee events. Queen Victoria, that is."

Jane handed David the most recent-looking twenty-pound note she could find and then looked at some more pictures. There was Riley with her mother at the Eagle and Child with two men, one who looked like C.S. Lewis and the other... Jane gasped. It was Harry, only he was dressed in 1930's clothes.

"What's wrong?" Colin asked. His phone started to vibrate. It was a text from Brittany:

A letter just came to Paul and Mayah's house from 1815. I think someone's trying to kill Isabella.

Chapter Twenty-Five

 HARRY WALKED UP THE stairs of Reddings House, returning to the guest bedroom to find Isabella pointing his hunting rifle at him. "Whatever is your problem?" he asked.

"I never told you Mr. Granger's Christian name."

Harry shook his head and simpered. "You really are the shrewdest of Gill's daughters. It makes your total blind spot toward me all the more hilarious."

"So you're really Nathan Arnold," Isabella said. "Our romance... our marriage... it was all just to get close to my mother?"

"After Riley stranded me in 1810, I joined the Royal Navy. The Napoleonic Wars have always been a fascination of mine, actually. I quickly rose up the ranks and got more and more prize money with my knowledge. The only thing left to do once I was honorably discharged was to find a place in Hampshire, meet you and Jane, and determine which was the stupider of the two of you. You both put up a pretty good fight for that, I have to say."

"Well, I'm sorry, but I have no idea where the time machine is," Isabella said.

Nathan pointed out the door where a man was riding away. "I just sent an express to my attorney in Bath that Mr. Phillip's coachman and I caught you at the bridge about to run away with Mr. Granger, your child's father. They warned me when I married you that you were the most determined flirt in Hampshire, but I thought I could reform you. It was sad, really, how you jumped off the bridge in despair rather than face the rest of your life isolated on some farmhouse in another county."

Isabella pointed the gun at him. "That's not loaded, you know," Nathan said.

"I'm not an idiot, Harry, despite what everyone thinks." Isabella jabbed the gun into his chest, then knocked him out in the head before he could regain his composure.

Isabella raced to Eleanor's bedroom and the bed-knob. "*Please* let there still be dust." She shone Torch on it. There was some, but not enough for a person. A letter perhaps... She grabbed the first piece of paper and pen she could find and scrawled a quick note.

Isabella folded the letter. Where could she send it to that would still be around in 2015? She remembered Edward's sister's house on Grosvenor Street. She addressed the letter and pounded it on the bed-knob. The letter disappeared as Nathan grabbed her.

"Please!" Isabella cried.

"Have some pity on me, please," Nathan said. "You think it was easy for me to pretend I cared about your insipid life for so long?" He carried her out through the house. "Make a sound and your family will be shot on sight."

"CASSY, PLEASE PICK UP..." Jane shouted at the phone. She, Colin, and David raced to the Oxford Station platform, only to watch the train speed away.

"When is the next train to London?" Jane asked, shaking.

Colin looked at the screen. "Not for another two hours."

Jane fell into David's arms. "I just want her to know I'm sorry for everything I said."

"Don't worry darling, you forget we have all the time in

the world," David said. He pulled out a pocket watch. "Well, almost all of it."

They raced back to the elevator. Colin made sure the doors stayed closed while David decompressed the pocket watch into the large clock and turned the handles. Jane took David's hand as dust started to swirl around.

Colin could hear his grandmother's voice in his head. *They are not worth risking your life, Colin. Think of Brittany, you selfish thing."*

Colin looked at Jane's pleading face. *Why not? he told his grandmother. Brittany would rather remember me as a hero than as someone who let Isabella die. That's how I would want to remember her or Eleanor.*

"You're too afraid, Colin."

"But I'm going to do it anyway!" Colin sang. He grabbed Jane's other hand the same second the dust was about to engulf her and David.

Colin, Jane and David reappeared in Paul and Mayah's living room. "I just hit *send*," Brittany said. "How did you… never mind." Brittany showed Jane the letter.

Harry is a liar and a murderer. Please do not risk your lives to rescue me. Just know that I am very sorry and I love you all.

Jane's phone rang. It was finally Cassandra.

"IT NEVER CEASES TO amaze me what they can do on the stage these days" Aunt Linda said as the curtain fell for intermission on Charlie and his chocolate factory. She turned to Eleanor. "How are you doing, darling?"

"Fine, thank you," Eleanor said. "Yes, it is quite amazing."

"Mum, can I get another soda?" Clara asked. "Kaitlyn drank all of this one.

"I did not!" Kaitlyn insisted.

"Stop arguing," Linda said. "Eleanor, do you need anything?"

"No, I am fine, thank you," Eleanor said. Uncle Gary left with them to visit the toilet, leaving Eleanor with Mr. and Mrs. Bates, her aunt and uncle's friends. The Bateses politely smiled at her and then went back to their conversation about their upcoming trip to the Lake District.

Eleanor looked at the program, and then checked her phone. There were two missed calls from Cassandra. Eleanor was just about to call her back when Cassandra rang her again.

"Nelly, you need to come back to Uncle Gary's quickly," Cassandra said, proceeding to explain the situation without stopping for a breath.

Eleanor took off her high heels and raced to the concession stand. She met her aunt and cousins at the doorway. "Isabella's in great danger! I'm so sorry, I must get to my mother."

"Of course, I'll go get the car," Uncle Gary said.

"Oh, no, you don't need to do that, there's still another act and your friends will wonder why we left so abruptly," Eleanor said. "I'll call a cab."

"Someone will have to stay with Fly and Gilly if you end up running off with David again," Uncle Gary reminded her. "We'll tell the Bateses your sister has car trouble. They can take the kids home."

ELEANOR, UNCLE GARY, AND AUNT Linda didn't say a word on the way back to Finchley. Eleanor would have loved some conversation to distract her from all the anxious thoughts swirling around her head, but everything she thought of saying sounded too flippant. She had never related to Colin more than in those moments.

Cassandra was waiting on the front porch. Eleanor ran into her arms. "Is Mamma all right?" Eleanor asked.

"Yes, she's in her bedroom, taking measurements on the ball," Cassandra said.

"Where's Fly?"

"Edward's putting him and Gilly to bed right now."

A few specks of reddish-gold dust flew in from the hallway, then a crash and a scream came from the guest bedroom. Cassandra, Eleanor, Uncle Gary and Aunt Linda raced upstairs, while Edward raced in from Jeffrey's room. Gillian was slumped in David's arms sobbing, holding the cracked ball. Jane fell into Cassandra's arms; Brittany and Colin standing behind awkwardly.

"I'm so sorry," Jane said. "We must have blown the ball out of her hands as we arrived."

"If I had only paid more attention to Isabella when she was blabbing on about her 'Harry'..." Gillian said.

Eleanor embraced her mother. "Don't be so hard on yourself, Mamma. He had us all fooled."

"Do you have any 23rd century pockets, Mr. Andrews?" Cassandra asked.

"This is the furthest I can go, I'm afraid," David said.

Gilly started crying too, from the next room. Cassandra and Edward jolted, only for Aunt Linda to stop them. "I'll take care of Gilly and Fly," Aunt Linda said.

"I'll go put on some tea," Uncle Gary said. "Nice to finally meet you, David."

"And you," David said.

"Is there anything we can plug in the hole to keep the dust in?" Jane asked.

Eleanor looked over at Colin. "Do you have any of that gum?" she asked.

"Maybe some in my pants pocket," Colin said. "What do you need gum for?"

"The time pocket is attracted to sugar, just like in *The Gate of the Year*," Eleanor said. She turned to David. "Wonderful book, by the way. I just finished it."

"And if we put some on the cracked ball, maybe we can keep it from floating away!" Cassandra said. "Will that work, Mamma?"

"It had better," Gillian said. David pulled Colin's pants out of the bottom drawer of the clock. Colin rustled through his pockets and found a package of Spencer's. Everybody chewed a piece and stuck it on the wall.

"David, please tell me you have a torch and a ball," Gillian said.

"In the drawer, Gill."

Gillian shone the light on the gum and captured the gathering dust. Eleanor, her sisters, Edward, David, and Brittany held onto Gillian as she tapped the ball. "Here this goes again," Colin said. He took a deep breath and took Brittany's hand.

"Mamma?"

"Francis Jennings!" Eleanor cried. "You're supposed to be minding your great-aunt!" Fly grabbed onto her before they completely disappeared.

Jane blinked as they reappeared in the middle of what looked to be a storeroom, filled with countless rows of translucent cases. Eleanor held on to Colin and Brittany as they collapsed again.

A man raced into the room. "Unauthorized time travelers!"

"For goodness sakes, Roberts, it's just my family and I!" Gillian said.

Roberts sighed. "What do you need now, Bennet?"

"We need someone and something that can take us to 1815!"

Roberts beckoned to the floor. "Help yourself. We're still trying to clean up from the last Red Scarf attack."

"That's probably my fault," Cassandra said.

Gillian squeezed her daughter's hand. "You did what you could." She and David grabbed several of what looked like small guns off a shelf. "Have you ever fired a gun, Edward?"

"Just my hunting rifle." Edward said.

Gillian handed him and her daughters the guns. "Fire these phasers only if you need to. There's no need to go all *Die Hard*."

Jane &c racked through the labeled balls. None of them were for anywhere close to 1815.

"Maybe we should try the time machine park, Gill," David said. He led them down the hall to what looked to be a large glass parking garage. Only one machine was in the park, a very familiar one.

"Riley?"

"Jane!"

Edward pointed his phaser at Riley. "Your face looks rather like a pheasant, did you know that?"

"No, no, it's not like that," Riley said. "I'm about to get the evidence I need to nail Roberts."

"Riley, for heaven's sake *stop*," Cassandra said. "Roberts is no more after you than my mother stranded you or Colin made you break up with Brittany."

"What did I do?" Colin asked groggily. Eleanor stroked his face and helped him up.

"Actually, Riley is completely right about this one," Roberts said, aiming his phaser. A man and a woman in red scarves, holding old-fashioned rifles, walked up behind him. "A shock, I know."

"Agent Keller?" Cassandra asked the woman in disbelief. "You mean you've never wanted to prosecute Riley?"

"Oh, we've wanted to prosecute him, all right," Roberts said. "This modern justice system is too pandering. A little Red Scarf justice is what this scumbag needs for murdering my innocent granddaughter."

The Red Scarves aimed their rifles at Riley. Gillian and David fired their phasers at them, grazing the man in the red scarf. He returned their fire.

Jane grabbed Riley's hand and they ran behind the cabinet where Eleanor and Fly were hiding. Agent Keller pursued them. Cassandra grabbed the nearest time pocket and threw it at her. Agent Keller caught it in her hand.

"You missed." Agent Keller looked at the label. "Guess I don't get a free trip to 16-" She looked down and realized time dust was swirling around her. Cassandra had thrown another one, this one labeled "Early Ice Age?" Agent Keller tried to grab Cassandra before she disappeared, but Brittany kicked her in the groin.

Edward and Colin embraced their wife and their sister, respectively. "We're surrounded by extraordinary women, aren't we, Darcy?" Edward said.

"Yeah, we are." Colin gave Brittany an extra hug.

"Finish this, Wohler," Roberts said. "I'll call for backup."

Wohler, the other Red Scarf, fired at Riley and Jane. Edward jumped in front of them and hit Wohler in the right arm. It wasn't enough to stun him, but it was enough to make him disoriented for a moment.

"Get to the machine!" Gillian cried.

Roberts picked up Wohler's rifle. "Maybe the old-fashioned way is best." Colin shone his Sonic Screwdriver in Roberts's face. He took Cassandra's hand while Brittany took Edward's and they raced to the machine. Gillian hit Roberts on his right shoulder, completely disorienting him, as Jane and Eleanor made it to the machine.

"Wait, where is Fly?" Eleanor helped Jane into the machine and turned around. Fly was playing with one of the flashlights. Wohler had come to and aimed his rifle at him.

"Don't hurt my son!" She fired her phaser in three places, stunning Wohler in his right hand with one. Fly outraced Wohler and ran into Eleanor's arms. Eleanor took Jane's hand and stepped onto the machine.

David raced to his clock. "Look at this brilliant time machine!" He tapped on his clock as Wohler grabbed onto him.

"Get that thing going, Gill!"

"But what about you?" Colin asked.

"Don't worry about me, I still have a novel to finish!" David cried as he and the Red Scarf disappeared.

"Where is that backup?" Roberts cried. He regained use of his arm and aimed the rifle at Riley. "What are you grinning about, you idiot?"

Riley took out what looked like a light contact. "I told you I almost had the evidence I needed. I taped your confession on my lens camera and sent it to every law enforcement organization in the area. They should be finishing rounding up your 'back-up' just about now." Roberts was caught in a force field as he tried to shoot Riley. Uniformed officers had appeared in the room.

Gillian turned to her family. "Everyone finally here?" She set the coordinates into Ziggy. Riley raced to grab Jane's hand as dust swirled around the machine.

"I can help you find Nate," Riley said. For Isabella's sake... Jane thought, taking his hand after a few seconds.

"Hold it right there, Granger!" one of the officers cried. The machine was gone before he could fire his phaser.

ISABELLA HELD ONTO HENRIETTA, finding the strength to resist Nathan as he tried to push her off Honeysuckle Bridge.

"My patience is wearing, Isabella," Nathan said. "Where is the drasted TIME MACHINE?"

"I told you, it's not here!" Isabella sobbed. "I don't know where Riley or my mother are. Harry... Nathan... please... what would Audrey think of you killing our child?"

"Don't you dare bring Audrey into this! That baby should have been hers!" Nathan was about to fire when Jane and Riley raced to the bridge. Jane stunned him in the crotch with her phaser so hard he fell to the ground.

"That's enough, Ant-Man." Riley jumped on him and

kept him down.

Isabella raced into Jane's arms. "You must think I'm so stupid."

Jane held her sister tightly. "Not that stupid."

Riley kept holding onto Nate as the drones materialized. "Any chance I can see you if I make it out for good behavior, Jane?"

Jane looked into Riley's eyes. As hard as she tried, she could not help but flinch.

"I'm so sorry," Jane said. "I know now your love wasn't the love I was looking for." She looked to her family. Nate tried to get up and Isabella kicked him in the forehead. "I will always be so grateful for your kindness, though. I'm sure most of it was sincere."

Riley smiled wistfully. "I did tell you a lot of lies, Jane. But I meant it with all my heart when I told you that you deserved much more than living the rest of your life at Reddings Hall watching all your dreams fade away." He held out his fist and Jane fist-bumped him back.

Riley kept smiling, even as the drones shot out their dust. "Wait, just one last question," Jane said. "Have you ever been able to change anything?"

"No, I haven't." Riley said.

"Then however did you save my fair copy when my aunt threw it in the fireplace?"

Reddish-gold dust swirled around Riley and Nate. "I didn't save it," Riley said. "I made a totally new copy by hand from your book..." Jane held on to her mother and sisters and watched Riley and Nate disappear.

Chapter Twenty-Six

JANE'S SISTERS AND EDWARD were standing in nearly the same places on the bridge they had the night they followed her and Mr. Granger to the future, Jane realized once Riley and Nate were gone. Jane almost wondered if the whole thing had been a dream, until she saw her mother and the time machine and Colin and Brittany.

Eleanor saw the Darcys too, and clasped her hand over her mouth. "I never noticed..." she said. Brittany looked at Colin and gave a delighted shriek. Brittany and Colin must have never changed out of their Chameleon Cloths. Colin looked like he was wearing an indigo coat and breeches, while Brittany was wearing a long red dress with a red bonnet. Eleanor looked down and realized she was still wearing her short, sleeveless black dress from the theater.

"This isn't the part where you're about to run me over, is it?" Colin asked. He and Eleanor laughed.

"So what do we do now?" Gillian asked.

"I want to get the children back to 2015 tonight, before any more Red Scarves or drones or whatever show up," Cassandra said. "Is there enough dust so we can return at a later time?"

"For at least one more trip."

"Good, we'll take care of Woodvale and Edward's sisters later." Cassandra and Edward took each other's hands and raced back to Woodvale Park.

Eleanor rubbed her shoulders to shield them from the cold January air. Colin tried to take off his coat.

"It's only an illusion," Eleanor said. "Reddings House isn't that far of a walk." Brittany followed behind, even more excited than Mr. Bingley whenever he saw a squirrel.

Gillian turned to Jane. "Well, I suppose I should get you back to your aunt and uncle." Noticing the quizzical look on Jane's face, she added, "For your things, I mean."

"Oh yes," Jane said. "Isabella, do you want to come with us?"

"I think I'll stay here for a while," Isabella said flatly. "I don't want... I'm not ready to face anyone yet."

"If you're sure," Jane said. She looked at Isabella again as she and Gillian walked away, wondering if she should have been more persistent.

"WHERE IS MY AUNT?" Jane asked Mrs. Troughton, the housekeeper.

"In the sitting room with Mrs. Parker, Miss Farnsworth," Mrs. Troughton said. She stared at Jane and Gillian like they were foreigners.

Gillian charged into the room. "CAROLINE JENNINGS! Explain yourself!"

Lady Jennings looked at Gillian and gasped. "You've been alive all these years, Cassandra?" she said.

"And you've remained a horrid witch all these years," Gillian said. "You ignored Cassy and Eleanor, bullied Jane, and indulged Isabella! James might have not been able to see through you, but you're as clear as a vial of dihydrogen monoxide to me. I'm taking Jane back to America with me and I will thank you not to interfere anymore." Lady Jennings stood there for a few moments and then walked out of the room, unable to utter a syllable.

"Mrs. Farnsworth?"

Gillian turned to Mrs. Parker. "Miss Finster?"

Mrs. Parker smiled. "I am Mrs. Parker now, thanks to your advice. I could not be happier."

"That's wonderful," Gillian said.

Mrs. Parker looked at Gillian's T-shirt and jeans with either disbelief or interest, perhaps both. "They dress quite strangely in America."

Jane and Gillian looked at each other. "She was like my mother," Jane mouthed to her mother. Gillian nodded yes. "We really came from the future," Jane told Mrs. Parker. "Your brother went there too." Jane took a deep breath and told her about the Colonel. "He was so brave."

"He had tenacity, I could never be more sure of that. You do too. That is what he loved most about you."

"Would you like to come back with us?" Jane asked.

"Oh, that is all right, my dear. At my age, I have accumulated too much to leave behind. I will make sure your sisters' servants are all comfortably situated, though."

COLIN WANDERED AROUND THE halls of Reddings House in a daze. "That's an original Turner..."

Brittany sat down on a couch. "This is like the ultimate Jane Austen museum!"

Colin turned to Eleanor. "Thank you."

Eleanor took his hand and they followed Fly up to the nursery. James was sound asleep, unaware his mother and brother had been away so long. Eleanor tried to cry too loud as she shook him awake.

"Mamma!" James cried. Eleanor scooped him into her arms.

"Colin, this is my youngest son, James," she said.

"Jamey, this is our new papa!" Fly said.

"Fly!" Eleanor cried. Colin laughed and hugged the boys.

CASSANDRA AND EDWARD WALKED into Woodvale Park, feeling like they had never left.

"Are you sure we can leave?" Edward asked.

"Yes, some new family can make memories here," Cassandra said. "We have Peavy Road."

Betsy, the nurse, was walking out of the nursery. "Mr. and Mrs. Phillips?" Betsy asked, looking at his beard, her cropped hair, and their strange attire in disbelief.

"Are the children all right?" Cassandra asked.

"I just got them to sleep..." Betsy said, but Cassandra and Edward raced through the door before she could finish.

Cassy leaped out of bed. "Mamma, Papa, you are home!"

"Oh, my little girl!" Cassandra cried. She held onto Cassy while Edward picked up Neddy and Charlotte. Edward brought the two of them back and he and Cassandra embraced all three of them.

"Guess what?" Edward said. "Your mamma and I have been visiting your grandmother in the most amazing magical land and she wants us all to come live with her there! Your new baby sister is there already." Betsy stared at Edward, convinced he had totally gone insane.

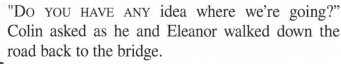

"DO YOU HAVE ANY idea where we're going?" Colin asked as he and Eleanor walked down the road back to the bridge.

"I... don't," Eleanor said with a laugh. James, who had fallen asleep in her arms, began to fuss.

"Here, I can take him," Brittany said. Eleanor handed him to Brittany, running her hands through his hair five times, and then took Colin's hand.

"Thank you for helping Isabella," Eleanor said.

"Of course," Colin said. "She's my family, too."

"You really think so?"

"I'm sorry about what I said at the train station. I love

you, and I love your family, and I know I won't get to have any of you forever, but I want to love you all with every moment I can."

Colin reached over. Realizing he was about to kiss her, Eleanor backed off.

"Colin! Not in front of the entire town!"

"Why not?"

Eleanor shook her head. "Why not?" She pulled Colin close to her and they kissed.

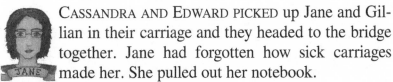 CASSANDRA AND EDWARD PICKED up Jane and Gillian in their carriage and they headed to the bridge together. Jane had forgotten how sick carriages made her. She pulled out her notebook.

Julia grabbed the time pocket as the Vikings attacked. Louisa held off the Vikings as Julia turned on the machine. Louisa raced to the machine as it disappeared. They didn't know where they were going next, but at least they were going together.

Jane set down her notebook. "I finished the first draft!"

"Congratulations!" Edward said.

"I'm so happy for you!" Cassandra said. "Charlotte, can you give Aunt Jane a fist bump?" Jane fist bumped Charlotte. Charlotte laughed; Jane gave her a kiss on the forehead and then Cassandra a hug. Jane knew at that moment Riley was wrong. Her family would always make time for her, like they had tried so hard to before.

Jane bolted out of the carriage as soon as it stopped. "Slow down, darling, we still have to wait for Colin and Eleanor," Gillian said. Colin and Eleanor, followed closely by Brittany with Eleanor's sons were coming down the road. Jane turned to the bridge... where Isabella was leaning over the edge.

"What are you doing?" she cried. Everyone raced to Isabella. Jane and Gillian, not encumbered by small children, made it first. Jane embraced Isabella as she broke down.

"I wasn't going to jump, you fools," Isabella said. "And don't bother with any your attempts at comfort, Jane. You're really happy, admit it. We're both the same again. I don't have a husband any more than you do."

"But you're going to have a child!" Jane said.

"A child who will have no prospects and be persecuted by Aunt Jennings and that wretched Mrs. Watson and the rest of the town her entire life for having such a degenerate mother," Isabella said.

"What are you talking about?"

"Har- Nathan sent a letter to his lawyer saying I was carrying Riley's child. No one will believe the truth, even if I could tell it."

Jane reached out her hand. "Isabella... I'm so sorry for all the hurt I've caused you. Come back to 2015 with us, please. Mamma and I will help you raise the baby, won't we Mamma?"

"Of course we will, darling," Gillian said.

A thoughtful smile came across Isabella's face. "Well, seeing as there are still plenty of shops in the future, I suppose it will be all right." Jane and Isabella embraced each other. Gillian joined in, as well as Cassandra and Edward. Colin, Eleanor, and Brittany joined in the moment they arrived.

"It's going to be okay, Is," Colin said. "We still got that picnic in the Wild West to go to, remember?"

"We could make a stop in 1875, if nobody minds taking a detour home," Gillian said.

Isabella smiled and nodded. "That sounds wonderful," Jane said. She took her last glance at Reddings as the machine disappeared.

Epilogue: 2025

JANE LAY IN BED in her apartment, trying to steal a few more minutes of sleep and quality musing. The latest book in her series about three plucky time-traveling sisters from the Regency era had spent fourteen weeks on the New York Times best-seller list. Now her agent was encouraging her to get the first draft of the next book in by New Year's.

"Get off, Bingley," she said, pushing the dog off her face. It was seven-thirty. Scott, her boyfriend, would be coming to pick her and Emma up to take them to Cassandra and Edward's house in less than an hour.

Jane went down the hall to Brittany's room where Emma was staying and gently shook her niece. "Wake up darling, it's Christmas morning!"

"Yay!" Emma sprung out of bed, giving her aunt a hug. Jane picked her up and spun her around the room. She knew an aunt couldn't have favorites any more than a mother could, but everyone could see her special rapport with Isabella's now nine-year-old daughter.

Emma giggled as Jane brought out the cereal. Jane turned around to find Scott sneaking up on her.

"Happy Christmas, Potter," Scott said, giving her a kiss. Jane gazed into his eyes, not wanting to look away.

"Happy Christmas," Jane said. She had recruited Scott to the project after he was cast, of all things, to play Riley in the upcoming film adaptation of her books. Scott had finally worked up the nerve to ask Jane out a few weeks later. "Are you nervous?"

Scott smiled. "Nervous? About Christmas with your time-traveling family? Not me."

Isabella and Gillian were having coffee with Edward and Cassandra when Jane and Scott came in the Phillip's living room. "Mommy!" Emma cried, racing into Isabella's arms.

"Hey, baby." Isabella and Emma kissed each other on the cheeks. "Did you have fun with Aunt Jane last night?"

"We made Christmas cookies and watched *Winging It* three times!" Emma said.

"Of course you did," Isabella said. "Thank you so much for taking care of her, Jane. I sold three paintings last night."

"Of course you did, they were beautiful!" Jane and Isabella hugged each other.

"Happy Christmas!" Cassy, Charlotte, Neddy, and Gilly came racing down the stairs and joined their aunts in the hugging.

"See my new tap shoes?" Charlotte said.

"Look at my new softball!" Cassy cried. She threw it at the TV stand, nearly knocking down the family portrait from Colin and Eleanor's wedding, which had occurred on one of Edwardian England's most luxurious ocean liners. ("Not the *Titanic*," Gillian had kept promising.)

"Careful!" Cassandra said. She gave Jane a hug.

"Look at my new camera!" Neddy said. Jane tried not to laugh. Neddy was looking and sounding more like a miniature Edward every day.

Gilly put a paper crown on Jane's head. "Aunt Jane, see what I got for Christmas?" Gilly showed Jane her new journal.

"A future writer, how wonderful!" Jane said.

"Christopher, Maureen, can you tell Aunt Jane and Aunt Bella Merry Christmas?" Cassandra said. She beckoned firmly but compassionately to the two orphans she and Edward had rescued from the Blitz.

"Merry Christmas, Aunts," Christopher murmured. Maureen stood back, frozen.

"Merry Christmas, darlings," Jane said, waiting patiently until they felt comfortable giving her a hug. "Merry Christmas, Edward."

"Merry Christmas, Jane." Edward gave her a hug. "How is the sequel coming?"

"Wonderful," Jane said. "How is Woodvale School?"

Edward took Cassandra's hand. "The finest in Dallas, as always. It helps that it has the finest principal."

Cassandra gave him a kiss. "And the finest English teacher."

"And the finest art and drama teacher," Edward said, beckoning to Isabella, who was getting her own paper crown from Gilly.

Two streaks of red and two of blond raced into Jane's arms. The Darcys had arrived. Jane bent down and kissed Fly, James, four-year-old Andrew, and two-year-old Sam.

"Aunt Jane, I'm almost fourteen!" Fly protested.

"That's impossible, I'm only eighteen," Eleanor said. Fly, still as fast as ever, raced to join Cassy and Neddy in the backyard.

"Guess what Aunt Jane!" James cried. "I'm going to have a have-sister!"

Jane laughed. "You mean half-sister, darling." She looked over at Eleanor, who was holding her large stomach. "Happy you're finally having a girl?"

"I love all my children, Jane," Eleanor said.

"Come on, I saw how ecstatic you were when you and Brittany were picking out Amelia Rose's little dresses," Colin said. "And I just spoiled that announcement, didn't I? Sorry."

"If we waited much longer, darling, she could have announced her name herself." Eleanor gave Colin a kiss. Colin stroked her belly as she sat down.

"David told me to tell you both Merry Christmas," Gillian said.

"Thanks," Colin said. Eleanor and Colin had met many time travelers since taking the vacant positions of research assistant and historical advisor, respectively, on Gillian's project, but they would always have a special regard for David Andrews for taking them on their first trip through time together.

Brittany gave Jane a hug as soon as she could get Mr. Bingley out of her arms. "Merry Christmas, roomie!"

"Merry Christmas, roomie," Jane said. "How did the final performance of *A Christmas Carol* go?"

"Wonderful, not a dry eye in the house. Especially not me, when I could finally take off my shoes." Brittany looked over to the appetizer table where Gillian was interrogating Scott. "You think we should rescue him?"

"I think he can manage." Jane flashed Scott an encouraging grin.

"Anyone thirsty?" Eleanor asked, struggling to get up.

"You stay right where you are, Nelly," Isabella said.

"For heaven's sake, I'm not an invalid."

"When I'm having the baby, you can fetch my drinks."

Eleanor laughed. "Oh, so you did accept the Roman senator's proposal, did you?"

Cassandra smiled. "Or the Viking chief's?"

"Or Henry VIII's?" Jane asked.

Isabella gave her sisters playful slaps on the shoulders. "Oh, stop it, all of you. I'm not letting anyone near my Emma and me until I know it's right." She stroked her daughter's hair as Emma and Charlotte played with Bingley. "And just when are you and Scott going to settle down at last, Jane?"

"No time for that now," Jane said. They probably would get married eventually, but for now Jane enjoyed having fun with him.

"No time?" Cassandra asked. "You have a time machine, for heaven's sake!"

"There's no point in getting out of the starting gate first, Cassy..."

"If you're not focused on finishing well," her sisters finished in unison. Gillian laughed and gave all her daughters a hug.

"Ready for presents?" Gillian asked.

Jane had the feeling everyone was concealing something huge from her as presents were unwrapped. Once the last present had been opened, Isabella took Jane's hand and led her upstairs to Gilly's bedroom.

"Is that my..." Jane examined the writing desk. Her initials were still there.

"Yes, it took us forever, but Colin and I finally found it in a shop in London in 1826," Isabella said. Jane sat down on the bed and cried.

Bingley rested his head on Jane's lap. Jane petted him as she looked at her sisters and mother and then around to Scott and Edward and Brittany and Colin and her nieces and nephews. She wiped her tears, feeling grateful to have them all by her side.

"Are you okay, Potter?" Scott asked.

"Yeah, it's just that I can't figure out if the next book should start with my characters rallying with some suffragists or watching Michelangelo paint the Sistine Chapel," Jane said.

Isabella grinned. "So we need to do some firsthand research?" They looked over at Gillian.

"Let me take the turkey out of the oven and then we'll fire up the machine."

Acknowledgements

To the timeless Jane Austen, if somehow you have utilized a time machine and are reading this, thanks to you and all the other creative minds whose influence permeates every page of this book. Whenever a story problem entrapped me, going back to Jane was always the solution.

Cara Daine and Hannah Daniel, thank you for giving your time and tenacity to helping me improve the manuscript and for all your inspiring suggestions.

To David Shapard (*The Annotated Pride and Prejudice*), Vic Sanborn (janeaustensworld.wordpress.com), Joan Klingel Ray (*Jane Austen for Dummies*), Daniel Pool (*What Jane Austen Ate and Charles Dickens Knew*) and the numerous other print and on-line sources that were invaluable in research for this story. Special thanks to the Austen Thesaurus (writelikeausten.com) for helping me capture the "Jane-ness."

To my own dearest sisters Kay and Jo, thank you for your help and enthusiasm. Special thanks to Kay for the fantastic cover and illustrations and graciously bearing my endless critiques.

To my parents, thank you for the encouragement and untiring support you have provided since I first conceived this story in the fall of 2013. And to my Heavenly Father, thank you for bringing every necessary person and event together at just the perfect time. *Soli Deo gloria.*

About the Author

A life-long Jane Austen and time-travel aficionado, Hannah Vale was inspired to write *Time & Tenacity*, her first novel, after wondering what would happen if *Pride and Prejudice* ended with Mary or Kitty Bennet running away with the Doctor from *Doctor Who*. Fascinated by the Regency period, but time machine-less herself, she was determined to write an exciting story that fused the two worlds together. She lives in the Dallas, Texas area with her family, her cat Georgie, and her gerbils Jane and Lizzy. Learn more about Hannah and look for special bonus content from *Time & Tenacity* on the Web at www.hannahvale.com

Coming Soon from Hannah Vale

When she sees a fire-breathing dragon flying over the skies of her quiet North Texas suburb, 16-year-old Rachel Mac-Donald quickly realizes that this is not going to be a typical weekend.

It turns out that Fabula, the magical land from her favorite childhood book which she has mentally retreated to via her own stories, is a very real place and now she and her family are in very real danger from those set on no less than literally re-writing history. With the help of a handsome prince, a dubious thief, and other characters she has known almost all of her life but has just begun to get to know, Rachel sets forth on a mission to save both their world and hers. Along the way, she'll have to face ruthless wizards, shifty mermaids, treacherous pirates, fickle fairies, and, perhaps most unnerving of all, the need to let a new chapter start in her own life.

Coming November 2018

Made in the USA
San Bernardino, CA
17 September 2018